Gangster Magic

By Charlie D. Weisman

First published by Charlie D. Weisman 2024

Copyright © 2024 by Charlie D. Weisman

All rights reserved. No part of this publication may be reproduced, stored or transmitted in any form or by any means, electronic, mechanical, photocopying, recording, scanning, or otherwise without written permission from the publisher. It is illegal to copy this book, post it to a website, or distribute it by any other means without permission.

This novel is entirely a work of fiction. The names, characters and incidents portrayed in it are the work of the author's imagination. Any resemblance to actual persons, living or dead, events or localities is entirely coincidental.

None of the descriptions or actions in this book are intended to inform or be replicated. All work is exclusively for the enjoyment of reading.

First edition

ISBN: 979-8-9878559-3-5

Cover art by Yvette Gilbert

Prologue

Humphry opened the door to Merideth's cabin. A cold draft swept through the room, threatening the set of flickering candles Merideth just lit and chilling her exposed ankles to the marrow. She jerked them under her many layers of blankets and nestled deeper into the couch upon which she lounged.

Humphry was slow to close the door behind him. His slow and deliberate mannerisms were at odds with his perpetually stained, ill-fitting clothing, which were more appropriate for a clumsy fool. The contrast was upsetting to Merideth. As was the general look of his face and sound of his voice. It seemed to her that his entire being was specially designed to irritate.

The two spent the previous weeks alone on a secluded commune that once held a dozen or more. Richard, the former leader of the commune, and Merideth's former closest friend, left to travel the countryside to sing songs about Charlando, a mysterious cult leader who seized control of her country. Richard was smooth and sharp, with a wicked wit and amazing talent. Humphry was a dull boy of seemingly no use. *Why did it have to be Humphry who stayed?* Merideth asked herself.

Humphry wobbled forth with a tray of cheese and set it on a table beside the couch. "Your cheeses, my lady," he said with a bow.

"Thank you," Merideth grumbled. Humphry was not actually useless, but it would be a convenient explanation of her disdain if he were.

"Is there anything else I can get for you, my lady?" Humphry asked, pulling out of his bow.

"No. Begone. And don't let the cold get in on your way out."

Humphry sighed and wobbled back to the door with his head held low. Merideth had hurt his feelings, and though it was one of her most pronounced talents to do so, it was not her intention or desire. He must have been lonely on the empty compound, as lonely as she was herself, and her continued refusal to befriend him bordered on brutality.

"Wait," she called out, realizing her error. "Do you want to eat the cheese with me?"

Humphry spun so fast he turned all the way around to face the door once more. "Merideth?" he asked in confusion.

"I'm over here." Merideth already regretted the invitation.

"Of course, of course." Humphry hobbled back to the couch. "I would very much like that," he said before plopping a chunk of cheese in his mouth. "May I sit?"

"On the floor."

Humphry took a seat, careful not to disrespect Merideth's personal space. "You know, my lady, you remind me of someone."

"Really? Who?"

"Her name was The Lovely Marlene."

"That's a beautiful name. What was she like? Did she also face great challenges and overcome them?" Merideth found it easiest to listen to Humphry when he was complimenting her.

"There was a time I believed she was too beautiful to be of this world," Humphry started. Merideth perked up. Humphry continued. "Not just in the way of her sparkling eyes and soft smile, but in her tender character. Though I am pitiful, she gave me respect. Despite my plumpness, she gave me love. I used to think she was surely an angel or at least a fairy of some sort. Now I am not so sure. I think she may have just been a prostitute."

Merideth winced. "You know there are more important things than being sweet and lovely, right?"

Humphry looked concerned. "Surely there are none, my lady."

"What about leadership and hard work? What about fighting for what you believe in and sacrifice?"

"Those are terrible things, my lady. I wouldn't trouble yourself with any of them."

"Excuse me? Don't you see what's happening in the world? We are living in tyranny. We need all those things and more. We must be fierce and enraged. That is the only way to break our chains. Being nice gets you nowhere." Merideth clutched her many layers of warm blankets and scowled. "Of course you don't see what's happening. You're just a regular, stupid boy. You've never been oppressed or told no. You've just coasted through life without a care in the world."

Humphry's face grew cold. "I beg your pardon, my lady, but you are wrong. No chain is more confining than that of our inescapable death and we each wear it all the same. I have known struggle. I fought for my life doing what I believed was right. It only brought me more pain."

Merideth laughed. "What could you have possibly been through? You're Humphry. You're the most boring person in the world."

Humphry whimpered like a wounded dog. He grabbed a piece of cheese and turned his back to Merideth to hide his woes.

Merideth had done it again. She hurt Humphry's feelings, and just as every time before, she hurt herself by doing so. "I'm sorry, Humphry," she said.

Humphry looked back over his shoulder skeptically.

"Do you want to tell me more about that woman?" Merideth offered. "The one I remind you of?"

"You want to know the story of The Lovely Marlene? It's a very long story, you know."

Merideth closed her eyes and inhaled for several long, arduous seconds. "Please," she forced herself to say.

Chapter 1

It began on a summer day in the northern town of Bethlahoom. At those latitudes, the summer sun was all too eager to rise, and none too committed to crest. It hung just above the horizon for all by the deepest depths of the night. I, for one, took no umbrage. More light to clean, I always said.

I awoke at the first glint of dawn and raced to tidy the mess I left from the brief night before. I fluffed my pillows to their maximum fluffiness and tucked my sheets so tightly around my mattress that a single tissue could not fit between them and the bed. Aside from the bed, I had a dresser and a desk. I polished both to a shimmer and straightened each with a protractor. The floor appeared clean at first glance, but I took no chances. I grabbed my magnifying glass and tweezers and went to work, plucking every speck of dust and stray strand of carpet I could find. A warm sense of accomplishment stoked within me.

A ray of sunshine caught the corner of my tweezers and shook me from my plucking. I stood and marveled at the light trickling through the leaves outside my window, dropping my tools to my feet. I thought for a moment that the heavens themselves had seen the cleanliness of my room and opened their gates to me as a reward. Oh, how I was woefully mistaken.

The door behind me flew open and my father barged inside. "Jesus, boy," he said, his serious, regimented tone laced with disappointment. He was not a tall man, but he was much taller than me, and while he was not particularly muscular, his hairiness was as intimidating as though he were. "Are you just going to stare at that sun all day? Make yourself useful and help your mother with breakfast. And for the love of God, pick up those tweezers. How did I end up with a filthy animal like you for a son? Why can't you be more like Jebediah?"

"Of course, sir," I said. "I was just using them to—" I tried to continue, but he turned away and slammed the door. The aged locking mechanism was too worn to latch in such a short time, and the door slowly crept back open. *Why can't I be more like Jebediah?* I thought. *Since when did Jebediah clean anything?* "Jebediah's not as great as you think he is," I muttered aloud to myself.

A cool cough came from just outside the door. *Jebediah!* His head drifted from the shadowy hallway into the open. A wicked sneer splayed across his teenage face. Jebediah was my older brother. According to my family, he was my better brother as well, though it seemed for little reason apart from him being older.

His body followed his head into the open doorway. He eyed me suspiciously and slithered into my room, his face full of knowing. He had three patches of hair growing on his chin that he spent more time grooming than an older man would a full beard. At the time, I found the hair intimidating, like it was a piece of the same power my dad had in the abundant groves sprouting all over his body. I was nearly hairless by comparison, and thus powerless.

"I know what you just said," Jebediah whispered into my ear. "I know all your secrets."

My eyes widened. *Does he really know all my secrets? Was this one of the powers of his hairy chin?* I could feel his perception beaming into me. "I didn't mean it, Jebediah," I sputtered. "I was just frustrated and it's so early in the morning and all."

Jebediah shook his head disapprovingly. "You know, Humphry, we're all getting pretty fed up with your attitude. Mom and Dad have wanted to get rid of you for years now, but I convince them to keep you. It takes so much effort, and if I stop for just one day, they'll kick you out of the house that same night." He paused to sigh and shake his head before moving to my other ear. "Or worse, I'm afraid," he continued in an even more frightful hiss. "I won't trouble you with the details. You couldn't handle the details. Just be grateful you have an older brother like me. It's amazing how much I do for you and how little you acknowledge it. Shame on you." He shook his head once more, hovering above my cowering stance. I could feel the weight of his creeping body as though it was draped all over me, though no part of us touched. Such was the power of his hairy chin.

"Thank you," I said begrudgingly. I had a nagging feeling that he was not telling the truth, and yet I couldn't disregard it. My parents probably did want to kick me out of the house. My dad certainly. My mom seemed to like me, but I couldn't help believing it was a lie like my brother told me. He told me that she pretended to like me because of how guilty she felt for hating me so much. Everything she did that made it seem like she liked me was only more proof that she really hated me. I was skeptical at first, but over time, I grew more inclined to believe it.

"Thank you,—" Jebediah said, gesturing with his hands to suggest that I needed to finish the sentence.

"Thank you, sir?" I suggested.

"Try again, boy."

"Thank you, almighty Jebediah," I said with my head held low.

"That's a good boy. Now go to the kitchen and make me my breakfast."

"Yes, almighty Jebediah," I said and began trudging to the kitchen.

"You walk like a caterpillar, boy," he said as I left the room. I turned back to look at him but said nothing. I wasn't sure what that meant, though I knew I should be ashamed of it.

My mom barely noticed me when I came into the kitchen. She stood over the stove sipping a mug of coffee the size of a large bowl. Her pained face disappeared behind it every time she took a sip. She was slow to react in the mornings. She needed to be warmed by this external source of heat before moving around. Just like a lizard. Also like a lizard, she stared at me with cold, unblinking eyes.

"Are you here to help me with breakfast?" she croaked, her voice slightly sweeter than the drone of the refrigerator.

"Yes, Mother. Is that okay with you?"

She smiled slowly, closing her eyes as she did as though it took all her concentration to smile so early in the morning. "Of course you can, Humphry. Just clean up your mess when you're done." She sipped her coffee once more and shuffled out of the room, not to be seen again until at least the afternoon, if not late in the evening. Jebediah was probably right about her.

I began making breakfast: bacon, sausage, eggs, toast, and sliced tomatoes. As I cooked, the frustration of my family went away. Maybe it was the smell, or maybe it was being productive. Whatever it was, I began to feel cheerful.

Cheer is a tricky feeling; as are the rest of human emotions. Cheer makes everything seem like it is going to work out as I hope it to. Maybe not exactly how I expect it to, but in a way that will make me continue to feel cheerful. That is the through-line of all my emotions: they make me think that the future will inspire more of that emotion and exclusively that emotion. My emotions are never right.

As I cooked, I thought about how happy my family would be eating their breakfast. If I cook this bacon just right, Mom really will love me! When Jebediah tastes this sausage, there won't be any more mind-reading. He will use the powers of his chin hair for good. And Dad won't throw these eggs against the wall in anger. No. He will throw his arm around me in pride. And when Tabitha, my sister, eats these tomatoes, she won't be disgusted at being related to me, but joyful that she gets to spend time with her loving family!

Pure delusion.

Tabitha paced into the kitchen and stopped right behind me at the stove. "I swear to God," she shouted in my ear, "if you burn my bacon, I will drag you down to Hell myself!" She slapped the back of my head and stormed back to her room.

"Good morning to you too, Tabby," I said to myself after she was long gone. Tabitha had not always been that angry. There was a time, long ago, when she was only controlling and mean.

Tabitha didn't act that way to other people. Just me. I had conflicting opinions about that fact. On one hand, she treated me worse than she did everyone else, and so it would make sense that she did not like me as much as everyone else. On the other hand, if this was truly who she was, then it was only with me that she trusted her innermost thoughts and feelings!

This was another folly of emotions. I feel them all no matter what happens around me. If there is nothing that warrants a particular emotion, I will have it anyway and contort my perspective to justify it happening. Even feelings as seemingly environment-dependent as trust and intimacy have little bearing on my reality.

I made five plates but set the kitchen table for four. I ran the fifth plate to my mom's room and set it at the door. I knocked twice and ran back to the kitchen, calling out as I did that breakfast was ready.

My dad and siblings crept out from each of their private spaces in the house to eat. Each of them would have preferred to take their meals back with them, but Mom made a rule that everyone had to eat breakfast together. Not even Dad dared to argue. Especially not Dad, in fact.

They grunted as they ate. Their heads tilted towards their food to better shovel it into their mouths. Their eyes darted around to each other and back to the food. I did the same but made sure to shovel just one bite slower than Tabitha. I didn't want to finish before her and be accused of trying to finish first to avoid doing the dishes.

Dad cleared his plate and stood. "Can you take care of my dishes, son?" he asked Jebediah.

Jebediah nodded without stopping his shoveling. Dad left the room, dusting off crumbs from his shirt as he did.

Jebediah repeated the exact same act with Tabitha, who responded just as Jebediah did. When Tabitha finished her plate, however, she smacked me in the back of the head again. "How did you get that fat eating that slowly?" she asked.

I had one bite of sausage remaining. I sat alone at the table and looked at it. Was I fat? I grabbed my belly. Leaning forward in my chair made it plump up into flabs that were perfectly sized to grab and feel shameful. I looked at the chunk of sausage. It was cold and covered in solidified grease. I did not want to eat it, but I did so anyway. I slouched for a few seconds before starting to clean.

Washing the dishes would have enraged any of my other family members, but it had a calming effect on me. In this way, it was right that I cleaned up after them. Why would I not do something that made my family happy? A smile soon crept across my chubby face. Yes, I thought, one day they will be happy for all the things I do for them.

I finished the dishes and frolicked back towards my room. I skipped along down the hallway, my arms swaying all around, and who approached? It was Jebediah! I waved and smiled. "Such a great morning we're having, Jebediah, and oh such a beautiful afternoon it will become!" I sang.

Jebediah shoved me mid-frolic, slamming me into the door to Dad's room. I crumpled to the ground. "Eat dirt, fairy boy," Jebediah said.

Dad's yells erupted behind the door. Even behind a wall, he was as loud as five regular men. I crawled away from the door as fast as I could. Jebediah sprinted down the hallway and out of sight. The door rattled. The yelling grew louder. The door shot open. A mountain of rage and hair towered in the doorway.

YOU WORTHLESS LITTLE RAT! GET OUTSIDE AND STAY OUT! I DON'T WANT TO SEE YOU AGAIN UNTIL THE SUN GOES DOWN!

I screeched and crawled on all fours down the same direction my brother just went. Dad followed, but his rage was too powerful to direct only in my direction. He turned every which way, yanking at his hair and yelling. In the confusion I escaped.

Once out of the hallway, I flung to my feet and ran out the front door. When I made it to the corner of the street, I turned back to see him on the front lawn yelling nonsense in his robe with his hands waving high in the air. I turned the corner and ran down the block before his yells were only as loud as one regular man. If he was only as loud as one man, then I was a safe distance away. I slowed down and caught my breath.

Though the sun had only been in the sky for a couple of hours, the summer heat was already making itself known. I began to sweat, but the humid air didn't allow it to evaporate. Sweating this early in the morning meant I would stink the whole afternoon. Fortunately,

Deedris was the only person willing to play with me, and Deedris smelled much worse than I ever could.

Dad's yells mellowed until they were no louder than the birds, just a lingering hum indistinct from the buzz of lawnmowers and screams of other neighborhood children getting forced outside to play. A skip entered my step, and I pranced over to Deedris's house, singing to myself the whole way.

Deedris lived just across the train tracks where Jebediah told me all the rats in the world were born. I didn't know if that was true or not, but I did know that not everyone born across the tracks were rats. Deedris was from across the tracks, and he was a friendly boy. He also happened to be my best friend! Would I be best friends with a rat?

Deedris left his house with none of the fanfare I experienced leaving my own. His parents would probably never know that he had even gone. They both worked long hours, even on a Saturday. As a result, he was free to do whatever he wanted. That used to mean playing pretend with me in the empty lot by the supermarket, but now he wanted to talk about girls and walk around trying to cross paths with them, or at least see them from down the street before scampering away in nervousness. As developed as Deedris liked to tell me he was, I could see he was still a nervous little boy.

Try as I did to hide it, I too felt the creep of lustful yearnings. I was a twelve-year-old boy and such awakenings were frightening. Rightfully so. Nothing good can come from the burgeoning loins of a twelve-year-old boy. Especially so in the town of Bethlahoom, where, by the dictate of public opinion, such burgeonings were condemned above all other burgeonings.

"Hey Hump!" Deedris called out while running down the path from his front door to the sidewalk. Deedris always ran to places if he could. He had the kind of lengthy, slender frame that somehow made running more efficient than walking. I had the kind of short, fat frame that made rolling down hills especially efficient, though the opportunity rarely presented itself.

"Hey Deeds," I replied with a wave.

"Did I tell you about Annabelle?" Deedris asked as he ran past. He circled me a few times before settling into a walk beside me. He had to fight the urge to leap into a gallop after every few steps.

"Annabelle Sternlicker?"

"I'm in love, Humphry. I was thinking about her last night. I never realized it before, but I've always loved her."

"Even when she ate that beetle and barfed on everyone's lunches?"

Deedris looked off somewhere in the sky recalling the event before nodding. "Even then."

"What happened to Molly Mucasine? I thought you were in love with her?"

"That wasn't real love. I was just a kid then." Deedris stopped walking and grabbed me by the shoulders. "Humphry, I'm a man now." He turned his face to the side and pointed to a mole on his jaw that had sprouted a thick, black hair.

"Deeds…" I was in awe. My best friend for my whole life was now a man. "How does it feel?"

"I can't even explain it. It's like I just know things now. You wouldn't understand."

He was right. I didn't understand. I wanted so badly to ask how he did it. How did he take that impossible step from boy to man? He looked down upon me with pity, as though he knew what I was thinking. Just like Jebediah! He patted me on the cheek. "I'm going to run ahead," he said, "and see if I can't spot Annabelle from behind the dumpsters." Before I knew it, he had galloped off out of sight. Deeds, a man now. I couldn't believe it.

I walked alone. Something had changed. The world had moved forward and I had stayed still. How does one catch up with something as big as the world? What do you do when there is nothing to be done? I didn't have any answers to give myself that day. I am not sure anyone did. Life had the answers, but life doles them out piecemeal over the course of a lifetime like a crooked employer offering subsistence wages. I would get the answers, but I had to wait. In hindsight, I wish I got to wait longer.

Lost in thoughts too big for my small brain, I wandered aimlessly on the far side of the tracks. Sometime in the afternoon, I came across two men in long coats holding up a rail-thin man in tattered clothes. One of them held the stringy man against a brick wall and berated him. "We ain't messing around, Jobo," he said. "If you don't have the money we got to take something else. Frankie don't like missed payments. Isn't that right, Sam?" The man pulled out a knife and waved it in Jobo's face.

"I got better than money!" Jobo laughed. He seemed unusually happy for someone being held at knifepoint. "I got a dragon. He comes at night and gives me kisses!"

Sam kicked the dirt. "Come on, Mitch," he said. "His head's gone. That's magic talk. Nothing we can do to get that money back now."

"I swear it!" squealed Jobo. "See, there's a dragon tamer right there!" The stringy man pointed right at me.

I stopped in my tracks. Sam walked towards me. "You friends with Jobo?" he asked.

I looked behind me to see if he was talking to someone else, but no one else was there. "Jobo? No, no. I am friends with Deedris. Do you know Deedris?"

"Who's Deedris? Look, fool, we work for Frankie. I don't know who this Deedris is, but if you're peddling magic that's not Frankie's, we got a problem."

"Be careful," Jobo said. "He's got dragons."

Sam hesitated for a moment. Understandably so, I thought. I would be nervous too if I heard someone had dragons.

Unbeknownst to me, a police car had rolled to a stop beside us. Mitch and Sam froze in place as though a spell had been cast upon them. The police officer stepped out of his car and strutted to the sidewalk with his hands clasped about his belt. Every step was intentional and confident. His confidence seemed to come from his mustache, which was thick enough to sweep a whole barn. There must be a lot of magic in that mustache, I thought.

"Good afternoon, gentlemen," he said. His burly voice broke the bonds cast upon the two cloaked men. Mitch released Jobo, put his hands in his pockets and started whistling innocently. I couldn't help but sway to the rhythmic tune.

"Good afternoon, Officer Flannigan," Sam said in a much more welcoming voice than the one he had used with me. "What can we do for you today?"

Officer Flannigan didn't appear moved by his generous salutation. "If you know my name, you know what I want. I'm looking for Frankie Fourfeet. Do you know where I can find him?"

Sam laughed. "You don't really believe in Frankie Fourfeet, do you? I mean, he's a myth. It's like believing in fairies or warlocks. Come on, Murphy, all that ain't real."

Officer Flannigan appeared offended by the use of his first name. He smelled the air. His mustache wavered from his powerful inhales. He scanned the scene, stopping briefly upon Jobo and then fixating upon me. "Is that true, kid? Do these guys really know nothing about Frankie Fourfeet?"

His powerful mustache compelled me to tell the truth. "That's not what they said," I began. "They said they work for Frankie, and that anyone selling magic that isn't Frankie's would be in a lot of trouble. Whatever that means."

Sam looked like he was about to pounce on me, but Officer Flannigan pulled out a pistol, and with one commanding step forward, froze the two cloaked men in their tracks. "Hold it right there. You're coming with me."

"He's lying, Flannigan! He's lying!"

Officer Flannigan growled, "We'll see about that." He stepped towards the two men and cuffed them both.

Mitch squirmed, but Sam showed no restraint. He just stared at me with cold, unblinking eyes as he was marched to the car. "You better watch out, kid. Frankie Fourfeet is coming for you. You're a dead man walking." He disappeared into the back seat of the patrol car. Officer Flannigan tipped his hat to me before driving away.

"You're in trouble now, dragon-tamer," Jobo cackled. "Frankie Fourfeet will kill you a thousand times! And your dragons too!" He laughed hysterically. He had the toothless smile and gray wrinkled skin of a ghoul. "Better run, dragon-tamer! Frankie's coming for you!"

Jobo's cackle slapped me like a whip. I ran away as fast as I could.

Chapter 2

In my haste, I ran well askew of my house, and into the adjacent neighborhood of Northwe. It was named for its position north of the creek that cut through Bethlahoom east to west, and west of the train tracks that cut through north to south. It was often confused in conversation with Northee, though they were quite dissimilar. I lived in Southwe. Of all the neighborhoods, Northwe and Southwe were the most alike, both being generally free of hooligans.

Such was not always the case. Some may have suspected me of being a hooligan that day. I certainly did not appear as an innocent young boy. I was drenched in sweat, panting heavily and looking over my shoulder every chance I could.

With my head turned firmly to my rear, I bounded straight into two girls of the neighborhood. They were none other than Annabelle Sternlicker and Molly Mucasine. A high-pitched yelp escaped my mouth as I fell upon my bottom.

"Oh my god," Annabelle said, sweeping her long blonde hair over her shoulder. "Can you believe that thing just touched me?"

"That's not a thing. That's Humphry," Molly said, pointing at me. It was hard to gauge her expression beneath the enormous frames of her glasses, but she didn't seem as disgusted as Annabelle, who clearly wanted to puke.

"You know his name? Eww!" Annabelle whipped her hair over her shoulders several more times before stepping over me on her way down the sidewalk.

"He's been in our class for six years," Molly called after her. She grumbled at Annabelle's lack of response. "Nice to see you, Humphry," she said to me before chasing down Annabelle.

Embarrassment was too weak a word. It felt like someone was vacuuming out my insides and pouring ice water down the back of my neck. It was one thing to bump into a girl, scream for your life then flop around like a fish, but I had failed to say excuse me.

I moped the whole way home. I had never moped before. It felt awful! The girls would surely share the story of my ineptitude with the whole town. Molly was probably blabbering about how impolite I was. It wouldn't have bothered me before, but something about the way her braces had shown that day made me deeply concerned with her perception of me.

Additionally, Deedris was becoming a man without me. I should have been happy that Deedris was a man now. If there was anyone who would use the power of chin-hair for good, it was him. Instead, I was bitter and jealous.

And, of course, there were the magical wizards and ghouls that threatened to find me and kill me. That wasn't good either, I thought.

All of it together was too much for a boy to handle. If only I were a man.

I arrived back at the house much later than usual. The smell of mushy green beans greeted me at the front door. My legs felt just like those green beans.

At least Mom was up and cooking. Everyone treated me better when she was around. For this, I loved her no matter how much she hated me.

I walked into the kitchen to see that everyone had already gathered at the table. Tabby held her fork and knife tightly in her fists and growled at me as I sat down.

"Just in time, Humphry," Mom said sweetly. "Did you have a nice day?"

"Yes, mom," I said. I didn't trouble her with my worries, especially knowing all the kindness she would surely show would be against her will.

"Well, that's good, sweetheart. Would you like to say grace tonight?"

My belly rumbled. I didn't want to, but it felt wrong to refuse. "Of course, Mother." I clasped my right hand in hers and smiled. I lifted my left hand to Tabby who promptly stabbed it with her fork.

"Don't touch me," she growled just soft enough so only I could hear. I obliged and hovered my hand off of hers.

"Dear God," I began, "thank you for this wonderful meal and this wonderful family. Thank you for the house that we live in and all the amenities we get to enjoy. And if you could please make me a—" I paused. Make me a man, I thought. Make me a man! But I couldn't say it aloud.

"Are you okay, sweetheart?" Mom asked, presumably out of guilt for her dislike of me.

I nodded, but it was not so. I continued my prayer with what I thought my family would want me to say instead. "And thank you, God, for bestowing my loved ones with ample amounts of body hair. Amen."

AMEN.

Dad and my siblings tore into their dinners, but Mom stared at me looking disappointed. I met her eyes and smiled. She smiled back feebly before pecking at her green beans and spaghetti. I may never garner her true affection, I thought, but at least she was an expert at pretending.

I started feeling better. Spaghetti and meatballs settled my demanding tummy, and I was no longer so anxious to become a man. Maybe my prayer had something to do with it. Praying always had that effect on me. Almost as much as spaghetti and meatballs did.

I would have finished my plate first but held off eating my last half a meatball until everyone else had finished. I took my last bite at the same time as Mother. She started to collect the empty plates as soon as she finished. I did the same. "I can take care of these if you want," I said.

"Oh, Humphry. How did I get so lucky with you?" She pulled my head close and kissed my forehead. For a moment I thought she was going to offer to do the dishes with me. I was a fool. She let go of my head and slugged out of the room. "Oh, Humphry," she snapped right as she was out of my line of vision, "make sure you really scrub those dishes. I don't want your father complaining in the morning."

"Yes, Mother."

Silence.

I scrubbed as hard as I could, imagining each plate was the person to which it had belonged. From my dad's plate, I scraped off his periodic rage. I wiped off all of Jebediah's manipulativeness. I rinsed Tabby's cruelty. Mom's indifference and lethargy. I got to my own. What was I scrubbing off of myself? A lack of hair? That couldn't be it. How do I remove the absence of something? And who needs chin hair when they don't even have a spine? Unattractive. Unpopular. Unmanly. I couldn't think of anything that I actually was. Just things that I wasn't. Finally, I clutched my plate and I washed off all the foolishness. Or at least I pretended to.

My bed was always welcoming. I lay straight and stiff as a board with my arms tight at my sides and the covers pulled all the way to my nose. The sooner I fell asleep, the sooner the day would be over. I closed my eyes, but sleep did not come. My mind hummed with worries. I tossed and turned to no avail. Finally, I opened my eyes and finished my prayer. The part of it I didn't want my family to hear. "Dear God, please make me a man. Please." I closed my eyes. A tingling feeling washed over me. I did not become a man, but the sense of urgency to become one was lifted off my shoulders. I fell asleep thinking fondly of Deedris and his chin hair.

I awoke in my dreams in what felt like an instant. I was in the school cafeteria. There was hardly anyone there. It was just me and Molly Mucasine. She sat on the bench next to me with her hand clasped in mine. It felt nice and soft! "Hello, Molly," I said to her. "You look very pretty today." She did. She always did, and it was only then occurring to me.

Molly smiled. Her braces were full of a munched-up beetle. A disgusted look spread across her face and she barfed all over my lap. Everyone from town stormed into the cafeteria. Deedris led the way with Annabelle Sternlicker under his arm. They all pointed at me and shouted in unison, "HUMPHRY LOVES MOLLY!" They repeated the phrase and danced in a circle about me.

I shot awake, my heart pounding through the sheets. What was that? It was just a dream, I told myself. I don't really love Molly Mucasine after all. I just needed to relax and go back to sleep. It was still the middle of the night.

I went to straighten my scrunched-up sheets, but something wet and sticky gave me pause. How did Molly's dream vomit end on my real lap? Was I still dreaming? I leapt out of bed. I hadn't had an accident in years. Not only was I not a man, I was devolving into an infant!

I tore off my pajamas and threw them onto the bed. Whatever was happening, I could not wait until the morning to clean it up. I grabbed each corner of my bedding and yanked it up like a sack over my shoulder, making for the hallway.

My door croaked like a frog, and the slower I opened it, the longer and louder it croaked. Waking my family would be a disaster. The door must be opened like a band-aid, I thought. I pulled it open as fast as I could. It slipped out of my hands and crashed into the wall next to me.

BANG

Oh shoot, I thought. But maybe nobody heard. Everyone was fast asleep, after all.

I tiptoed down the hallway to the basement. A chilly draft washed over my bare bottom that made me clench my cheeks as tight as I did the sheets. I had to continue.

Once inside the stairwell to the basement, I relaxed. It was safe down there. Dad often started yelling in the basement, and nobody would know until he made it to the top of the stairs and opened the door. If the basement could silence Dad's yells, my tiptoes would be as silent as snow.

I flipped my sack into the washing machine, threw in some detergent and hit start. I had been washing my own clothes for years at that point, as well as the rest of my family's whenever they forgot to wash it themselves. They were much better at remembering when I forgot to wash their clothes than when they forgot to wash their clothes. Memory is a funny thing like that.

The basement was full of forgotten knick-knacks and doo-dads Dad was too cautious to throw away. He had a way of foretelling impending disasters and reacting to them ahead of time in a fashion that someone who didn't know about his premonitions might see as completely insane. There were stacks of newspapers going back decades and boxes of coupons long since expired. You would think we were a family of Olympians with all the deteriorating gym equipment lying around. Jostling through it all was a nice way to stay busy as the wash ran.

A headline caught my eye on an old newspaper I was thumbing through.

Dark Magic Makes it to Bethlahoom
By Rudolphus Slim

Gone are the days when Bethlahoom was a refuge from the debauchery of the modern world. First, in 1947, came the cinema, broadcasting filth and charging our children to see it. Next was the dance hall, where unwed singles met to fornicate. Now, there is a new onslaught to our sanctity, worse than any before: Dark Magic.

Jacob Glump, local hooligan, age 27, was apprehended for sunbathing in the nude just outside Tiddlylumps in Paltry Square. Upon examination, he was found to be under the influence of Dark Magic. That's right, Dark Magic.

Where did it come from? Will there be more cases like it? Will Bethlahoom fall like its southern neighbors? This reporter wants to know.

Dark Magic? In Bethlahoom? Why hadn't I heard about this before? The magic of body hair was one thing, but this sounded more like the kind of magic only a wizard could wield.

The wash ended with a ping. I moved the load into the dryer and went back to the stack of papers to learn more. The papers were more or less in chronological order, and from the headlines alone I made out a grim story.

Two More Hooligans Expose Themselves

Dark Magic Sweeps Through Bethlahoom

Dark Magic Takes Its First Life

Charlie D. Weisman

Scores Murdered, Dark Magic Presumed

Dozens Dead, Hell in Bethlahoom

Flannigan Fumbles Frankie Fourfeet

The picture was clear, but it didn't make any sense. According to the paper, a dark wizard had taken over Bethlahoom and destroyed the town. But I lived in Bethlahoom. While some parts were disheveled, namely all the parts outside my neighborhood and the one immediately to the north of mine, it certainly did not appear to be under the domain of a dark wizard.

The most recent article was only a few months old. I took it atop the washing machine and began to read.

Dark Magic or Police Incompetence?
By Rudolphus Slim

Rumors about the spread of Dark Magic have reached a fever pitch. Beginning some months ago and cresting just this weekend when dimwitted Officer Murphy Flannigan made claims that the recent uptick in crime is associated with a global cartel run by a mysterious man named Frankie Fourfeet. Murphy Flannigan claims Frankie, a four-legged freak of nature, was at the scene of what he claimed was a quadruple homicide. But I didn't see any bodies. Did you?

The police department has not corroborated Flannigan's claims, but have yet to announce any disciplinary action. Step it up, Police Department. Murphy Flannigan is a loon. Don't fall for his spun tales. There is no such person as Frankie Fourfeet and we should all just mind our own business!

What in Bethlahoom? This Rudolphus Slim wasn't tracking. First, he talked about Dark Magic every chance he could, saying it was the worst thing to ever happen to Bethlahoom. Then he turned on a dime and said there was nothing to be worried about. He even said doing such a thing made someone a loon!

And that name: Frankie Fourfeet. It was the same name the hooligans had warned me about. They told me Frankie Fourfeet was going to find me and kill me. According to Murphy Flannigan, Frankie Fourfeet was the dark wizard behind all the dark magic in the world! What did I do to get his attention?

It was all too much to think about. I jumped off the washing machine and grabbed the dryer. The shaking coursed through me and rattled my brain enough to drown out the rest of the world. I didn't hear the basement door open or the heavy footsteps behind me. I just held on to the dryer with all my flabs and dangles jiggling like jello.

"Hey, fairy boy," a voice called out behind me.

Jebediah!

I spun to face him, covering my dangles as best I could. "What are you doing here, Jebediah?"

"I would ask the same of you if it weren't so obvious."

"What? I'm not doing anything. I swear!"

"The one thing I don't understand is why you still try to keep secrets from me. I know everything you do, boy. You think you can get away with what you're doing down here? Not a chance."

"Jebediah, please don't tell anyone. I know you know all my secrets, but I don't even know what I did!"

Jebediah squinted and looked me over head to toe. He slithered up to my ear and hissed. "You don't know what you did, huh?"

I shook my head no.

Jebediah pondered this fact for a moment and then smiled. "It's for the best that you don't. Just know that it is worse than you could possibly imagine. Mom and Dad would kill you if they knew, and rightfully so. Using the family washing machine for this?" He shook his head and put his hands at his hips. "I won't tell anyone about this. Okay? But you have to do something for me in exchange."

"Anything, Jebediah! I swear! I'll do anything! Just, please, keep me safe."

"Alright, fine. I'll let you be my servant if that's what you want. You can do my chores, my homework and everything else I ask. I'm going to be on you, boy. It's for your own good."

"Thank you," I cried. "I promise I'll try not to do whatever I did again."

"Thank you—?"

"Thank you, almighty Jebediah."

Chapter 3

The summer was strangled by the torment of Jebediah's oppression. Morning until night I waded at the shores of his feet. His commands bit at my soul. His name-calling lashed at my spirit.

"Hey fairy-boy, where are my pancakes?"

"Hey fart-breath, what am I doing clipping my own toenails?"

"Hey bum-licker, why can't I see my reflection in this toilet seat?"

The end of summer had never before been anything other than the greatest dread. Now it was my only hope.

At long last the day came. The first day of 7th grade. Middle school.

There were three stages of school in the town of Bethlahoom: elementary school, middle school, and high school. Elementary school was for children. Once a student made it to middle school, expectations changed. This was the time when a boy became a man, or defaulted to a loser. There were no other options, and there was nothing that could be done to correct course in high school. At that point, if you weren't a man, you were done for.

Much was done on the part of the teachers to minimize the students' concerns over this reality. I never understood why. There was no sense denying it. Doing so only left one completely vulnerable.

Some kids, like Flammery Bootwinkle, bought it up. Flammery was in Jebediah's class. He believed that everyone grows in their own time. That to shoo out the child within was a loss greater than any gain the social hierarchy could provide. Flammery was found on the edge of town wrapped in toilet paper, dangling from his underwear and crying for his mother. He was never seen again.

The bus was always late. I was on the last stretch of stops before school, and by the time it got to my house, it had already spent ten or fifteen minutes waiting for straggling students. Frank, the bus driver, would always wait for the students to come out before kicking up speed and making them sprint a block or two before coming aboard. If he didn't like the effort shown, he would just keep driving out of reach of the running student until he had to stop for someone else. This may have been why Deedris was so much better at running than me. His stop was first, and he was always running late.

Tabitha and Jebediah didn't wait for the bus. Jebediah had Dad's old pick-up truck to take to school. The high school was just down the block from the middle school and elementary school, but Jebediah and Tabitha both agreed that it was not worth jeopardizing their scholastic endeavors to take the extra minute to drop me off in the morning. I once suggested that I could easily walk from the high school to the elementary school, but they agreed this would be a violation of principle. I didn't understand, but that was acceptable to me. I didn't understand much of anything they did, and the more they said that I didn't understand, the more easily I could accept that my inability to understand was a reasonable excuse for anything.

The bus screeched as it whipped around the corner to my street. I stood and made sure Frank could see how quickly I meant to jump aboard. The bus door unfolded as it approached, but the bus didn't slow down. I took a few shallow breaths to calm my nerves and I leapt into the passing bus. I hadn't made the jump for months, but jumping onto a moving bus is like jumping onto a moving bicycle.

"Hi, Frank!" I said after peeling my face off the floor. "It's good to see you again. Did you have a good summer?"

"Oh, hey kid. Not bad. The seats are that way."

"Thank you, sir." I followed the path of his jabbing thumb to my classmates. The bus was so full and rowdy, I could barely hear the howl of its rusty engine.

I wobbled down the center, doing my best to balance as the shockless tires dipped in and out of potholes. The kids with glasses and headgear sat in the front. Judy was the first to acknowledge me. Judy had more metal strapped to her skeleton than tendons. "Hello Humphry," she slurred through her headgear. "You can sit here if you want!" She pointed to the empty seat next to her.

"Hi, Judy! I would love to," I started to say before a particularly rough patch in the road sent me airborne. I crashed to the floor and got to my feet to find Judy's face stuck to the seat next to her. A spike jutting out from her headgear had impaled the spot where my head would have gone had I sat down.

OH NO!

I grabbed her by the headgear and tried to pull her free with all my might. I yanked and yanked. Finally, the seat cushion tore open and Judy was freed. She smiled at me with a mouthful of chrome. "Thank you for saving me," she said sweetly. "Would you still like to sit next to me?" A large portion of the seat cushion still hung from the side of her face.

I didn't want to hurt Judy's feelings, but it was too dangerous to sit next to her. "Oh, I would love to, but I think I'm going to find Deedris. I haven't seen him for a while and we need to catch up. It's really good to see you though, Judy."

Judy's smile faded and she tilted her head as far forward as her bent headgear would allow. I wish there was something I could do to make her feel better. My heart broke for her, but at least my face was still intact.

I hadn't noticed before, but Molly Mucasine was sitting right behind Judy. She had a book covering most of her face, but her eyes poked out from the top. They were wide like those of a frightened squirrel and flew behind the book as soon as my own eyes made contact with them. Was she looking at me? My heart pounded. A profound urge ignited in me. I both wanted to be as close to her as possible and run as far away as I could.

"Hi, Molly," I shrieked in a pitch as high as a tea kettle, before throwing my hand to my mouth to keep more from coming out.

Molly's eyes reappeared from behind the book, even wider and more fearful than before. They darted from side to side, the book inching down her face. I caught a glimpse of her button nose. Her nostrils flared open and shut like a hippopotamus. Was she going to speak to me? No. She flung the book back up and curled into a ball, almost managing to conceal her entire body behind the standard-size paperback. I mumbled some sort of 'goodbye' and continued down the aisle.

What had just happened? Was that love? Was it something more sinister? Is there anything more sinister than love? I had been thinking about Molly more than usual during the preceding weeks. Even dreaming about her. There was, of course, the time Molly had managed to merge my dreams with reality. Every time I dreamt of her since then, I had awoken in fear of what else she could do. Molly had always been a strange girl. Was Molly a witch? I wondered.

I kept creeping down the jostling bus. The cool kids populated the middle seats. The girls sat in front. Four rows of them. There was a complex hierarchy within this group that I was not privy to. They were all so far out of my reach that I could barely tell them apart. All I knew was that Annabelle Sternlicker was their leader. Annabelle had hair down to her knees. It didn't have the same kind of magic that Dad and Jebediah's hair had, but it was just as powerful. She usually sat next to Molly, but their friendship now appeared tenuous. The socialization of girls was far too complicated for me to have speculated why.

The cool boys were more obviously delineated. There were not one, but two boys who held positions of power: Barnaby Butterchin, and Anatoly Teeniweenie. Barnaby was the prettiest of all the boys. The girls giggled every time he walked past. The teachers all doted upon him. He was the glue that held the class together.

Anatoly was a different sort of leader. His power came from a ferocious set of sideburns that had grown in during the summer before fifth grade. He was always the grumpiest boy. Tall and fat and grumpy. The combination demanded respect.

I thought of them as the summit of two mountains. Beneath each peak was a small faction of lesser boys who were totally loyal to their leader. Further down the mountains was a larger group that made up the base of both peaks. I was somewhere in the valley between these two mountains. Both towered above me, but neither held particular sway. I liked Barnaby much better than Anatoly, but it did not mean I could ever be his friend. It was hard to connect with someone whose social standing was so different from my own.

Anatoly never noticed I existed. I was fortunate in that regard. Deedris was not so lucky. Anatoly used the threat of violence to control his underlings, and Deedris was the preferred subject for demonstrating the seriousness of those threats. Deedris was a boy of many qualities, but resilience was what I admired most about him. Seeing him get pelted by spitwads and dangled by his underwear gave me the strength I needed to face my siblings. I don't know what I would do without him.

I stopped a few rows from the back of the bus. The remaining seats were home to the dweebs, fellow outcasts without notable distinctions. The smelly kids. The quiet ones who preferred to go unnoticed. Deedris should have been sitting amongst them, but I couldn't see him. Had I missed him along the way? I turned back to the cool kids' section. He wasn't there either. I knew things would change now that he was man and all, but I didn't think he would disappear entirely. My heart sank.

What did I think? He didn't want to play with me after he told me about his chin hair. He ran off and let me spend the rest of the summer alone and miserable. Our friendship was just a matter of convenience for him. He left me the moment he got the chance. So much for the school year saving me.

I trudged to the empty seat in the back of the bus. It was the seat for the ultimate loser. My head was hung so low I didn't see that someone was already there, curled in a ball facing the back. "Deedris?"

Deedris flailed in fright before righting himself. He moved to a seated position but still cowered with his face covered under his arm. "Oh, hey Hump. How'd your summer go?"

"It was alright, I suppose. I spent most of it polishing Jebediah's toilet seat. How's being a man?" I couldn't help but sound upset.

Deedris groaned like he had been punched in the gut. "Humphry, I have to tell you something."

"What is it, Deedris?" The sadness in his voice made me realize I may have been too quick to judge him. I took a seat next to him.

He lowered his arm. "I'm not a man anymore." There was a clump of gauze taped to his chin where the hair once grew.

"What happened?"

"Doctor Shuttlerberry said the mole looked cancerous."

"Oh, no! Tell me you'll be alright!"

"I'm afraid it doesn't look good for me."

"Deedris! You have cancer?"

"I wish. Doctor Shuttleberry took my manhood for nothing." Deedris kicked the seat in front of him and yelped as his foot connected with a metal beam.

"Oh, Deedris, you'll be a man in no time. I promise." I felt joy for the first time in weeks. Relief feels sweet no matter how much suffering remains. Sometimes not being alone is all it takes to make a sad situation bearable. I was as lost as Deedris when it came to being a man, but all I cared about was having my friend back.

"Thanks, Hump. Maybe you're right."

We took the remaining time on the bus to recount the details of our last weeks of summer to one another. Deedris had gone to his annual physical the day after we last spoke. After getting the news about his mole, he was instructed to stay out of the sun until the results came back. By the time they did, summer had nearly ended and he was too upset to leave the house anyway. It didn't sound like Deedris to react that way, but everyone has a breaking point and I suppose that was his. Hearing about his experience erased my concern about my own. Hearing about my summer seemed to have the same effect on Deedris. By the time we rolled into school, we were laughing again.

My classmates unloaded from the bus. We walked in rank and file to the auditorium for the opening ceremony. I was curious how this one would differ from the one at the start of elementary school. In elementary school, we spent the whole morning singing songs about the virtues of kindness and do-goodery. This would be more of the same, I hoped.

Two adults stood guard beside the door to the building. Their eyes, stern with suspicion, cast fear on the hearts of all who passed. A chill swept through my clothes as I stepped into the vestibule. Two more scowling teachers funneled us through to the theater room. Pale lights flickering on the domed ceiling kept the room a shade brighter than complete darkness. All I could manage to see in front of me was the outline of Deedris bobbing like a horse resisting the urge to break into a gallop. I was not in elementary school anymore. This was middle school.

A spotlight burst onto a portly, gray man in a well-worn suit pacing to a podium at center stage. The crowd erupted in whispers. "Who's that?" I asked Deedris in a whisper of my own.

"He looks like a bear who works at a prison."

The grizzly man tapped the microphone in front of him.

BOOM. BOOM.

The crowd fell silent.

"G'mornin'," the man bellowed. "My name is Arnold Smellington. I'm your P.E. teacher and your groundskeeper. You'll call me sir, or you'll call me Mr. Smellington. If I catch you callin' me Mr. Smelly-town, I'll have you hanged by your britches." The crowd gasped. Mr. Condork, my old P.E. teacher, would have never said such a thing. "Now in a minute, Dr. Chewbooger is gonna tell you some things. You're gonna wanna listen. You're gonna wanna make sure you hear every word and understand what they mean. 'Cause if you don't, you might just find yourself hangin' by your britches!"

A girl's scream came from somewhere in the crowd. Everyone else held their breath, myself included. A scrawny man in glasses stumbled out of the curtain behind the P.E. teacher and raced to the microphone.

"Thank you, Mr. Smelly-town," he shouted into the microphone. "Mr. Smellington, I mean, of course." Mr. Smellington's cheeks grew as rosy as a pig. "Now, now students, there is nothing to laugh at," Principal Chewbooger continued, but the damage was done. The entire student body was laughing at Mr. Smellington, and he ran off looking like he was about to cry. Poor Mr. Smellington.

"Alright, that's enough now," the Principal said to quiet the crowd. "I hope you all enjoyed your summer and aren't too disappointed that it's over."

"School sucks!" Deedris shouted next to me. I couldn't believe my ears. What was he doing? Deedris was a dweeb! A handful of giggles followed throughout the crowd.

"Well, now, that's not a very nice thing to say." The principal straightened his posture and adjusted the microphone to match his new height. "It's also not true. You know, I was like you once upon a time. When I was your age, I thought that summer was the greatest time of the year and that school was a bore. That's right. I didn't want to be in school either. But looking back on it now, all my fondest memories were at school. It was in school that I saw all my friends. It was in school that I learned the valuable life lessons I still use today."

"You suck!" Deedris called out again. I shot up from my seat in shock.

"Alright, who said that?" Chewbooger's eyes ignited with rage. "I swear to God you little rat, you won't regret anything so much in your life." The spotlight moved over the silent crowd. Deedris sank into his seat like a turd in the pool. The spotlight stopped right over me.

"There! It was you."

"Me? No, sir! I, I, I, I..." I looked to Deedris for help, but he was lying motionless on the floor.

"Come up to this stage, little boy."

I started to inch by the knees of my stunned classmates. I didn't want to, but I couldn't help it. It was like my body moved without my control. I could barely breathe, but I somehow made it all the way to the stage.

"Tell me your name, boy."

"It's Humphry, Mr. Principal Sir."

Principal Chewbooger grabbed me by the shirt and yanked me close. "Well Humphry, consider joy to be a thing of the past." He forced me to the front of the stage. "Everyone look at Humphry. See how weak and pathetic he is. Does this look like a man to you?"

NO, PRINCIPAL CHEWBOOGER.

"No, he does not. This little rat is barely a boy! And a boy he shall remain for the rest of time." He shoved me to the floor and kept talking to the crowd. "I was going to tell you how wonderful you all are. I was going to tell you to embrace this time in your life, as you will never get it back. Well, that would have been a lie. It is time for you all to grow up or perish. Life is a river. Some of you will swim, but most of you will drown. Little Humphry here is a sack of lead. Don't be like Humphry. Be a man, or die."

Chewbooger dropped his mic and knelt down to my ear. "I am going to be on you, boy. If you try anything at all, I will make you suffer like you never knew was possible." He kicked me once for good measure before exiting the stage.

Mr. Smellington came over to me and knelt down into a squat as well. "You done make a mistake, boy. I'm going to take you into the back and give you a whippin'. I'ma be on ya like gravy on a biscuit. Like a--"

BOOOOM

He was interrupted by his own rambling fart, amplified by the microphone he was squatting over. The building shook as it rumbled.

"Hey! Smelly-town farted," someone in the audience shouted. I turned to see Molly Mucasine standing and pointing. Did Molly make Mr. Smellington fart? Where was this power coming from?

"I did not!" Smellington pleaded, but the students were unconvinced. A chant rang out as loud as the fart.

SMELLY-TOWN FARTED! SMELLY-TOWN FARTED!

Smellington's cheeks glowed like embers in the wind. "I didn't fart," he cried as he ran off the stage with tears in his eyes. Poor Mr. Smellington.

Thunderous cheers roared from the students. I rose to my feet and marveled at the attention. Surely it was misguided. That kind of approval isn't meant for people like me.

Chapter 4

I met Deedris outside on the way to our homeroom class. He looked more jittery than ever. "I don't know what happened back there, Hump. I was just so angry and I couldn't help myself."

"That's okay, Deeds. I suppose it happens to everyone." I was still riding high from the applause. If anything, I wanted to apologize to Deedris for stealing his spotlight. He was the one who should have been up there getting farted on by Mr. Smellington.

The walk was short. The middle school consisted of two buildings right across from each other, the theater and the main hall. It also shared a gymnasium with the elementary school. The High School had its own facilities. Occasionally there would be events for the students of all the schools at the high school gym. Today was not one of those days.

Deedris and I were lucky to be sorted into the same homeroom. Unlike the lower grades, 7th-grade classes were split into small groups at random. It was possible to share every class with one person and no classes with someone else in the same grade. This was unheard of in elementary school and was a great source of discussion on the first day. It was devastating to find out that you would not be with your friend in any class for the entire year.

Our schedules were released to us in the summer. Deedris and I shared four out of a possible seven classes. Homeroom, History, Science and P.E. were all with Deedris. Math, Grammar and Art were not. It was as much as we could have hoped for. It was enough to ensure that we would have at least one class together every day. We would spend recess and lunch together, of course, but the more time I spent with my best friend, the better. Middle school was a dangerous place, and there is safety in numbers.

Everyone had homeroom scheduled at the beginning of each week. Our homeroom teacher was Mr. Snottworth, who also happened to be the art teacher. He was young as far as teachers go. He was unmarried and had no children either. Bachelors in the town of Bethlahoom were not uncommon, but it was uncommon for them to be as well groomed as Mr. Snottworth. Usually, unmarried adult men hung around in alleyways, seemingly so satisfied with having giant bushy beards that they neglected to take showers or have friends. Mr. Snottworth was as far away from the norm as possible in this regard. There was hardly ever a trace of stubble on his face and there wasn't another man in town with less grime on his clothes or skin. Most anomalous of all, Mr. Snottworth was kind to me.

The main hall was laid out with classrooms arranged in a rectangle around an open seating area called the patio. The building was two stories tall, and the second story was laid out the same way as the lower level with a balcony around the inner edge overlooking the patio. We didn't go up there often, because it was mostly faculty office space. High above the patio was a domed glass roof that shielded it from the elements. The roof was covered in dead leaves and dirt that gave the whole school a musky tint. It felt right to learn in a place like that. It was like the building itself had been acquiring knowledge for millions of years, or however long it had been around, and that hard-earned knowledge was passed onto the students. I could feel the walls breathing. The school was a living thing, and only something that abided by truth could live for as long as that building had. A clean school can't be trusted.

Mr. Snottworth greeted us at the door to the art room. "Welcome. Take a seat wherever you're comfortable."

Each homeroom teacher used their own classroom, and as soon as I entered the art room, I couldn't be happier with my placement.

Deedris and I sat at the end of one of two long tables in the middle of the room. There were eleven people in our homeroom, including Deedris and me. Some I recognized from my years in elementary school, but five were unfamiliar to me. People from the surrounding areas would often transfer to Bethlahoom Middle School from their neighborhood elementary schools or from home-schooling. The influx of students was seen as a potential new start for those like Deedris who had been designated as the class punching bag by the bullies. One of the five looked like he had the potential to take that position. Deedris nudged me and pointed at him. "Look at that doofus," he said.

"Deedris!" I exclaimed.

Deedris looked down at the table grumbling to himself.

"Alright everyone, time to start," Mr. Snottworth said. He had the soothing, mellow tone that comes from doodling all day. "My name is Mr. Snottworth, but you can all call me Norman. How about we all go around the room and introduce ourselves and say our favorite animal? I'll start. My name is Norman Snottworth and my favorite animal is a rooster. You want to go next?"

A girl to his left looked around nervously before introducing herself as Shirley Nottaman and her favorite animal as a beaver. The doofus Deedris pointed out was next. "My name is Scrotumus Spitwallow and my favorite animal is the reticulated armadillo of Gorgmont from the Shadows Of Sermanthia series."

"Anatoly is going to kick his butt so hard," Deedris whispered to me with a big smile.

I understood why Deedris was happy about this, but I couldn't help but shake my head. Scrotumus seemed like a good boy. I just wished there was a way that good boys didn't have to get beaten up all the time.

It came around to Deedris and me. Deedris's favorite animal was an eagle and mine, of course, was the tender koala. The next few people had their answers prepared and shouted them out in succession faster than the previous students. I thought everyone had shared, but when it got back to Mr. Snottworth he stood and looked to the back of the room. "And you, young lady?"

Molly Mucasine appeared from behind an easel in the back corner. I could barely believe my eyes. "My name is Molly Mucasine and my favorite animal is the bat." She faded back behind her easel. I spun away from her. How did I not notice her before? She must have the power of invisibility, I thought. Sounds an awful lot like a witch to me.

The rest of homeroom was a blur. My mind held nothing but thoughts of Molly casting spells behind me. Luckily, there wasn't anything of importance that took place in homeroom. It was intended as a time for teachers to convince the students that they really did like school after all. Mr. Snottworth would have to try again next week to convince me.

Deedris had to yank me off the bench when homeroom ended. "What are you waiting for? It's recess!"

"Oh, splendid," I muttered back. Recess was twenty minutes of freedom. Unlike lunch, which lasted forever, recess was a mad dash to start and end a complete game of something. Or at least it had been in elementary school. Middle school turned out to be different. No one was sprinting to the field for a game of kickball or to the swing set to secure a swing. Everyone just flowed out of the classrooms like syrup and coagulated into tight circles around the patio. Deedris and I flowed to our own dark corner and formed our own circle.

"I think I have a plan for our new friend Scrotumus," he said.

"You've warmed up to him! That makes me so happy, Deeds. Should we go find him and see if wants to play?"

"I am going to beat him with my shoe."

"What?"

"At lunch, I am going to beat him with my shoe. It's rubber, so I don't think it'll hurt him much. But at the same time, he'll be getting beaten by a shoe on his first day of school. That will definitely get Anatoly's attention."

"But that will make you a bully! You'll be just like Anatoly. And if you don't like Anatoly, how could you like yourself?"

"You know Hump, this might sound harsh, but I think it's time you grew up. We aren't kids anymore. At least, we better not be. The world is a rough place, and you can either let it sharpen you like an ax, or whittle you down like a pebble. I have to do this. This year is going to be different for me. I've been thinking about it all summer. Anatoly is going to find someone else to torture, and Annabelle is going to fall in love with me. I just know it."

Deedris looked off across the patio. His eyebrows lifted and furled like he was looking at a puppy. I turned to see Annabelle twirling her hair around her finger in the distance. There was a crowd drawn around her like planets around the sun. I had no fondness of violence, but I could see Deedris was motivated by something pure. I couldn't fault him for following his heart. "Be gentle with him," I said. "Hit him with the soft end and keep away from the nose. He doesn't need to smell your feet to get your point across."

Deedris placed a hand on my shoulder. "Thanks for understanding. I'll do my best."

The bell rang for the start of the next class. It was history, so Deedris and I walked together. We found seats near the back, closest to the door. The teacher was Mr. Fylack, a portly man with a mustache thick enough to distract from the shocking smoothness of his bald head. He gave the same customary introduction as Mr. Snottworth and asked the class to share their names and favorite historical figures. A familiar twangy voice called out with confidence. "My name is Scrotumus Spitwallow, and my favorite historical figure is The Serpentine Emperor of Galindrone from The Phalicoon Prophecies."

"I think I want to use the hard end," whispered Deedris.

I frowned at Deedris.

The class went around sharing their names and favorite historical figures. Deedris's favorite was Hercules, and mine, of course, was Saint Flartingfoot, the patron saint of rabbits and all the animals that eat them.

Just when I thought we were through, Mr. Fylack pointed to the other back corner. "And you, miss?"

"My name is Molly Mucasine and my favorite historical figure is Merlin."

"Where did she come from?" I squeaked.

Deedris swiveled back to me. "You didn't see her before? She was staring right at you when we came in."

My mind blurred yet again. This girl had to be a witch. How else could she have the power of invisibility? The dreams were one thing. Maybe there was another witch nearby causing those, but why would another witch choose to make Molly invisible in class? It just didn't add up. Molly had to be the witch.

"What's gotten into you?" Deedris asked as we walked out of class. I was never any good at hiding my feelings, and I was feeling an unease like I never had before.

"What do you think about witches?"

"You mean the wrinkly old hags with warts and yellow teeth?"

"Well, obviously that's what they're like when they're twenty or thirty, but what are they like when they're our age?"

"I don't know, Hump. I never gave it much thought."

"Yeah, me neither."

"Why do you ask?"

I checked all around, looking for Molly. I didn't want her to overhear that I discovered her secret. She had already taken notice of me, and I didn't want to give her any reason for her to punish me further. She was nowhere to be found, but I decided it wasn't worth the risk to say anything out loud. "Oh, I don't know. It was just something that popped into my mind." I had never lied to Deedris before. I felt a cold wind through my chest as I did.

"Well, whatever it is, it will have to wait. There's Scrotumus right over there. Everyone's around. I won't get a better chance than this."

"Be careful, Deeds."

Deedris laughed. "You think Scrotumus is going to fight back or something? This was meant to be, Hump. This is destiny calling. I just have to pick up the phone." Deedris slipped off his shoe and pressed it against his ear. "Hello, Destiny," he said before turning towards Scrotumus.

Maybe it was destiny. Maybe this was just how the world worked. If you wanted to get higher up, you just had to find someone weaker than you to stand on. I would have been honored to hold up a friend like Deedris if it didn't mean getting beaten by a shoe.

Deedris limped across the patio. His uneven gait from his one shoe-less foot amplified the essence of cynicism floating in the air around him. Students took notice and began to point and whisper. The whole patio grew dark.

Deedris singled out Scrotumus with his eyes and drew him into the center with nothing but the power of his gaze and the slap of his shoe against his hand. They circled around each other. Scrotumus could barely stay on his feet from fear. Finally, he stumbled to the ground and Deedris pounced. He held his shoe aloft and looked up to the crowd. "Hey Anatoly, check out the new kid!"

Anatoly made his way to the front of the crowd. "What are you doing to my cousin?"

Deedris lowered the shoe. "Your what?"

Anatoly rushed in, tackling Deedris to the ground.

"No!" I yelled, but it was too little too late. Anatoly took Deedris's shoe and beat him with the hard end. Scrotumus pulled off Deedris's other shoe and joined.

"Everybody look at Deedris," Scrotumus called out with a heavy lisp and gasping for breath. "He's as pathetic as the peckering willowbees of Merrathryl!" He continued beating Deedris with his own shoe.

The crowd grumbled collectively. Destiny is a real tease.

Chapter 5

Deedris was slow to recover from his beating. When it was his turn to say his favorite shape in science class, he said it was the shape of a hole in the ground. Poor Deedris. I felt embarrassed just sitting next to him. I couldn't imagine how embarrassing it would be to be sitting inside of him.

Molly appeared just as she had in my previous classes to tell everyone her favorite shape was the silhouette of a wolf howling against the full moon, but after seeing my best friend get beaten half to death by a shoe, I wasn't as worried about Molly casting spells on me. Sure, she was a witch, but she didn't seem to want to do me any harm. For all I knew, she was a friendly witch and only wanted to be my friend. The idea was appealing, and my resistance to her charms failed me.

The following weeks were marred by a series of Molly-centric dreams. I dreamt we sat together for lunch and rolled down hills together all afternoon. I even had a dream in which we held hands at the park under the stars. Why she was so intent on haunting my dreams, I could not be certain, but I relished our nightly reunions enough not to care.

Though confident in my dreams, I was too afraid to speak to her in person. Reality could only tarnish the fantasy in which I chose to live. Yet by some otherworldly spell, I couldn't restrain myself from staring at her every time she was near. She drew upon my body like a siren. It was sorcery.

At the very least, Jebediah's demands of me had lessened since the start of school. Both my siblings were fully absorbed into their own lives and barely noticed me. Tabitha especially so. Her health had become a growing concern. She spent the mornings stuck in the bathroom sick to her stomach and had missed a full two weeks of school in the first month of classes before being taken to the doctor. The results of the visit were due at any time.

...

I wished Deedris a good afternoon and went to the front of the bus to prepare for my jump. I held on to the rail as the bus whipped around the corner to my house. The door unfolded in front of me and I leapt onto the sidewalk, somersaulting onto my back for a soft landing. The blue sky sprawled above me. The weekend was finally here. I could breathe again.

I skipped to my room to set my backpack on my bed. The smell of roasting meat filled the house. It was a rare treat for Mom to be awake early enough to slow-roast something in time for dinner. Per usual, I remained perfectly quiet to ensure my family was undisturbed by my presence.

Mom finally called out that dinner was ready. I sprung into the hallway hoping to be the first one to the kitchen, but my dad and siblings were already stampeding. I hugged the wall just in time to avoid being trampled and followed behind them.

Steaming plates of beef, potatoes and vegetables awaited us. A basket of freshly baked rolls were snuggled in cloth right in front of my plate. I could feel their warmth on my face. I was so hungry, I could barely wait to say grace. By the ravenous looks on everyone's faces I could tell I was not alone.

"Would you like to say grace tonight, honey?" Mom said to Dad.

My dad started to answer but was interrupted by the phone ringing behind him. "Who in God's name is calling at this hour?" He stood in a huff.

"Calm down, honey. It might be the doctor."

"I'll shove his stethoscope up his sphincter."

"Rodger!"

"Alright, I'm calm." He grabbed the phone off the wall. "This is Rodger speaking... Do you know what time it is Doc?" He looked over at Mom and shook his head. "Well, it would have to be big news considering the time... What the hell are you talking about? You call me at dinner and try to tell me my daughter is pregnant? I'm going to march down to your house and impregnate your ass with my foot!"

"Rodger!"

"Oh, settle down, woman. This quack says Tabby's pregnant. I'm not about to be insulted in my own home at this hour by some quack who doesn't know a nostril from a butthole." Dad picked the phone back up. "You listen here you disgusting freak, you're going to keep your filthy mouth shut about my daughter or you're going to lose your tongue. Do you understand me? Good." Dad slammed the phone back on the wall. "Let's eat."

"Tabby's pregnant?" I mumbled.

Dad swatted me hard in the back of the head. "You'll be slurping beef through a straw, boy."

"Rodger!"

"Settle down, woman. It's time for grace. God, thank you for the restraint you have given me tonight. Amen."

AMEN

Dad grabbed the roast and sliced off about half for himself. Jebediah grabbed some potatoes and I inched toward the rolls. Tabby and Mom didn't move.

"Tabitha," Mom said coolly, "Is there something you want to tell us?"

Everyone looked at Tabby who turned beet red and sank into her chair.

"You don't really believe that quack, Judy," Dad said with a mouthful of meat.

"I think Tabitha is going to speak for herself about this." I had never seen Mom look so serious. She looked at Tabby the way she felt about me, with the complete absence of respect.

"Umm..."

"Tabitha Jean..."

"It was God," Tabby spit out.

"God?" Mom didn't look pleased.

"He came to me in a dream. I swear it! I didn't think much of it at the time. Just a silly dream, but he said that because I was good and pure, he chose me to have his baby."

A chunk of half-chewed beef fell out of my dad's mouth and onto the table. "Is that true, Tabby?"

"Of course it's not true, Rodger. She's lying."

"It is true! I promise."

"You will not lie to me, young lady!" Mom raised her voice like I had never heard before.

"Now wait a minute, Judy. I think she's telling the truth. She's my little sweet butter cake. She wouldn't tell a lie if it meant getting a million dollars. I think it makes perfect sense that God chose her."

Mom looked too angry to form words.

"Humphry," Dad said proudly, "get Father O'Flacity on the phone."

"Yes, sir," I said and bounded for the phone.

Mom crossed her arms. "Rodger, we need to talk about this before it leaves the family."

"Nonsense, woman. This is the will of God. We will share it with the world."

A delicate voice answered the phone and I handed it over to Dad. "Father O'Flacity," Dad started, "good evening. I have wonderful news about my daughter. Nay, the world. She's pregnant, Father. My daughter is pregnant with the lord's child." Dad held Tabby's shoulder as he spoke. Tabby looked like his hand was made of liquid nitrogen. "I meant what I said, Father. The lord came to her in a dream and chose her to carry his child. Now, I want you to announce this to the congregation on Sunday. Yes, Father, this Sunday. No, Father, you do not have a choice. Good, Father, and congratulations." He handed me back the phone looking thoroughly pleased. "Well, dig in everybody. And make sure the baby gets its fair share."

Chapter 6

The following day was a whirlwind. Dad barely took a breath dialing everyone he knew to tell them the news. I had never seen him so excited. Tabby looked especially pleased with herself as well. Dad instructed me to serve her in whatever way she wanted and she was quick to exercise that right. Some of her instructions made sense to me. I could understand why she wanted me to massage her feet, but other requests were beyond my comprehension. Why she wanted me to stick my head in the trash and say I am garbage, I may never be privileged to know.

The following day was Sunday. Sundays are an enigma. They are the end of the weekend, but the first day of the week. They have as little school as a Saturday, but as much school the next day as a Tuesday. The range of happenings on a Sunday is limitless. The only thing that was certain about Sundays was that everybody went to church.

Church was the most powerful force I knew of in the world. It subdued even the most magical of people. It forced Mom to wake up early. It turned Jebediah into a well-groomed gentleman. Perhaps most impressive, in all the countless long hours I spent in church, Dad never yelled a single time.

"This is the start of a new age," Dad announced in between bites of pancake. "From now on, we will be the most respected family in Bethlahoom, maybe even the world."

"The world?" I marveled.

"That's right son. The world. As such I want everyone to be on their best behavior. That means when we get to church, there will be no laughing, no smiling, no expressions of any kind."

"I'm always well-behaved, Daddy," Tabby said before sticking a pancake-crusted tongue out at me.

"I know you are sweetheart."

"But Daddy, I think it would be even easier to be well-behaved if I didn't have to smell Humphry in the car. Can Humphry walk to church today?"

Mom came to my defense. "Humphry is not walking to church and you are not to say mean things to him. Apologize to your brother."

"But Mom, I'm special!"

"Tabitha Jean--"

Tabby was silenced. She smiled at Mom, but when she turned to me, her eyes ignited with a red flame. "I'm sorry you smell bad."

She had never apologized to me before. I was so honored a half chewed-bite of pancake fell out of my gaping mouth.

"Eww!"

Dad smacked me in the back of the head. "Best behavior boy!"

"Daddy, can I *please* not go with Humphry."

Mom sighed and put her face in her hands. She knew as well as I did the power Tabby had over Dad.

"Of course, sweetheart," Dad fawned. "Humphry, you're going with Jebediah in the truck."

Jebediah threw up his hands. "How did I get dragged into this?"

Tabby tugged on Dad's shirt. "Humphry should walk, Daddy. Look at how fat he's getting! He needs the exercise. I think it will help the smell too."

Dad patted Tabby's head. "There just isn't enough time for him to walk, sweetheart. Jebediah will take him."

"But--" Jebediah started.

"I said you will take him." Dad's command shook the room. He took the power of everyone else's voice and put it into his own. Nobody made a sound for the rest of the meal.

Exhaust slowly filled the cabin of the truck as we idled in the driveway. Jebediah kept fixing his hair with his hand and flossing his teeth with his fingernail.

"What's wrong, Jebediah?" I asked. "Aren't you happy for the coming birth of the lord?"

He snorted. "You're a moron, Humphry."

"And that makes you sad?"

"You really believed her? Unbelievable. That's the devil's baby if anything." He reversed out of the driveway and off we went.

Tabby was pregnant with a demon baby? I would have never guessed. My mind raced with questions, though I was hesitant to ask them aloud.

In an age gone by, Jebediah and I spent entire days playing together. In those days, I asked him all sorts of questions about the world, and he would give an answer whether he knew one or not. I longed for those days and thought maybe for just a moment they could return.

The church parking lot was empty and we had to wait for the others to arrive before going in, otherwise risk having a conversation with Father O'Flacity. It was the perfect time to ask him my questions.

"Hey, Jebediah, what do you know about girls? There is a girl in my class named Molly who I've been thinking a lot about lately."

"Pshh. Girls are witches. You're probably already screwed and you're just too dumb to know it."

"I knew it!" Molly really was a witch, I thought. And Jebediah knows everything.

"You know nothing, you moron."

"Indeed I don't. But maybe you could help. As you know I've been worried a lot about magic recently. Maybe you can explain to me how Tabby got pregnant with a demon?"

Jebediah looked disgusted. "How stupid are you, kid?"

I thought hard about the question but had no answer.

"Unbelievable." He shook his head a few times. But then his expression changed. A sly smile slithered across his face. "You don't know anything do you?"

I shook my head. I don't know why he asked the question, seeing as how he regularly told me the answer.

"You got her pregnant, Humphry. It's all your fault and if I were you, I would keep your mouth shut about it and hope to God nobody else finds out."

Dad pulled his car into the spot next to us. Jebediah snorted again and hopped out of the truck, slamming his door behind him. Dad knocked on my window and waved for me to hurry along. "Best behavior, boy," he said. His voice was muffled through the glass but still biting. I trembled. This was all my fault.

We made our way to the front pew on the left of the aisle. Father O'Flacity bounded out from behind the altar. "My dear child!" he exclaimed on his approach. "God's chosen one. And who did he choose to be your priest, but me. Oh sweet child, Archbishop Fondler is going to be so jealous. Come tell me everything that happened." He led Tabby by the head towards the altar and waved for Dad to join.

The townspeople trickled in slowly at first, but as it got closer to 11:00 AM, a steady stream flowed through the back door. Once Mrs. Murflock and her seventeen home-schooled children squished into the back two rows, the church felt uncomfortably full.

The bells rang and a hush overcame the audience. The echoing walls of the church had the odd effect of making an isolated cough or shuffling of someone's bottom as loud as boisterous conversation. Father O'Flacity, whose voice was otherwise easily overshadowed, benefited from this effect mightily. The clops of his galloping sandaled feet brought everyone's attention to the front. He skipped into a two-footed jump stop on the top stair of the nave. A string pressed into the widest section of his rotund belly, keeping his flabs from jiggling.

"Dear Bethlahoomians, God's favorite children, we are coming together on a very special day to celebrate a very special girl and her very special priest. This is no ordinary day. This is the day we have all been waiting for." He smiled at the sudden eager whispers that bubbled in the audience. "Let me speak, children." The crowd quieted. "Some of you will be skeptical of what I have to say. It is not your fault. We all have moral failings from time to time. However, you must fight the devil's influence and trust wholeheartedly in what I have to tell you. My dear followers, one amongst you has been chosen by God himself to carry his child!"

The church erupted in chatter. Father O'Flacity made no immediate attempt to quiet the congregation, but instead closed his eyes and basked in the enthusiasm.

I looked around at the church. Jebediah looked solemnly at me and shook his head. How could I have messed up so badly? Mom looked equally upset. Her left arm was crossed over her chest and her right hand covered her whole face. Did she know too? I felt sick to my stomach.

The rest of the church looked like a flock of chickens after seeing a fox. They swiveled their heads all around clucking nonsense at each other. I saw Deedris in the middle of it all doing the same. There was Annabelle Sternlicker clucking away off to the side. Anatoly was not far behind. Then I saw her. Molly Mucasine. She was not clucking like the rest, neither was she swiveling. Her mouth was pressed firmly into a thin line and she stared straight at me with her brown, owl eyes bulging. Of course! This was Molly's doing.

I tried looking away, but I couldn't break my stare. She had me trapped. Every muscle in my body grew weak. My resistance quickly crumbled. I felt as though my body lifted from my seat and floated towards her. I didn't care that she was a witch. I wanted to do whatever it was that she told me. My will was hers to command. I mustered every bit of strength I had to reach my hand up to touch her but she was out of reach.

SMACK!

Dad slapped me back into my seat. "Best behavior, boy."

I wiped a stream of slobber that was dangling from my chin and checked the back of my head to make sure it had not broken open. There was no blood. I was safe.

Father O'Flacity quieted the crowd and brought Tabby out from the back. I was too dazed to follow everything that was being said. My thoughts were all about Molly and how she could possibly be involved. Try as I might, my tired mind couldn't piece it all together. Before I knew it, we were kneeling for the closing prayer.

Townspeople began pacing to the exits. Their lower bodies moved quickly, but their upper bodies remained stiff out of respect for God. It was not in good taste to sprint out of church, no matter how much everyone wanted to. The most devout members of the congregation, a scattering of octogenarians and Mrs. Murflock and her seventeen home-schooled children, stayed where they were. Some even crept towards us and away from the exit. I had never seen it before. Tabby was perplexed. She tugged on Dad's sleeve. "Daddy, why aren't we going home?"

"We'll go home eventually, sweetheart. We just need to say hello to some of your supporters. Why, here's Mrs. MacDoodle! Good afternoon, miss. How are you doing today?"

"Out of my way," Mrs. MacDoodle croaked, shooing Dad with her walker. She scooted up to Tabby and grabbed her by the cheek. Her grip had been strengthened from clinging to life several decades longer than anyone hoped she would. "You need to fatten up for that baby, girl. I had six of my own by your age with nothing to eat but the cabbage I grew and the rabbits I caught. You fatten up and get to work. I didn't come all this way for some skinny girl to mess it up." She let go of Tabby and scooted past me, down the side of the church towards the exit, muttering to herself as she went.

A line had formed to talk to Tabby. She looked to be on the verge of tears. I don't think she realized that carrying God's child wasn't a free ticket to absolute power. Who knew having a baby would require so much responsibility?

Interlude 1

Merideth threw up her hands, stopping Humphry mid-story. "What does any of this have to do with the Lovely Marlene?"

"The Lovely Marlene?"

"Oh my god. Please tell me you're telling the right story."

"Of course I am!" Humphry squeaked at a frequency not well known to communicate the truth. "It is a long story, my lady, and the beginning is not like the ending, otherwise there wouldn't be much of a story. If the ending is of the Lovely Marlene, then surely the beginning won't be."

Merideth closed her eyes and prayed desperately for patience. "I'm sorry for interrupting. It just didn't seem like you remembered what you were talking about. Just to clarify, I remind you of the time your brother convinced you that you got your sister pregnant and you blamed some poor girl in your class that you clearly just had a crush on?"

"Yes, my lady," said Humphry, though the blush of his cheeks gave him away. "I will admit that I may have forgotten what got me started on the story, but the story I tell is indeed the one you seek."

"I didn't seek this story. I was willing to tolerate it, and you are welcome to continue." She took a deep breath in. "Your poor sister!"

she yelped before catching herself. "No. I am going to be tolerant. Please, continue."

"Excellent. Now, where was I? Did I get to the part where I lived in a trash can?"

"You didn't." Merideth rubbed her temples and redoubled her prayers for patience.

Chapter 7

"Hump! I have to tell you something!" Deedris nearly bowled me over outside of church. He hopped in circles around me as we walked. I was so tired I could barely track him with my eyes.

"What is it?"

"I have a plan for Scrotumus."

"Scrotumus Spitwallow?"

"That's the one. I'm gonna get him in P.E.. Anatoly won't be there to protect him and I don't think Smelly-town will care." Mr. Smellington had proved to be neglectful at best. P.E. had thus far been an exercise in humiliation for everyone, including the athletes. Mr. Smellington was intimidated by their abilities and made them drag him in a cart while he cried. Mr. Smellington cried more than any teacher I ever knew.

"You're not going to try and beat him with a shoe again, are you?"

Deedris guffawed. "Come on, Hump. I am too old for that now. That's child's play. I'm gonna get him in front of all the girls and I'm gonna pull his pants down."

"Deedris!"

"I knew you'd act this way. Look, I'm trying to be a man, here. You can't just mosey about not pulling down other boys' pants and expect to turn into a man."

I sputtered for an answer, but I knew he was right. Becoming a man is not a passive chore and I was doing nothing to see its completion. Still, I refused to believe humiliating another boy was the only path. There had to be another way. Besides, I had more pressing issues. A witch was haunting me and a demon baby gestated like a ticking time bomb in my own home. What hell awaited me was beyond comprehension.

I couldn't formulate my thoughts into words, in part because of sleep deprivation and also because of my hesitancy to speak Molly's name aloud. Deedris circled around me a few more times waiting for me to speak, but pranced off as soon as he realized I wouldn't. As much as I wanted to confide in Deedris, it was for the best that we parted ways. I needed to focus on what was important.

It was fruitless. I tried to come up with a plan, but it was impossible without knowing what I was even up against. Sure, I knew Molly and Frankie Fourfeet were trying to destroy me, but why? What was their goal and how did I factor in? Could the church and school be binding their magical powers to harvest body hair? I had no idea. The only thing I knew was that Molly attacked while I was sleeping and therefore, I shouldn't sleep.

That night I stood on one leg while holding a lit light bulb to stay awake. It didn't work. Sleep snuck up on me and froze me in place. I awoke the next morning with a seared hand and one thigh that looked like a bodybuilder's. And yet, I had no dreams! Molly must have used up all of her power to make that demon baby, I thought. There was time to investigate before her powers were restored.

I tried asking Jebediah again that morning but was unsurprisingly met with a barrage of insults to my intelligence. That was okay. I had already written him off as a source of information. Though he held all the answers, he held them so tightly as to be useless. I was lucky to have squeezed any information from him at all.

I passed Molly on the bus. Out of the corner of my eye, I could see that she was concealing herself behind a book again. I kept my eyes straight ahead and my gait unaltered by her presence.

I continued down the aisle. Everyone went silent and stared at me as I passed. Even Annabelle Sternlicker took notice of me. Deedris was there, but we had little to say to one another beyond a standard salutation. He was obviously focused on his pending bout with Scrotumus. Our next P.E. class wouldn't be until Wednesday, so we would likely have at least two days of this respectful distance. Hopefully by that time I will have discovered something that I could share with him.

Mr. Snottworth ushered us into the art room. I did my best to fight the relaxing energy of the room. I had to stay vigilant for any clues to what was really happening. I scanned the room. Without her magic, Molly was clearly visible hiding behind the easel in the back corner. I trembled slightly and kept looking. I caught some of the students staring at me. They each turned away when I locked eyes with them and whispered to whoever was next to them. What did they know?

"Welcome everybody," Mr. Snottworth announced in his perennially mellow voice. "I hope you all had a wonderful weekend. I myself went with my friend Jared to pick peaches out in Smashtown. Should we go around the room and say something interesting that happened this weekend?"

Scrotumus leapt in out of turn. "The new Parables of Penacles comic came out on Saturday, and I got a signed first edition with matching underpants."

"We'll see about that on Wednesday," Deedris whispered to me.

"That's wonderful Scrotumus. And I suppose we can just start to your left."

Jezebel Chopsky looked around before speaking. "Well, God got Humphry's sister pregnant. Then my mom and dad got in a fight because Dad called her a skank and Mom kicked him out of the house and so now I have to feed him leftovers out the window again."

"That's wonderful, Jezebel. And you, Tommy?"

I didn't hear what Tommy had to say. Jezebel had just dropped a bomb I had to diffuse. What was a skank and how did her dad know what nobody else did?

The circle came around to Molly. Her powerful voice snapped me back to attention. "Umm... Well... A plan years in the making turned into motion. What will come of it has yet to be seen, but the fate of all rests upon its success or failure." She slipped back behind her easel.

The fate of all? How could I have been so stupid? I had been thinking the whole time that I alone was the target of this evildoing, but of course, this was folly. Why would anyone do all of this for me? I was just a pawn in a game of kings and queens.

The lineup circled around to me. I just caught the last of what Deedris was saying before it was my turn. "Suffice it to say, I'm gonna be a man soon," Deedris finished.

"And you Humphry?"

I wasn't prepared. I had so many thoughts but so little to say.

"Humphry?"

"Well, I think life as I know it has come to an end."

"That's great, Humphry. Alright everyone, let's get out our notebooks and doodle for the rest of class."

Doodling did much to settle my nerves. By the time the bell rang for History class, I was as sedated as Mr. Snottworth. It wasn't until well into History that my fears resurfaced. How was I so easily subdued? Does Mr. Snottworth not want me thinking about this either? How could someone so placid have sinister motives boiling within?

History flew by. The lesson was something about the Philandrines' capture of Arbuckle in the 1100's. We had been studying the Philandrines for the last two weeks. I could only assume that like the captures of Wickerton and Paldermore before it, the capture of Arbuckle involved copious rape and pillaging, whatever the heck that meant.

I followed Deedris out for recess. Though we were each locked into our own heads, it was understood that we stuck together. I only made it a few steps outside the door before a cold hand clutched my shoulder from behind. It spun me mid-step. A tall, spindly man stared back at me with a hell-born sneer. Principal Chewbooger.

"Good morning, Humphry," he said in a low, chilling drone reminiscent of a prowling panther.

"Uhhh..."

"Don't be frightened, boy. This is not about your tirade on the first day of school. I have chosen to show you mercy. I hope you will recognize that in my character without feeling the need to test it further?"

"Ummm..."

"I want to see you at lunch today. Come straight to my office. It is on the very end of the top floor. It will be the one with the purple streamer that says 'Happy Birthday' on it."

"Is it your birthday?" I was trembling so much I could barely mutter the words.

"It was last year. I just like the way it looks." He bent down to whisper the rest in my ear. "And I like the way people treat me when they think it's my birthday. Do you understand?"

"Yes, Principal Chewbooger, sir."

"Good. I will see you at lunch. Begone." He spun me back around by the shoulder and pushed me slightly forward.

I found Deedris hiding behind a fern. "Oh hey, Hump. What was that you were saying to Chewbooger?"

"Apparently he wants to see me in his office at lunch."

"You're not gonna tell him it was me that yelled in the assembly are you?"

"Of course not! Besides, he said it was about something else. Look, Deeds, I think there is something big going on here. I can't say too much because I don't want anyone to hear, but--" The bell rang signaling the end of recess. "I'll try to fill you in later, okay?"

Deedris nodded from behind the fern.

Paying attention in math was challenging enough on a normal day. With a meeting in the principal's office hanging over my head, there was no chance in Bethlahoom. The clock's digits were the only numbers I could focus on. I tried using a bit of my own magic, if I had any, to make the hour hand jump ahead to the end of school. By the time class ended, my unblinking eyes were red and watery, and my knuckles were stuck in balls from clenching my desk so tightly. I couldn't tell if my attempt at magic had any other effects. If anything, the hour hand had moved more slowly than usual.

I remained seated while the rest of the class raced out to lunch. Ms. Trudy, my ancient math teacher, noticed that I hadn't left. "Oh my," she croaked. "I finally have a student who wants to stay after class! Oh, thank goodness. I was beginning to think that I would spend the rest of my life alone. But here you are to keep an old woman company. Your family really is special, isn't it? Tell me, Humphry, is that why you are here? Did God send you to me?" She wobbled over to me with her cane flapping at her sides. "You are here to make me walk again! Oh, Humphry!" she yelled as she collapsed to the floor. Dead as dirt. I screamed and ran out of the classroom. Poor Ms. Trudy would be missed.

The patio felt distant, like I was seeing it through binoculars from a far away hill. Everyone was laughing and chatting, but I heard none of it. It was not my lot in life to participate in the froths of adolescence. It was my job to thwart whatever evil schemes were being hatched to destroy this sanctuary of youth. I had to be strong.

I marched away from my innocent classmates and up the stairs to the second floor. I looked down upon the patio once more to remember my purpose. I felt I was in heaven, resting on the glass dome above the earth, seeing God's children play amongst themselves, mistaking their petty trifles for something more, unaware of the cosmic forces raging and the sacrifices being made to ensure their continued squabblings.

I passed office after office. Each one carried a plaque more suspicious than the last: 'General Administrative Director', 'Senior Custodial Officer', 'Head of Accounting'. Who were these people? What kind of sick operation was this?

Finally, I saw it at the end of the path: 'Principal Chewbooger'. His door was framed by birthday streamers, just as he said. It chilled the spine. To flaunt a known lie with abandon was an undeniably potent display of power and pride. My power was nothing compared with this man. What could he possibly want from me? My doubts were raging. I had to quiet them and focus on finding answers.

The door was unlatched. I knocked on it with respectful ease, but it swung open even under my light pressure like it knew I was there.

"Come in, Humphry," an eerie voice rode the cold draft blowing from within. I followed it. Principal Chewbooger sat behind his desk. "Take a seat." He motioned to a plain, wooden chair much smaller than his own artfully crafted throne. I did as he said.

"Hello, Principal Chewbooger, sir." I could do nothing to hide my fear.

"Hello, Humphry. You can relax, you know. You are not in trouble. I invited you here to talk and have lunch. Would you like some meat pie?" He slipped on two oven mitts and pulled a steaming pie from a toaster oven on his desk.

What was happening here? Was this some test? What was in that pie? Who was in that pie? I had too many questions to have an appetite. I trembled and shook my head 'no'.

"Are you sure, Humphry? I grew up on weasel pie. It was a source of shame growing up that we could only afford weasel, but I have come to find that there is no tastier dish." He tore open the crust and heaved a spoonful of brown mush into his mouth. A single drop of goop slicked slowly down his chin. "I suppose we sometimes lack the perspective needed to appreciate what we have. Maybe in the future you will have similar changes to your attitude about me and this school. What do you think about that, Humphry?"

"I don't know what you mean, Sir. I don't think I would ever like to eat the school."

"You know what I mean." Chewbooger's guard slipped, exposing his hidden menace, but he recovered quickly. "I mean that one day you will have more appreciation for your education. You are a troublemaker, Humphry. You made that clear on the first day of school."

"I don't mean to cause any trouble, sir! I promise. It was... It was someone else who called out that day. I just took the blame."

"Humphry, Humphry. I don't care who it was. I am willing to let bygones be bygones and seek a sort of, *friendship* with you. A proclivity for disobedience is not without value."

Something about the way Principal Chewbooger said the word 'friendship' made me stir. It was like that word was toxic to him. If he said it more than once in a great while he might succumb to poisoning.

"Tell me, Humphry, how is your family doing? I hear you have a sister. Tabitha, was it?"

"Oh, yes sir. Tabby, or Tabitha I should say. She is good I suppose. She is having God's baby it turns out."

"Oh is she now? Fascinating." Chewbooger leaned over the desk and tapped his fingers together eagerly. "Such a proud brother you must be."

I groaned unconsciously. Surely I should have been quick to declare my pride, but suppressed anger from years of abuse was the first to show itself.

"Oh, you are not so pleased with her after all."

"Of course I am! I just..." I sputtered. How was he so quick to pick up on my mixed feelings? I wasn't even aware of them until now. Did he put them there? No. Those were my own. I really was angry with the way I was treated and Chewbooger had to wait for me to show that anger to know it existed. He was not in my mind.

"It's okay, Humphry. This is a private conversation. Student-master confidentiality is important to me. Secrets do nothing but burden the soul. So unnecessary. Is there a secret about Tabitha that you would like me to know? Let me be your-- *friend*." He hissed and recoiled at the word.

There was something wholly untrustworthy about this man. I had to keep my guard. He was clearly more powerful than me, and maybe he would eventually overwhelm me regardless of any resistance I showed, but as of yet he could not infiltrate my mind as thoroughly as Jebediah or Molly. I would not let him in. I would resist. "No," I said defiantly.

Chewbooger growled. "I know your type, boy. You think you're so smart. You think you're so cool. You think everyone will bow down to you just because you are you. Well, you're nothing, and I'll never do such a thing. I run this town, and if you're not with me, you'll never know freedom again."

The bell rang. I was happier to hear it than ever before. I bounced off the chair, grabbed my backpack and ran out of the office.

"I own you boy!" Chewbooger's hiss followed me out the door and spurred me to run faster.

. . .

My meeting with Chewbooger gave me plenty to think about over the next couple of days. He was clearly invested in the outcome of whatever was happening. He wanted to know more about Tabby and gain access to my mind. Was that an attempt to further the control he already had or stake a claim on the territory of some other magical force? I couldn't be sure. He was undoubtedly powerful and evil, but the connection between him and everything else was tenuous at best. How Molly was connected to him was completely unclear. As scary as Molly was, she did not seem like an agent of the school.

That Wednesday morning brought the first taste of the coming winter. Frost clung to the grass well past the sunrise. I could see my breath even in the bus. Deedris looked frozen solid in the back seat. I couldn't tell if the grave look etched on his face was from the bitter chill blowing in from the broken window to his right or the resolve of his cold-hearted quest for manhood.

Tension built the entire morning. Deedris had not confided his plans to anyone besides myself, but middle schoolers' senses for controversy are beyond the need of explicit notice. The rumors had begun. Something was going to happen in P.E.. Only I knew what it was. An innocent boy was to be sacrificed for the sake of another.

Whispers mounted into choruses of chatterings and squeals. Deedris's icy resolve was enough indication that he was the central figure involved in the unfolding event. By lunch, it was nearly a matter of past recollection for the students that Deedris was to mount a furious attack on another classmate or otherwise flash his bottom to Mr. Smellington and dance on the highest step of the bleachers just out of his reach. Equal odds were given to both outcomes.

The bell rang for the end of lunch. It echoed under the vaulted ceiling of the patio. The chattering stopped. All bets were placed. Everyone turned to Deedris who stood at his highest height and stoically marched out of the patio towards the gymnasium. Those who shared P.E. with us followed. Those that didn't, watched from the gate of the main hall for as long as they dared risk being tardy.

"In ya come, kids. In ya come," Mr. Smellington said. He liked to exert his rule as quickly and longly as possible. He gathered us to the center of the gym to make his regular announcement. "Alright, kids. As you know, my name is Mr. Smellington. My family has a long and proud history in this town. My Father was Mr. Smellington. His father was Mr. Smellington. And so on and so forth. At no point were any of their names Mr. Smellytown. Do you understand?"

YES MR. SMELLINGTON

"Good. Good. Alright everybody on the wall. I'm picking teams for Groberball." Groberball was a favorite of Mr. Smellington. It combined the brutality of dodgeball and the orderliness of baseball. There was a pitcher and a hitter, but unlike in baseball, the pitcher was on offense. He or she would throw a tennis ball filled with rocks as hard as they could at the hitter, who would, of course, get hit.

"Up first we got Mallory and Peter. Peter, you're gonna throw the ball at Mallory."

Peter and Mallory exchanged somber looks. Nobody liked throwing the balls at the girls, except maybe Scrotumus. He alone seemed to understand the importance of the game. He understood all of Mr. Smellington's games and rules and would often compliment him on his genius.

Peter and Mallory slumbered to their respective positions. Peter wound up and pegged Mallory clean on the left arm. It was a perfect pitch. There was no risk of severe internal damage, and as a right-hander, no risk of extended disability. The class applauded the effort. Peter bowed to Mallory and Mallory hid her tears until she had slunk to the back of the class.

"That's a beautiful game of Groberball, kids. Alright, let's see here. Next up we got Scrotumus and, uh, he's gonna be throwing at Billy."

Scrotumus skipped to the cone marking the pitch while Billy moped to the hitter's box, also marked by a single cone. Scrotumus lifted his groberball into the air and shouted, "for the scourging of Tantamoon!" He lunged well past the pitcher's cone, twirled several times to build up momentum and released the ball underhand only a few paces from Billy. It was a direct hit to the sternum.

"Good form!" Smellington cheered. "Good form! Well done, Scrotumus. Everybody tell Scrotumus he did a good job."

GOOD JOB, SCROTUMUS

"And Billy, I saw you flinch. Go to the back and think about what you did."

Billy hobbled to the back and the process continued. I was fortunate enough that day to be on the receiving end of one of Bethany's feeble tosses. I barely had a mark where she pelted me on the thigh. Others were less fortunate and the sour mood typical of a day a groberball made everyone forget that Deedris was planning something special. Everyone except Deedris himself.

Just after the last students limped off the Groberball court and Mr. Smellington made his usual declaration of victory for the pitching team, Deedris made his move. He gave me a stern look that I understood to be a request for moral support. I nodded gravely. Deedris would always have it no matter my opinions of his actions.

Time seemed to slow to a tenth of its normal speed. Scrotumus was cheering for victory. His love handles, bulging from his sides, jiggled thrice for every time he jumped in the air. His arms were raised and his defenses lowered. A better pantsing target couldn't be imagined. It appeared to me as proof that Deedris was doing the right thing. Such perfect circumstances were surely a signal that fate had fixed this moment in time. This was destiny.

Deedris thought so too. He looked back at me, not with the stern look of a desperate boy, but with the relaxed smile of someone looking at the end of a long and painful journey. I smiled back. I was so happy for my friend. The yellow light from the filthy sunroof shimmered on the thick dusty air surrounding Deedris and Scrotumus, a scene worthy of painting by one of the great artists whose works could only be displayed in churches.

Deedris approached his sacred lamb. Each step spun the sparkling dust clouds in ever more elaborate spirals.

Deedris was just one step away when it happened. A crow flew above the skylight. Its shadow ripped across Deedris's face. A cloud followed and the heavenly beams disappeared entirely. A stifling chill swept over us all. Time rushed back into motion. The changing tide was unmistakable. I could see recognition on Deedris's face, but he had already committed to his course. Time now raced too fast to navigate.

He grabbed the sides of Scrotumus's shorts and pulled, but they were caught in the flabs of Scrotumus's hips. Deedris's pull was not nearly enough to take them down. Scrotumus jumped once more in cheer and Deedris redoubled his effort. He yelled out in a cracking voice as he pulled down as hard as he could. The shorts broke free of flab and glided unimpeded down Scrotumus's legs. Deedris had put his full force into the pull and was unable to keep himself from falling forward as swiftly as the shorts. He smashed his face into the ground and promptly spun to a supine position. Scrotumus spun as well in midair. His feet flung forward by the force of Deedris's pantsing and he fell bare-bottomed directly onto Deedris's weeping face.

The story was retold several million times. Poor Deedris.

Chapter 8

I walked alongside Deedris to the bus. I didn't care that he was the laughing stock of Bethlahoom and that I would be similarly named by keeping his company. Deedris was my friend, and when a friend takes a butt to the face in front of the girl he is trying to impress, you stick by them. I tried telling him such, but Deedris refused all my attempts at encouragement. He took the stance that his life was over and that I should save my breath. I wouldn't give up on him that easily, but I did agree to walk in silence.

A police car flashed its lights beside the bus. Principal Chewbooger was speaking to two officers on the sidewalk, one tall and round and another short and wiry. Both had mustaches as thick as an otter's pelt.

"Deedris, look. The police are here. Why do you think they're talking to Chewbooger?"

"I hope it's for me. Going to prison would definitely make me a man."

"Deedris!" I shouted. My voice traveled far and wide. Chewbooger spun his head toward the sound and lifted his gangly finger straight at me. I felt a strike of electricity jolt through my body. "I think they're here for me, Deeds."

"Pshh. It's always about you, isn't it?" Deedris shook his head and kept walking towards the bus.

I stayed motionless for a moment before taking off across the lawn. I didn't know where I would go or what I would do when I got there, but I had to run. I hated running. If only it were a hill so that I could roll down it.

Barely five seconds passed before the bony shoulder of one of the officers crashed into my side, sending us both to the ground. He pinned my face to the dirt. "Who you running from, bucko?" he spat. "You got that magic on ya? Huh?"

The second officer lumbered over shortly after. "Cuff him, Croney," he said. "We'll question him down at the station."

Officer Croney slapped a pair of handcuffs on me and hoisted me to my feet by the armpits. "I've got you now, bucko," he whispered in my ear. "I got you for keeps."

"Is this the one, Chew?" the larger officer asked Principal Chewbooger who stood watching from the sidewalk.

"Ah, it is. Humphry. The most troubled boy in Bethlahoom. What have you gotten yourself into now?"

"I don't know," I whimpered as Officer Croney prodded me back to the sidewalk. "I think this is all a misunderstanding."

Chewbooger lifted his arm to stop our progress and leaned into my face. "Understand this," he whispered, "you mess with Chew, you get the shoe. Take him to solitary, boys."

"Well, we have to question him first," said the tall officer. "Submit a report to the district attorney. Stand trial. It's actually mostly just paperwork that we do."

"Well then do that!" Chewbooger lifted both arms and groaned in frustration before storming back to the school.

Every student, parent and faculty member stared at me as I was marched to the police car and shoved into the back seat. I could only imagine how boisterous the gossip grew once I was out of earshot. What had I gotten myself into indeed?

The police were one of the most powerful forces in Bethlahoom. Their magic came from a combination of city-issued immunity and thick mustaches. They were the ultimate hired guns. They made sure whoever was in power stayed there. The mayor used them to show how much crime he was stopping. Crime bosses used them to get an edge on their competition. It seemed Principal Chewbooger had use for them as well.

The police station was an old building of thick metal pillars and thin stucco walls. Its outside was caked in grime just like the school, a sign of its enduring power. The insides were faded beige paint and stale, recycled air.

Officer Croney prodded me through to an interrogation room deep inside. He unlocked my cuffs and pushed me in. This room had no paint. Every surface was of polished stainless steel except the one-way mirror in the back. I saw my reflection in every direction I looked. The reflection of a weak, helpless boy.

"Well, bucko, we got ya. Tell me everything you know about dark magic."

"Dark ma--magic?"

"Don't play dumb with me, kid. We already got you pinned for Ms. Trudy's death. Who else are you dealing to? Huh?"

"Ms. Trudy was killed by magic?"

"And it was you who killed her. Wasn't it? You were failing math so you offered old Trudy a bit of your stash. Next thing you know she was begging you for it. At first you took advantage, but then you got embarrassed at romancing an old lady and you decided to get rid of the evidence. Gave her an extra potent dose. She wouldn't refuse. That's what happened, wasn't it?"

He slammed the metal table with his hard plastic baton. The crack echoed against the steel walls. I covered my ears and buried my face in my lap. I was too shaken to speak.

The door behind me creaked open and the other arresting officer entered. "Why don't you take a break there, Croney. I'll take it from here."

"Heavy Jim is here to save the day. Alright, but don't be afraid to get your hands dirty. This one likes it rough." Croney hissed at me once more before leaving.

"I'll remember that," Jim said while ushering Croney out of the room. He closed the door gently behind him and took a seat at the metal table across from me. "Do you want anything to drink? Coffee? Tea? Lemonade?"

I shook my head. I didn't want to owe anything to this man.

"I'm Officer Cornwell, by the way. You can call me Jim if you'd like."

"No, thank you."

"I hope Croney didn't scare you too much. He can get a little carried away sometimes."

"He said Ms. Trudy died of magic. Is that true?"

"I'm sorry to say it is. You know, she was my teacher too once upon a time. Nobody is more surprised than me that she died a raving junkie. I'm sure you didn't mean for it to happen that way."

"I had nothing to do with it!"

"I believe you, Humphry, and I want to help. I really do. The problem is that there is just so much evidence against you. The best we can hope for is that you admit to killing Ms. Trudy and supplying this town with dark magic. If you just admit to it, I can convince the judge that you didn't mean to do any harm. Just say it clearly and into this recorder."

Jim pulled a voice recorder out of his vest pocket, clicked a button on its side and placed it in front of me. A red light blinked on and off in sync with my racing breath. Officer Jim looked so nice sitting in front of me and a part of me really believed he was only trying to help.

Another part of me knew that I couldn't trust anyone anymore, not with such a powerful witch or wizard on the loose. For all I knew Officer Jim was under the control of magic right now. It all clicked into place. I saw a flash of red in Jim's eyes. The reflection of the blinking recorder, maybe, but I thought otherwise. He was no friend. I was being targeted because I had shown a desire to resist. It was up to me to stop this evil force.

"I am innocent," I said.

The flash in Jim's eyes spread to his whole face. "It will be much easier if you tell the truth."

"That is the truth, Officer. You have taken an innocent boy and berated him for nothing. Continue if you wish, but know I will never submit to your lies."

Jim snatched the recorder off the desk and stowed it back in his pocket. "You have confidence, kid. It's the kind of confidence that comes from having too few failures. Just know this, in my time I have met countless people just like you and every one of them is rotting in a jail cell. You've never met anyone like me. If you had, you too would be in a jail cell. Enjoy your last days of freedom. They'll be over sooner than you wish." Jim stood and pushed his chair under the desk before calmly leaving the interrogation room.

Another officer came in shortly after. He was of medium height and build with slumped shoulders, a sulking face of bashful cheeks and a forced smile. "Humphry Bulgerdeen," he said, "you're free to go. I can escort you out."

I leapt to my feet. "I'm free?"

"Of course. You were just brought in for questioning. You can follow me." He led me out of the room and through the station the same way I had come in. He walked ahead of me with his head held low. I suppose I wasn't the only one having a bad day.

Three officers were entering the station. The biggest of them bumped into the officer leading me right before we reached the exit. "Watch it, buddy," he said as though he wasn't at fault. "Oh, look who it is everybody. It's Murphy The Moron."

The other officers snickered. "Murphy The Moron. Ha. Good one, Chip."

Chip straightened his belt and lifted his chest. "I heard you got taken off the Frankie Fourfeet case. I wonder why!" The three officers started laughing uncontrollably.

A lady at the front desk stood and shouted. "It was because he was too good for it. So you animals should go bug off!"

"Oh, little Murphy Moron got himself a mother! Come on guys. Murphy's mother is too tough for us." The three officers walked away but their impressions and laughter lingered.

The lady moved out from behind the desk. "Don't listen to them, Murph. You're ten times the detective they are."

"Thanks, Babs, but I think they might be right."

"Don't say that! You just made a mistake is all. How could you have known that those shoe prints came from two people with two feet and not one person with four. It could have happened to anyone."

"It wasn't a mistake, Babs. I saw what I saw."

"Oh, Murph. I believe you. You know I do."

Murphy Flannigan walked towards Babs. His somber mood disappeared in front of the woman. He held his head high. With his confidence restored, I was able to recognize him as the same officer I had met at the beginning of summer.

For a moment I thought the two would embrace, but he stopped short. He looked longingly into her eyes. "You don't have to believe me, Babs. I know what everyone thinks of me, but if I can't trust myself, who can I trust? I'll never believe something just because everyone says it's so. A man doesn't exist without beliefs of his own."

Murphy left the station with a look of determination and the unmistakable air of manhood. Babs fell back in her chair staring at the spot where the man just left. Neither paid any attention to me.

I ran out the door looking for the detective. He had said that to be a man one must have beliefs of his own. I had to find him and ask him what that meant. I needed to become a man if I had any hope of fighting the powerful wizard plaguing Bethlahoom and something told me I could trust this detective. He was not of the same cloth as those who apprehended me earlier. He worked on behalf of his conscience.

"Wait!" I yelled, but he was already in his cruiser and halfway over the hill towards the setting sun. The twinkle of his tail light slipped behind the horizon, followed quickly by the last sliver of sun. Sunset. I would be late for dinner!

I looked around to get my sense of direction. The police station was downtown about a two-hour walk from home. I didn't have that kind of time! I tightened the straps of my backpack to keep it from jostling and I ran. I ran as fast as I could all the way home.

Chapter 9

I stumbled through my front door an hour and fifty-five minutes later to find my family waiting at the dinner table. Getting arrested proved to be an ineffective excuse for tardiness. Dad nearly flipped the table in rage and suggested I get sent to military school to whip me into shape. He would have whipped me right at the table if it weren't for Mom's guilty conscience saving me. She held Dad back and asked me what happened.

"The police tackled me outside of school," I told them. "Then they drove me to the station to ask me about how Ms. Trudy died. I was the last person to see her alive, after all."

"You killed your teacher, boy?"

"Of course he didn't, Rodger."

"Well, why couldn't he have done it?"

"We're talking about Humphry here. How would he kill anyone? Clean them to death?"

"God dang it, Judy. It's not about what we think. It's about what the public thinks. I say we send him away. We can't let this come up when the Gazette's here."

"We're not sending him away."

"Fine. Humphry, you're grounded for a month."

"A month? But, but, but--"

"Do you want two?"

"No, sir. Thank you for the grounding, sir. Much deserved." I stared straight at my plate for the rest of dinner, silently eating my beets and carrots.

Being grounded was among the worst punishments a kid could face. The weekdays were somewhat tolerable. School took up most of the time and by the time it was over, the solitude was welcomed. The weekends, however, were downright inhumane. A person needs fresh air to breathe. They need the sky above their heads and the grass below their feet. They need a friend to talk to and laugh with. A game to play. A goal to reach. Locked inside for an entire weekend was torture. Getting locked up four weekends in a row could kill a boy.

My first day in captivity proved a hard lesson. When unfortunate circumstances arise, it is the shunning from others that breaks the human spirit. I was a pariah. I was used to people not noticing me. It was actually preferable to anything else, but this was different. Everyone on the bus noticed me and conscientiously averted their eyes. Their parents must have instructed them to do so. This was the standard practice in Bethlahoom for anyone deemed a troublemaker.

To make matters worse, Molly had no such respect for this tradition. The only person at the school who I wanted to ward off was more observant of me than ever. Her gaze followed me from the front of the bus to the back. Her power was returning to her. In combination with my compromised state, I was surely in trouble.

In hard times we find forgiveness for the faults of others. Deedris had been on a streak of selfishness and embarrassment that rivaled my own poor luck, but my growing frustration with him subsided with a few simple words he told me on the bus.

"I'm sorry I was a jerk," he said.

"What? Oh, Deedris. That's okay. I think everyone might be a jerk."

"Well, duh! That's why I thought it was so important to becoming a man."

"Is that why you have been so mean?"

"I haven't been that mean, have I? Oh, you don't have to have to answer that." Deedris looked ahead with the wide, shameful eyes that I used to know. "I can't believe you got arrested. Last night I thought I would never see you again, and it got me thinking about what's important. I have been so miserable trying to be a man, and if that's how it feels, I don't even know if I want to be one."

"Maybe we've been going about it all wrong. I saw a man yesterday who wasn't a jerk. At least I don't think he was. He said that a man needs to have beliefs of his own. I tried to ask him about it, but he left in a hurry. Do you know anything about that?"

"Beliefs of my own? Sounds like sissy garbage to me."

"This was definitely a man. I think it was true. Look Deedris, I need to be a man as soon as possible."

"You and me both, brother."

"No Deeds, I need to become a man so I can stop dark magic from taking over the town."

"Dark magic?" Deedris said it loud enough to get shudders and glances from two rows ahead of us.

"Shh! Deedris, don't tell anyone what I'm doing." I looked up to the front of the bus. The top of Molly's head was sticking out into the aisle and she was still staring straight at me. "I can't tell you everything just yet, but it's for more than my own sake."

"Let me help!"

"I think this might be something I have to do alone."

"Come on, Hump. You can't take on something as big as--" Deedris paused to look around before trying unsuccessfully to lower the volume of his chronically loud voice, "dark magic."

I winced at the words, but he was right. I needed the help, especially since I was grounded for the foreseeable future. I had no idea how to become a man, let alone how to fight magic. "Thanks, Deeds. Do you have suggestions on how to become a man?"

"Nope. I've tried everything in the world and none of it works."

I cupped my face in my hands. "I am very happy to have you on my side, but that is not very helpful."

"Well, becoming a man can't be all you need to do. We don't even know who's using the magic or what they're after! We should find that out first. Maybe we'll learn something about manhood in the meantime."

"Deedris, you're a genius. There's just one problem I haven't told you about yet. I got grounded for a month for getting arrested."

"A month! We're screwed."

"Well, maybe not. How about you investigate on your own? I'll get out eventually I suppose. You can tell me what you learn at school."

"You mean you want me to go around the streets looking for magic?" Deedris trembled.

"Well, at least until I'm able to join you again." It was a lot to ask of him. I wouldn't blame him for saying no. I had come to terms with the fact that my life was probably over. Deedris wasn't being haunted or targeted by the cops. He was just a regular kid. There was nothing forcing him into this trouble.

"I'll do what I can. If I make it through the weekend, I'll tell you everything on Monday."

"Thank you! Deeds, I'm really glad you're my friend."

"I would have agreed with you yesterday."

. . .

That Saturday couldn't have been a more beautiful day. It was like summer returned just to taunt my imprisonment. Breakfast was the usual affair, everybody racing to finish their eggs and toast, but I had no reason to rush. I took every bite knowing it would be the best part of my day. I savored each one, trying my best to appreciate the time I got to spend outside of my room.

I still had half a plate left when Tabby slapped my head and called me fat. It didn't hurt as bad as usual knowing the complete void of human interaction awaiting me. I eventually finished eating and cleaning and took the solemn march to my room. The door thudded shut behind me. It shut out more than the hallway air. The door to freedom and joy had closed.

Time moves slowest when it's not being used. The mind screams loudest when the body is silent. I had started my sentence at 9:02 that morning, and by 10:22 my tethers to sanity grew taught. My grip on the ropes strained. My will began to crumble. By noon my strength failed me. I fell through the backdoor in my mind where sorrow reigns.

A rustle in the branches outside my window awoke me from my tomb. Someone was out there. I stepped to the window and lifted it as gently as possible to better find the source of the sound. There were birds chirping, kids laughing, and the slicing of shears. The slicing was coming nearer. An enormous pair of blades came out of nowhere and sliced off a stray twig on the hedge right below my face. I shrieked.

A man outside yelped. It was Paulo, our gardener! Of course, I thought. He was always here on Saturdays. "Little Hippo," he said in his thick Bulovian accent. "I haven't seen you since you were a small child. You have grown much, but you still scream like a little girl."

"Hello, Paulo! I didn't mean to scream at you. I have just been locked in my room all day and wasn't expecting anyone to come by."

"Do you have the pox?"

"No, no. I am just grounded. I have to stay in this room now as punishment."

"I see. But how did Little Hippo get in trouble? I have known you since you were a baby. You were a sweet boy and you still are as I can see."

"Thank you, Paulo. The truth is that I was wrongfully arrested and am being punished for it."

"In Bethlahoom? Oh, Little Hippo. I have come so far to get away from injustice, only to see it is as close as ever."

"There were problems in Bulovia?"

"Yes, little hippo. There were many. I was in a situation much like yours before I came here."

"What happened? Why were you arrested? How did you get free?" I put my face against the window screen. I had to hear his story.

"Oh, it was a long time ago now. It started when I was a very young child. My family lived on the streets in a shanty town, and when I was old enough to stand, I began work as a scraper."

"A scraper? What's that?"

"They don't have many scrapers in Bethlahoom. A scraper is someone who goes through the rich people's trash and scrapes out the good stuff that they throw away. Sometimes it was bunnaberry jelly, and other times it was something less sweet. Whatever it was, I scraped it out. Sixteen hours a day so my family could eat."

"That is awful!"

"Pardon? I have not gotten to the bad part."

"Oh, I'm sorry. Please continue."

"One morning I was scraping like usual. A reporter man came to ask me what I thought about politics and things. As it happened, I was outside the mayor's house, scraping a jar of prescription strength foot fungus cream. It belonged to the Mayor. It had his name on it. There was a photographer with the reporter man who took a picture of me. Though I only had nice things to say about the mayor and his many creams, my name and image was used for the article they were writing. The article wasn't about his creams, but about his ties to the cartels terrorizing the country!

I saw the article in print the following week. It said the mayor bathes in creams while the people drown in screams. The picture of me holding up his foot cream became the new symbol of rebellion. I knew I was not safe. They would sentence me to life in prison or kill me. I barely escaped my shack when the policia arrived. I didn't get far. They captured me just outside of town."

"Oh no! They didn't kill you, did they?"

"Uhh, no Little Hippo. They did not kill me, but they did capture me. In Bulovia they have trials just like here. But in Bulovia they are merely for spectacle, for there are not any verdicts drawn against the government. I was to be an example for the rebellion. They would make my trial as public as possible and plant evidence against me, saying it was really the rebellion behind the drugs and violence. I was only a scraper. It was all lies."

"How did you win the trial with all that against you?"

"Little Hippo, your intellect is not so big as your belly. I did not win my trial. I escaped my jail and I ran to the water. The Bay of Buterro is dangerous for boats, let alone swimmers. I knew that I must take the most difficult path possible because that would be the last path they would search. It proved to be wise. I would like to say that I took that wisdom and used it elsewhere in my life, but I have done so seldomly. Maybe it is only for the desperate to pursue such paths or maybe it is only once in a lifetime that we have that opportunity. Whatever it was, that swim, from the Bay of Buterro to the shores of Goopland, continues to reward me every day of my life."

"Oh, Paulo. I had no idea you had such an amazing story. I thought you just grew up a gardener."

"Oh, Little Hippo. We have children like you back in my home country too."

"Paulo, do you think I should escape here too?"

"I don't know the details of your story. What exactly happened to you?"

"Well, I was arrested the other day for the suspected murder of my teacher, Ms. Trudy. Apparently, I was the last person to see her alive. They say she died of magic, but the thing is, I don't know the first thing about magic! It wasn't me, I swear."

"I worked for Ms. Trudy. She was a strange lady. She liked to expose herself to me when I was trimming her hedges. I am sorry that she has passed."

"Me too."

"Do you believe that there is anyone trying to set you up for her death?"

"Yes! But I am not sure who exactly. There is one girl, Molly, who... Well, I shouldn't say more about her. Then there is Principal Chewbooger. He hates me."

"I work for him as well. He does not expose himself like Ms. Trudy, but he is also a strange man. He reminds me of the mayor in my hometown. I would be very careful not to get into trouble with him. Who else are you concerned about?"

"Well, the last one is a bit more difficult to describe. You've heard of dark magic, right?"

"Of course I have, Little Hippo! Dark magic ruled my home country. It corrupted my government and destroyed all I knew and loved! What are you getting at with this evil?"

"Well, I think I am being targeted by the wizard who is bringing it to Bethlahoom. Frankie Fourfeet. I think he knows I am trying to stop him and is sending his henchmen to stop me."

"My poor Little Hippo, I could not have guessed it was this bad for you. I always thought you were just another spoiled Gooplandian kid who could not wipe his butt without complaining. I was wrong."

"Well, what do I do?"

"The magic trade is not something you can easily defeat. Many have tried and all have failed. This government is much stronger than where I am from, and I do believe it will resist the power of the magic cartel, but I don't believe it will be able to prevent its influence on others. Those who live in the world of magic are not confined by the government's laws. I don't worry of your arrest, but if these people are after you like you say, you are in more trouble than I ever was."

"What do I do?"

"I am sorry. I don't think I can help you in finding your path, but I do believe there is one who can. If you are like me, it will be the most difficult path. It will be the one no one else dares to tread."

"Please, tell me more about dark magic. I don't know what I am up against, only that it is terrible."

"I can not tell you more, Little Hippo. There is a wise lady who lives down the street. She helped me when I arrived in this country. She looks for goodness and honesty in a person and helps those she finds in a state of need. Her name is Betty Plumpkin. Look for Betty Plumpkin. She will help you."

"Thank you!"

Paulo snipped one more deviant branch from the hedge and slipped away out of sight. I leaned back from the window and took a seat on my bed. Paulo would have been the last person I guessed had a story so powerful and resonant. The most difficult path, I repeated to myself, thinking about what that meant in my situation. It was certainly not sitting inside, ignoring the town's destruction. The most difficult path was straight into the fight. Grounding be damned, I would act. I would see Ms. Betty Plumpkin no matter the odds.

Chapter 10

I spent the rest of my Saturday planning. Hope and action kept my mind safe from spiraling. The following morning I would be let outside for church. Tabby, being the future mother of the child of God, would demand the time and attention of the churchgoers. Dad, not wanting me to spoil such attention, would be receptive to the idea that I stood outside during the proceedings. Ms. Betty Plumpkin, if she is in fact the good person that Paulo suggested, will also be at the church. I would find her and discuss my situation in private. What could go wrong?

The eggs and toast were especially tasty that morning. "Thank you for the wonderful breakfast, Mom," I said to boorish growls of agreement from my siblings and dad, none of whom stopped shoveling food in their mouths to make such sounds.

"You're welcome, Humphry. I am always happy to make you breakfast."

I smiled and went back to eating, but a thought occurred to me. She never wants to make breakfast. My mind, sharp and fearless as it had become, was unable to see past the truth. My smile faded. The path Paulo spoke of would not be lined with satiating falsehoods.

"Daddy," Tabby whined, "Can Humphry walk to church today? I think his smell is getting worse."

"He'll ride with Jebediah again, sweetheart. Don't you worry." Dad patted Tabby's shoulder with a loving warmth that I would never receive. Jebediah exhaled disapprovingly. My value in the family came into focus. A flash of rage pulsed through me and came out in a growl. My fork scraped across my plate at the same time. My family turned suddenly to me.

"Watch your tone, boy," came Dad's punishing retort. I gave no response. I just kept eating my eggs. I was the first to finish.

. . .

Jebediah slammed his car door shut. I made sure to slam mine even harder.

"What the hell's wrong with you?" he asked.

"I'm sick of the way you all treat me."

"Maybe if you took a shower things would be different."

"If that's what you all want, then I'll never take a shower again."

"You are the dumbest kid I've ever met."

He slid the truck into gear and off we sped in silence. Jebediah had an acid tongue, but I had seen the inside of a jail. I had seen the claws of death take a life right in front of me. His power was not so impressive to me anymore. It couldn't be. Not if I were to face the full force of Freddy Fourfeet.

The church was busier than would be expected for how early we arrived. Word of Tabby's miracle had spread through Bethlahoom, and some curious members of other congregations came to see for themselves. The additional crowd meant finding Betty Plumpkin would be more challenging. I reassured myself that the additional people would also offer better concealment from the watchful eyes of Dad. The exchange might ultimately prove prosperous.

We reconvened in the parking lot and walked in as a family to project the wholesome image to which Dad so desperately clung. His head was held so high it was surprising he could navigate the church without bumping into a pew or an old lady. Pride is a strange thing. It is the greatest sin according to every teaching, yet it is the backbone for all who consider themselves virtuous. It is the veil that all other sins hide behind.

Father O'Flacity met us at the front pew. He shook Dad's hand and kissed Mom's. Tabby, he held by the shoulders and adored. His eyes passed over Jebediah and for a brief moment, landed upon me with an unholy disdain uncharacteristic of his usual priestly disposition. The moment was so brief I was left wondering if it had even happened.

Churchgoers continued to file in. The pews filled and a small group remained standing in the back, an occurrence usually reserved for holidays. Father O'Flacity seemed delighted about his growing flock. He started his sermon with gusto.

"Welcome! Welcome! We rejoice in the dawn of a new age!"

The old ladies of the church oohed and aahed as Father O'Flacity twirled around making grand proclamations. "Everyone here is vital in the plans of the lord! But what then about the people who aren't here? They are not important! It is us who were chosen!"

Father O'Flacity showed remarkable stamina, sustaining his flamboyant song and dance for the full hour of church. He told stories of biblical heroes fighting biblical foes as though he was there watching it happen, listening to God's inner voice and shouting at us with his one chance to share the knowledge beaming into him from above. "And God said to himself, 'You don't mess with me! I am God! I built this planet!' and God smote the sinner! He smote that sinner straight to hell!"

He touched on the blessed people as well. He called them 'lambs'. "God is our shepherd! We must trust his protection as we accept his blessing. He will fight the evils of the world if we come under his shield and obey his teachings. Fear not the coming doom. So long as you are pure in the eyes of the lord, the lord shall save you."

Father O'Flacity raised his hands and lowered his head, basking in the thunderous applause. I couldn't join, for I knew I was not pure. God would not keep me safe under his shield. I was a demon boy, and as such, I needed to defend myself.

Jebediah wasn't applauding either. He turned to me and shook his head disapprovingly. He alone knew my secret. I wondered if keeping it was also keeping him out of God's good graces. For a moment I thought he was making some kind of sacrifice for me, but then I remembered who he really was. Surely the years of torturing me had already doomed him. I couldn't waste time on those thoughts. I pushed them to the side and recommitted to my plan to find Ms. Betty Plumpkin.

Father O'Flacity announced that Tabby would be available at the front of the church to bless people, and a long line formed. Dad shooed Jebediah and me off and we left without question. I took a last look at the altar where Father O'Flacity had his sweat-drenched arm around the shoulder of the deeply disturbed Tabby. Maybe God was smiting her after all.

"Hey, Jebediah," I said right outside the church, "I'm going to walk home."

"But you're grounded? You better get home before Dad gets back."

"I'll take my chances."

"Whatever, fairy boy. It's your butt getting kicked." He strolled away leaving me to my plan.

I stood outside the church and waited for people to come outside. With everyone spending a few moments with Tabby, there was a manageable trickle out the exit for me to ask.

"Excuse me, mam," I said to the first lady leaving the church. She clutched her purse close to her chest. "Do you know Ms. Betty Plumpkin by any chance?"

"No I do not, and I don't have any change either." She turned up her nose and flew by me.

I asked the next person the same thing and got a similar response. Same with the next, and the one after that too. Did anybody know Betty Plumpkin? I began to lose faith. I must have asked three-quarters of the congregation before it occurred to me that I had to leave before Mom and Dad came out. I asked two more people before giving up. It was useless.

I head down the stairs to the sidewalk with my eyes at my feet. Hope had all but disappeared when I bumped into a tall, shrouded figure on the sidewalk. It was a man in a trench coat. His upturned collar and wide sunglasses hid his face. "I heard you're looking for Ms. Betty Plumpkin," he muffled.

"You know Betty Plumpkin?"

"Hey, keep it down!" He looked around making sure nobody had heard me. "I might know who you're looking for. It all depends on who's asking."

"Who's asking? I am asking. My name is Humphry. I am in a lot of trouble and my friend Paulo told me to find Ms. Betty Plumpkin."

"You're friends with Paulo? He is a good man. He helped me plant a bumbleberry bush in my nana's tea garden. If you are a friend of Paulo, then I will help you. Take this." The man in the trench coat handed me a note. I started to open it, but he slapped my hand. "Not here! Go somewhere private and tell no one about our meeting."

"Thank you, sir. I owe you a great debt. How may I repay you"

"I have too many debts myself to accept your offer. When the time comes, help the next man in need." The man turned away and sped off down the sidewalk.

"What's your name?" I yelled after him, but he did not stop. He just kept walking, disappearing amongst the other people leaving the church.

I stuffed the paper in my pocket and ran home as fast as I could. I had to make it back before my parents. I ran faster than I ever had. The way was long, but my excitement from making progress finding Betty Plumpkin was enough to temporarily mask the searing pain in my feet, calves, thighs, butt, lungs, sides and arms.

I finally came around the corner to the house. The driveway was empty. I made it back in time. I raced inside, grabbed the biggest cup of water I could and tumbled to my room. The screech of brakes let me know the others arrived. They made a loud fuss about the wonderful lunch they enjoyed on the way home. Good. Let them pamper themselves, I thought. The more they thought of themselves, the less they would think about me.

I heard a second car pull into the driveway. My window didn't have a clear view of the front, but if I stuck my head outside as far as it went, I could make out the very edge of the driveway. A second car had indeed pulled in. A woman in a fancy pair of dress pants and a blouse got out of the passenger seat and dusted herself off. She looked around the neighborhood and then spit on our lawn in disgust. "God chose this crapheap?" I heard her say. "I swear, Jordan, if they keep giving me these ridiculous feel-good bullshit stories I'm going straight to channel 6. Ruberta Calderone gets to talk about dark magic and I don't? That skank has less talent than your fat, hairy ass."

"You'll get yours, Beth. And hey, just pretend these nutjobs are telling the truth. Maybe it'll be your big break. The biggest story of the year."

The woman gave an icy laugh. "If I make these freaks believable they should build me a statue. Let's go."

I yanked my head back inside. I couldn't believe it. There was another person in my house, an adult even, who wanted to take down dark magic, and I was locked in my room without a chance to talk to her. She even used that word. 'Skank'. What did it mean?

I went to my door and pressed my ear against it. I might not be able to go outside to talk to the woman, but I could do my best to listen to everything she had to say.

"This is such a lovely home," I heard the woman say. Mom thanked her and began giving her a tour of our house like it was a famous museum. She was always excited to have another woman in the house to show off her trinkets and such. I was always amazed at how well women could pretend that they were interesting.

"Come on, Judy," Dad interrupted. "I don't think the great Bethany Blooberman cares about your collection of spoons. Let's go to the living room and get started."

Bethany Blooberman did an amazing job pretending that my dad wasn't right. My mom said nothing, but the hiss of her deep, infuriated breath was loud and clear.

The group moved into the living room, where their voices were too muffled to make out. I thought about opening my door and sneaking my head outside, but it was too risky. Jebediah might come by and snap my head off. Or worse, Dad could find me.

I looked around my room. I could still hear their muffled voices. The sound must be coming in from somewhere else. I traced the source to a vent high on the wall. I stacked my chair on the bed and put my face to the vent. It was remarkably clear. Tabby was telling the story of how God came to her in a dream. I had heard it several times by now. It was so rehearsed, I could say it along with her word for word.

"And I can only suppose," we said in unison, "that I must be God's favorite person in the whole world."

"That's so sweet isn't it," Bethany said. "And you Mrs. Bulgerdeen? How do you feel about us filming your unwed daughter's pregnancy and broadcasting her story across the world?"

Mom hissed and growled for about ten seconds before righting herself. "There is nothing that could happen to make me love my kids any more or any less than I already do. I love Tabby with all my heart. I did before and I do now. Nothing has changed."

"That's just beautiful. You must be so proud. And that's all the time we have for now. I'm Bethany Blooberman signing out from the small town of Bethlahoom, where big things are happening. All right, shut it off Jordan. Thank you so much for your time. We'll be in touch."

"Of course!" Dad responded. "And when did you say this will air?"

"If it gets picked up, sometime in the week. Probably a Thursday. Wednesdays are slow, too. Come on Jordan."

The group left the living room. I fell off the wobbly chair on my way to the door and by the time I got there to hear what else was said, the news team had left. I went instead to the window to catch any last bits of information.

"So what do you think, Beth? The story of a lifetime?"

Bethany laughed. "At least until we find out the real father is her cousin."

I pulled my head inside. My heart was racing. How did she guess that? It wasn't the truth, but it was too close to be a coincidence. I thought I had until the end of Tabby's pregnancy to fix this magical ailment, but now with an investigative reporter close on the tail, who knew how long there was until the damage was done?

Gangster Magic

I pulled the crumpled piece of paper from my pocket. I nearly forgot it was there. I unfurled it.

'You will find Betty Plumpkin at 318 W. Cornblower Lane. Knock on her door once at exactly noon and tell her you are in need. Do whatever she says.'

I crumpled the paper back into my pocket.

Chapter 11

I wasted no time that following morning meeting Deedris on the bus. I had no patience for idle speech. "Good morning, Deeds. Did you go out looking for information like I asked?"

"Oh, Hump. I, uhh, did my best, I suppose." He was hiding something.

"Well, what did you learn?"

"I learned that I don't want to go looking for magic anymore." Deedris curled into a ball in his seat and began swaying back and forth. It suddenly occurred to me that I had sent Deedris on a potentially fatal mission.

"Are you okay? What happened?"

"They tried to eat me, Hump. The alley-men. I slipped away when they were buttering up my arms."

"Oh, Deeds, I didn't mean for anything like that to happen. No information is worth you getting eaten by the alley-men." I put a hand on his shaking shoulder.

Deedris lifted his head from his knees. "It's okay. I know you didn't. And I did get some information out of it. I don't know how useful it will be. They told me about a man named Blane."

"Who's Blane?"

"They said he's the one who supplies them with their magic. It wasn't until I told them that I didn't know Blane and that I didn't have any magic of my own to give them that they decided to eat me."

"Deedris, this is exactly the kind of information I was looking for. Thank you." I patted his shoulder as affectionately as I dared under the watchful eyes of our nosey classmates, who surely already thought Deedris was a pansy for crying on the bus.

. . .

On my way to homeroom, an unwelcome hand grabbed my shoulder and spun me backwards. Principal Chewbooger looked down upon me with contempt. Deedris yelped and scurried ahead to the art room.

"Good morning, Humphry. A word?" Chewbooger asked with a conversational style that mocked the astounding power differential between us. I had no choice but to agree. "I just want you to know," he continued, "that I will be watching you every moment of every day, and if you take one false step, I will send you to prison for the rest of your life. Do you understand?"

Drawing on the sliver of dignity I had left, I kept my composure. "Yes, Principal Chewbooger. I understand."

"Good. Begone." He spun me back around and pushed me down the walkway.

Chewbooger kept his promise. Perched on the ledge of the second floor overlooking the patio, he cast his stare upon me from the moment I left one classroom until the moment I entered another. Recess and lunch, once the ultimate experiences of freedom, were now painful displays of my captivity.

Classwork felt meaningless. How could I possibly care about the pretend problems Ms. Abernathy used to teach us algebra when I was facing such monumental problems in my real life? Bethlahoom was being overrun by dark magic. People were dying in the streets and it was up to me to stop it. How did Molly Mucasine connect with the alley-men, and the alley-men to Father O'Flacity? Was Chewbooger working for Frankie? What did Tabby have to do with it, and why won't Jebediah share his secrets? These were the problems I cared to solve and they were impossible to answer while sitting in a classroom. My only hope was to find Ms. Betty Plumpkin, and even that was impossible without risking being grounded for the rest of my life.

Each day chipped away my concern of regaining freedom. My desire for the life I once lived was all but lost. That is the real cost of imprisonment. The mind habituates to torment and powerlessness. Eventually motivation atrophies and dies. Once completely gone, motivation is seldom, if not never, regained.

There is but one contradictory occurrence. The mind is made of conflicting motives. For those bound by self-imposed restraint, be it against good or ill intent, the uneven melting of competing motives can unleash a pressurized surge of directed action unbelievable to those unaware of the cosmic forces that had been previously battling to a stalemate within the tortured soul. It was such an imbalance taking shape in me. As the final bell rang on Friday, signaling the weekend had begun, my restraint took its final breath.

Dinner was meatloaf and asparagus. I finished first and excused myself before Tabby could even get the words 'little fat fairy' out of her mouth.

The crumpled paper had been stored in my desk all week. It had been so frustrating knowing where to go and what to do, but being unable to do it. That was no longer the case. I pulled it from the drawer and flattened it against the desktop.

318 W. Cornblower Lane. That's where I'd be tomorrow at noon.

. . .

I decided to eat breakfast slowly that morning, not wishing to arouse suspicion from my family. It was reckless to break from my typical behavior the night before. If I was going to get caught breaking the rules, it should be for something worth getting punished for.

"Are you alright, sweetie?" Mom asked me after the others had left.

"Of course. Would you like me to clean your dishes?" I tried to emulate my typical eager tone, but I couldn't keep a subtle glint of my rage from creeping in.

"Are you sure? You know you can always talk to me. I'm sure you have a lot of questions about everything that's been happening with Tabby and around town. Is there anything you want to ask?"

I didn't know how to respond. Of course I had questions. Questions I was willing to give my life to answer, but my mom was not the person to ask and now was not the time. I was to find Betty Plumpkin and ask her at noon. Any indication that I was in a troubled state would only increase the chances of Mom checking in on me while I had snuck out.

"No thank you, Mom. I am okay."

Mom's smile wilted. "Give me a hug then." She pulled me in tight and swayed side to side. As cold as I knew her soul to be, her hugs were as warm as any on Earth. "Thank you for doing the dishes. And if you could sweep a little too that'd be great." She left the room.

I took the next hour cleaning the kitchen. I made sure it sparkled before going back to my room. Maybe when everyone came back for lunch they would be so intimidated by my cleaning that they wouldn't dare disturb me.

Jebediah left the house right as I finished cleaning. Tabby was in her room, presumably on the phone with one of her bratty friends. She didn't go out during the day and would stay there until the evening. Mom was of course locked in her room for the foreseeable future. The only person posing a threat was Dad.

Dad was in the garage, with the garage door open, hammering away at a shelf he had been building for weeks. He kept an eye on the sidewalk outside and would stop his work every time someone passed. Dad lived to talk to people about himself. He talked about the shelf he was building, he talked about his work down at the mill, but most of all, he talked about his two wonderful children, Jebediah and Tabitha. This incessant need for jabbering was my greatest obstacle in leaving the house.

At exactly 11:00 AM I climbed into my open window and listened for the sound of Dad's hammer. The pounding was regular enough to time my steps to his swings. I could picture him looking up after every hit, hoping there was someone to talk to.

Getting into the window was less of a challenge than getting out. The hedge beneath the window was thick, and the gap between it and the house was not wide enough to fit my fully extended belly. I had to hold my breath and slide my way down as gently as I could. My feet touched the ground right as another ping of the hammer rang out. I paused for a moment, terrified my dad heard the snapping twig beneath my toes. Another ping of the hammer quelled my fear. I waited a moment and took my first step in rhythm with the next swing.

I crept to the back of the house, and from there sprinted to a line of overgrown trees that separated our yard from a concrete-lined creek that cut through our block. Jebediah and I used to search the creek every day for frogs, buried treasure and dead bodies. We never found any of them.

The creek could have taken me almost all the way to Betty Plumpkin's address, but I decided to get on the street as soon as I could. The creek smelled, and it would have only been a matter of time before my clothes absorbed its fumes. There were also sections of the creek that were no longer safe. At some point people began moving into tents alongside its banks. They looked much like the alley-men, but had a slightly different hue to their essence. It was like the difference between a frog and a toad. You would know it when you saw it, but I couldn't say what it was beyond that one lived by the creek and the other on dry land.

I made it to the address on the paper. I checked it a dozen times just to be sure. It was a wooden, two-story house just like the rest in the neighborhood. It had an unassuming white picket fence and a red brick path lined with rows of mulch that were presumably overgrown with flowers in the summer. This led to a covered patio and a double-wide front door with a brightly painted welcome sign overtop.

The note said to go to the house at exactly noon. It looked like a friendly place to enter, but this was too important of a meeting to sour over poor timing. I didn't have a watch. I stopped wearing one after Jebediah and Tabby made fun of me for pretending I had places to go. *'Hey look! Little Humphry thinks he's better than everyone else!'* They probably just didn't know how to tell time, those rotten little sacks of nothing.

I caught myself squeezing the fence so hard it might break. I looked around to make sure nobody saw. The street was clear. My anger had never made it that far to the surface before. I waited and listened for my inner-voice to tell me all the reasons I shouldn't be mad, but there was no rebuttal. I waited a little longer. Finally, a thought came to me. Don't waste your anger on a fence.

I looked up to the sun. It was as close to noon as I could ever guess. I opened the fence gingerly, but it was so well-built and maintained, it swayed open with the slightest effort. I approached the door and reached for the doorbell. If it wasn't noon, so be it.

The doorbell sounded like chimes, mellow like a trickling stream, but loud enough to be clearly heard through the closed door. Big, lumbering footsteps soon followed. The porch beneath my feet shook. Locks and latches clanked and the door opened inward as smoothly as the gate.

A heavyset woman in a thin, pink dress appeared, taking up nearly the entire doorway. Her hair was tightly knotted in a bun. Her feet bulged over the sides of her overtaxed slippers. She looked me over from head to toe. Her glasses covered nearly a third of her face. They were of such a powerful prescription that looking through them from my vantage point shrunk her face to the size of an average woman. It was like a glimpse into a different world in which Ms. Betty Plumpkin was not as round as a pumpkin.

"Can I help you, son?" she asked with a heavy drawl.

"Hello, Ms. Plumpkin. I hope so. I have been having some problems and my friend Paulo told me to find you. He said you helped him when he was in a similar position."

Ms. Plumpkin lit up at the name Paulo. "You're a friend of Paulo, you said? What a sweet little gingersnap he is. What's your name, sweetheart?"

"My name is Humphry, mam."

"I'll tell you what, Humphry, I'm on my way to get some lunch. You're welcome to join so long as you never call me 'mam' again. My name is Betty, and you can call me Betts."

"That would be wonderful Ms... Betts." It felt odd to address an adult in such a casual manner.

"Well, don't start our friendship by keeping me from my food. Here are my keys. Do you drive?"

I held out my hands to accept the keys. I had never driven before. It was profoundly illegal for a boy my age to get behind the wheel. Yet Paulo told me to do whatever Betty told me. If I wasn't willing to follow this direction, why bother asking her what else she should have me do?

"I can try if you want."

"It's the blue van right there."

We walked to the van. I made sure to be a gentleman and allowed her to use me as a walking cane.

"You remind me of Paulo," she said. "He's such a sweet little muffin, isn't he?"

"Thank you. I've never thought of Paulo as a sweet muffin, but I've always held him in high regard."

I helped Betty into the van and got into the driver's seat. There was a lever underneath that I pulled, correctly guessing it would allow me to move the seat forward. Unfortunately, I slid so fast I bumped my head on the steering wheel, honking the horn.

"Is this your first time driving, son?"

"Yes, mam."

"The name's Betty. Just put the keys in the ignition. The gas is on the right. The brake is on the left. Remember to only use your right foot, and when you start her up, you need your foot on the brake. Can you manage that?"

"It sounds simple enough." I pressed my right foot on the brake and turned the ignition. It rumbled to life. The car felt more powerful behind the steering wheel. I looked at the gears and back at Betty.

"Move it so the arrow points to the 'D'."

I did as she said. I felt the gears click into place like the car was an extension of my body. I looked out the driver's side mirror. It was slanted at an odd angle, but I could still see that no one was coming. I lifted my foot slowly off the brake. The car lurched without me touching the gas. It startled me at first, but I quickly regrouped. If Jebediah could drive, so could I.

The ride was far from smooth, but I managed to get us to the diner. I parked at the curb at Betty's direction. She said she didn't want me scratching her van, but I guessed it was also to allow her to more easily get in and out. The gaps between cars in the parking lot were not accommodating for a person of her dimensions.

Betty was a regular at the diner. She was well acquainted with the whole staff and spoke to each by name. Likewise, they all referred to her as 'Betts'. The hostess took us to a special table in the corner with a booth on one side and a chair on the other that was twice the size as the rest in the restaurant.

Our waitress came by as soon as we sat down. "Good afternoon, Betts," she said, "Can I get you two started with some drinks?"

"Oh, hi Sue. I love those earrings on you! I'll take a large sweetened iced tea, please. And let's see here. Throw in a gin and tonic while you're at it. You want something to drink, Humphry?"

"I suppose some water would be nice."

Betty leaned in towards Sue. "He's a bit on the shy side. Better just bring him a gin and tonic too."

The waitress jotted the order down. "I'll get those right out," she said and left us to look at the menus.

Betty looked natural in a diner. She commanded the staff with the full confidence of knowing that it was proper to do so. It was their job to take orders, of course, but I always felt like I was inconveniencing them by being there. Betty had no such qualms, and I admired that. She acted as if the world was hers to enjoy.

"So, what's troubling you son? You look like a scared little squirrel."

"I often feel like a squirrel, but that is not why I came. I am afraid it's more serious than that."

"Well, spit it out then."

"Okay, well," I looked around the diner to make sure no one was listening. "It's a long story. I suppose it all started this summer. Are you familiar with dark magic?"

"I've dabbled a bit, but it's really not my thing."

"Oh, well, I don't like it much either, but it seems to have taken quite a bit of interest in me."

"Here's that iced tea you ordered." The waitress seemed to pop out of nowhere. It occurred to me that when I looked around for people listening, I didn't take into account that Betty was taking up half my view of the diner. "And here are those gin and tonics. You have any questions about the menu?"

"You know, I haven't even looked! But I'll be quick, Sue, I promise. Let's see here. You know my doctor says I should really be eating more salads. I don't know why. Salads, salads, salads. Oh, this one looks good. It's got lettuce, tomatoes, onions, a little bit of bacon for flavor. Yeah, I'll take the double bacon cheeseburger, please. And if you could just bring some extra butter and gravy on the side, that'd be great."

"And for you, son?"

"I'm not too hungry, thank you." I hadn't come to eat, and I didn't have any money even if I had.

"For goodness sake, get this boy a ham sandwich. I swear, Sue, these boys just become bigger sissies every year."

Sue finished jotting down the order and looked back up. "They're less fun that way, but easier to control."

Betty laughed. "You're a bad girl, Sue."

"I'll be right back with that salad of yours." Sue disappeared behind Betty once more.

Betty waited a few courteous seconds before jumping back into our conversation. "So, you're hooked on the dark and don't know how to stop? Is that it?"

"What? No. I've never used magic before. The problem is that it's being used on me. I seemed to have angered someone named Frankie and now he's destroying my life."

"You're not talking about Frankie Fourfeet, are ya?"

"You know about Frankie Fourfeet?"

Betty's eyes widened. "Of course." She leaned over the table. She no longer looked like she was relaxing at home. "Son, I didn't mean to imply that your problems weren't serious. If Frankie Fourfeet is after you, then you've got your work cut out. How did this start? And how come you're not dead yet?"

"Dead? I can't answer that part, but how this all started is easy enough." I continued to tell her the story of finding the three men in the Summer. I spared no detail. Betty listened to every word. I had wanted her to take me seriously-- I thought having her help would make me more confident--but she was so serious that it gave me chills. I should have hoped she didn't take me seriously at all. My real hope lay in finding my paranoia had overtaken me. Every time I shared another detail and her icy expression remained unchanged, the magnitude of my troubles grew clearer.

I told her about Jebediah keeping me as a servant for the rest of my Summer and Tabitha getting pregnant with what she believed to be the baby of God. I told her that it was really me who got her pregnant while under the spell of Molly, and nobody but Jebediah and I knew. I told her about my run-ins with Principal Chewbooger and the police. The turmoil with Deedris and the Alley-men. Finally, I told her of my escape from the house and how much trouble I would be in if my parents knew where I was at that moment.

The blood drained from Betty's drooping jowls. She opened her mouth but closed it again without making any sound. She tried once more. Nothing. She tried a third time to speak. Sue the waitress appeared behind her with our food.

"God dammit, Sue," Betty yelped. "You scared the daylights out of me."

Sue recognized the tension between us. "I'm sorry, Betts. I just got your salad here, and the butter and gravy. And here's that ham sandwich for you. Anything else I can get?"

"Sue, this right here is a ramekin of gravy. I'm gonna need the boat. You understand me?"

"I'll be right back with that." Sue ran off. Betty stared silently at me until her return moments later. "Here's that boat of gravy for you. Just let me know if you need anything else."

"We won't be needing anything, thank you." Betty kept her eyes locked on me. Sue, trembling slightly, stepped backwards into the abyss behind her.

Betty dipped a fistful of French fries into the gravy and swallowed them all while maintaining eye contact. "You have your work cut out for you," she said between bites. "I'm not gonna sugar coat this, so brace yourself if you need to. You need to kill Frankie Fourfeet."

I nearly choked on my ham sandwich. "Ms. Plumpkin, I really don't think I can do that."

"For the last time, the name's Betty, and you don't have a choice. When Frankie gets someone in his sights, he never stops chasing 'em. Now, you can run away if you want, go to another country, change your name, do whatever. You might be able to outrun him for a while, but he'll find you."

"Is there no other way?"

"None."

"How do I find him? And if he's that powerful, what chance do I stand against him?"

"Frankie is strongest from afar. He has spies everywhere. His strength lies in his long reach. Keep your distance, and you'll be ripe pickings for a haymaker. You've got to get inside his inner circle. Start working for him. That's how you'll find him and that's how you'll keep him from finding you."

"But what about…"

"Killin' him? That I can't say. You won't be the first to try. I'll tell you that. Jumper Jack tried choking him with a bungee cord. He ended up being turned into a bungee cord. He now keeps Frankie's luggage tied together on road trips. As for Salty Sally, when Frankie caught her trying to poison his food, he fed her to the alley-men. The trick for killing him seems to be doing it without him killing you."

"What about my family?"

"What about them?"

"Well, are they in any trouble? And how can I start working for Frankie while I'm grounded?"

"You're not gonna do it living with your family, I'll tell you that. Don't go thinking you're staying with me either. We can't be seen together ever again after this meal."

"But, where does that leave?"

"That leaves damn near the whole planet. You stupid, boy? I'm not putting my money on you if you're stupid, boy."

"Can I stay with Deedris?"

"I don't think that's a good idea. You need a new identity. Something with no ties to your current life. Staying with your friend would be too big of a connection to who you really are." She narrowed her eyes, searing the idea into me. The thought of not being Humphry was both alluring and hollow.

She continued. "I've heard some interesting things around town. Frankie is dealing with a little rebellion in his ranks. There are always upstarts trying to make a name for themselves by overthrowing him. You should try to find out who they are and join them."

Neither of us spoke for a minute or so. Betty took the break in conversation to polish off her plate. She drained her iced tea and gin as well. She started looking around for more. I slid my own drink towards her. I had tried alcohol before and couldn't stomach it.

"You sure you don't want a drink after what I just said?"

"I'm sure." As difficult as this news was to take, there was no part of me that resisted. I felt no need to quell any grief or shame. The discomfort I felt was from needing to know the next step to kill Frankie. Alcohol wouldn't help with that feeling. I needed action. I needed to know more about Frankie Fourfeet.

"Betty, tell me everything you know about Frankie and dark magic."

Charlie D. Weisman

Chapter 12

Betty raised her empty cocktail glass above her left shoulder and twirled her free hand above her right. Moments later, Sue returned with two more gin and tonics. She disappeared again without saying a word. Betty took a long drink from one and set it back on the table.

"I can tell you everything I know, but you need to promise me that you won't tell anyone who told you this."

"I won't tell a soul." It was a reasonable request.

"Good. Frankie's real name is Sam and we used to be lovers."

"What?"

"This is going to be easier if you don't interrupt me every time I say something."

"I'm sorry. Please continue."

"We grew up in East Brookings, just outside Caddermore. It was even less developed then than it is now. There was nothing to do there but make trouble, and Sam did it best. He had a way about him from the beginning. Always a smooth talker. He was the first boy to really develop, if you know what I mean. Strong. Independent. Hairy."

Betty scowled and took another sip from her drink. I took the moment to think about my own attributes. They were far from Frankie's.

"I was a catch back then too, if you can believe it." She raised her eyebrows, daring me to question her. "This was forty years ago, mind you, before you go thinking I'm crazy. A lot can change in that time. A lot always changes in that time. Try not gaining 300 pounds in that time.

Anyways, Sam asked me out the summer before High School. I of course said yes. It was probably the best time of my life. We met every morning at the top of Cob Hill and spent the whole day sharing our secrets. How in the world two kids have so much to tell each other is beyond me. There were so many things I never told anyone and every time I shared something with him, we got a little closer. We started bumping shoulders together. Then we started holding each other's hands. Then one day in late August, over by the creek, he kissed me. If all of life could be like that kiss...

Well, it turns out it can't. That was the best of Sam. I don't know if we just ran out of secrets, or if you just can't talk and kiss at the same time, but our relationship peaked that day as far as I'm concerned. Sam might say otherwise. We disagreed about what made that summer so nice. He thought it was the touching and kissing. I thought it was all the talking we did. From his perspective, our relationship was just getting started. Even though I knew he was wrong, I was willing to do whatever it took to feel that special moment again. He got me hooked. And as it turned out, nobody was better at getting people hooked than Sam." Betty scowled and took another drink before continuing.

"He got into a bad crowd. It was expected for boys to go out smashing mailboxes, but his crew was out stealing tires off parked cars. He got caught for the first time as a sophomore in high school. I hoped it would scare him straight, but he had some wires crossed in his head. All it did was convince him that he was a criminal. He seemed to think jail was a place to learn and school was a prison. He got caught a few more times, and every time he came back from juvie with a new hustle to try. That's where he learned about magic from a boy named Grant Filmore.

Grant was a boy from the city. Magic had been making its way through the underground scene for a few years over there. Apparently he was making good money as a dealer. Good for a kid, anyways. Grant was small time. Sam saw that right away. Sam was the smartest boy around, despite always making the dumbest decisions. Go figure that one. He figured if he was the first person in East Brookings to be moving magic, he should be higher up on the food chain. You see Grant had a boss so to speak, and his boss had a boss, and they were all in the same city. If Sam was the only person in East Brookings, he should hold the highest title there. I guess you call that ambition.

Sam was obsessed. He started ignoring me and focusing all his attention on getting his magic. He needed to get a connection straight to the source and that took him some time. I still don't know how he did it. He wouldn't tell me. He wouldn't talk to me at all. You'd think I'd catch on to how little he actually cared about me. In retrospect it's clear as day, but at the time it wasn't so obvious. I think sometimes you care about someone so much that you just assume they feel something towards you even though every sign says they don't. He still expected a physical relationship with me, but anytime I would ask something of him, it would bring out his bad side. It's funny, his bad side seemed fine when it was directed at other people. I don't know why I didn't see that's just who he was, and the closer I got, that's what I would find. Dumb, Betty. Dumb." She shook her head and drank some more. There was a far-off look in her eyes that made me trust what she was saying. It was like she was reliving the experience while she spoke.

"I wasn't the only stupid little girl in town. I caught him feeling up Marissa Dumbleberry by the dock one day and I damn near killed them both. That little lying bastard. I was so angry I couldn't believe it. I hate being angry. There's nothing that feels worse to me, and I knew it was him making me feel that way. I could pretend that when I was sad, it was just because I'm a sad person. I could believe I felt alone because nobody wanted to be with me. I could believe a lot of things that weren't true, but I knew then as I know now that I am not an angry person. That anger was from dealing with him, not me." Betty dabbed her eyes with her napkin and took a few deep breaths.

"I'm so grateful that I felt that way." She laughed through her strained breathing. "This was right before he finally set up his connection. Had it happened any later, I probably would have been the one he tested it all on. Instead, I hated him so much that I never touched the stuff. Poor Marissa died that same week. The coroner didn't know what magic was, so the cause of death was just heart failure, but I know what really happened. You know what Sam did after that?"

I shook my head.

"He celebrated because he knew he had the good stuff. Isn't that just something else?

The magic obviously destroyed the town. Nobody had heard of it in East Brookings before and no one was prepared for it. We had your typical booze bags living in the gutter, of course, but that was it. People just thought it was harmless fun. When you're young and strong, killing yourself can take so long you don't even notice you're doing it. And then when it finally happens it's just that much harder to trace back to the source. The whole town went to shit."

Betty slurped the last of her drink. She looked into the glass, judging if it were worth trying to sip again. She opted to just set it back on the table. She didn't gesture for another one either. Instead she leaned back in her chair looking defeated. I was sympathetic to her anguish, but she clearly had much more to say, and whatever lack of desire she had to say, I had more than enough desire to hear it to compensate.

"What happened after that?" I asked. "Why did Sam change his name?"

Betty looked at me with tired eyes. "You know something, son? You're real' good at getting people to talk. I was watching you earlier, wondering what skill you could possibly possess. I'll tell you right now, it's not driving. But now I'm starting to see it. You look vulnerable and that makes people feel comfortable saying things around you that they wouldn't say otherwise. You're not vulnerable though. That's the thing that makes it odd. You're just honest, and that confuses people."

I thought for a moment about what she meant. She clearly did not understand my relationship with Jebediah. "That's an interesting thing to say, but I am afraid people are more than capable of holding their tongue around me."

"Of course they are. I don't mean you're all-powerful with it. Clearly you don't even know what I'm talking about, which means you've never used it consciously. That's for the best, I guess. I think people who start using their gifts young do so because they don't question their own quality. That's why you should never date a boy. If they have the confidence to talk to girls at a young age, they're a goddamn psychopath." Betty scowled and twirled her right hand above her head again. Sue dropped off another round in mere moments. Betty gulped one down and delved back into the story.

"Sam was riding high for a while. He's the type to only be satisfied by getting more. East Brookings wasn't big, but it still took some time to take over, and all that time he was getting richer and more powerful. He got some of the police on magic. He got the city council. The mayor was shit to start with; that was an easy get for him. But once East Brookings was his, he soured. Again, he doesn't care about having something, he cares about getting more than he already has.

It took a different level of evil to get more after that. He couldn't just throw around some magic and expect to take over Caddermore. Magic was already there and the people supplying it weren't about to give up control. He had to kill them. He had to kill all of them."

"But what about Grant Filmore? Wasn't he one of the people supplying magic in Caddermore."

"He sure was. Sam pretended to be his friend. He said that he wanted to be a dealer just like Grant and get to know everyone he worked for. The problem was that the people he worked for knew that a man named Sam was running East Brookings. You can't do everything Sam did without making a name for yourself. That's where Frankie came in. Sam said that it was really a man named Frankie who was controlling East Brookings, and that he was the scapegoat in case they ever got caught. He said that Frankie had built an army and was planning an attack on the Caddermore Cartel. Sam was just there trying to give them a heads-up so that they weren't caught unaware.

Grant believed him. Everyone believed him. He met with Grant's boss and told him. Then he was taken one step higher. And so on until he had met everyone, convincing them that Frankie was going to attack. They were obviously paranoid to begin with.

Meanwhile, Sam was taking the time to get his hands on as many explosives as he could. He learned about all their safe houses. He knew where everyone lived. And he knew that the night before Frankie's supposed attack, they would all be filled with members of the cartel shipped in to defend Caddermore. He blew them all to pieces. Hundreds of people died. Not even half were actually in the Cartel. And that was the last thing Sam ever did. Kill hundreds of innocent people, including his best friend."

"He killed his best friend?" I thought about Deedris. The thought of doing anything to hurt him was beyond comprehension.

Betty gave a solemn nod. "You know, I never met Grant, and I really have no reason to feel anything for him. He's just another guy, but knowing that Sam killed him the way he did after pretending to be his friend, it makes me feel really sad for him. Just like Marissa. I hated them both for what they did, but the truth is that Sam is the evil one. I don't know if either of them were anything special, but they weren't like Sam either, I don't think. Nobody is that evil."

"How did Sam get away with it? Surely if you know, others do too? Where were the police?"

"Well, like I said, that was the last thing Sam ever did. He went missing, and if you go missing at a time when hundreds of people die in an explosion, people just assume you were one of them. The police never even looked for him."

"But then what? If he disappeared, how is he still around?"

"Sam planned it all out. He had been telling his workers in East Brookings about Frankie, too. He set up lines of communication to Frankie before he left that way his minions could continue operating for him if he ever disappeared. Mail, telephone, messengers, that sort of thing. Like I said, Sam was a really smart guy. By the time of the explosions, he had already taken himself out of all of the operations of the business. When he disappeared, nobody really cared, because at that point everyone thought it was the mysterious Frankie who ran the show. I think I still might be the only person to know the truth. And you too, of course." She took a few more sips of gin. Acknowledging that her secret had been shared seemed to lighten her mood. She was no happier or more confident, but the edges of her nervousness were dulled. She seemed content.

"Is that still how it works? Frankie rules from afar through secret messages? How will I find him?"

"I don't know, kid. That all happened a long time ago. It was pretty obvious to me what he did in Caddermore, but after that, who knows? I know he wasn't satisfied, obviously. He went to conquer new territory, starting in the southeast. I ran as far northwest as I could, all the way to Bethlahoom. How he went about taking over Goopland is something I chose not to think about. Sometimes we have that choice and I made it as long as I could. I never thought he would make it this far."

Betty twirled the ice in her cup with a short straw in her drink she had yet to touch. She seemed to have reached the end of her knowledge of Frankie. It was much more than I expected her to have, and yet so much of it seemed inconsequential. She didn't know where he was, what he was doing or who he was doing it with. She just knew the boy he once was and the danger he posed as an adult. It was a good start, I suppose.

"Thank you for telling me this," I said. "There's little I can promise you in the way of results, but I will do everything in my power to make things right. I will find him and I will kill him for what he has done."

"Thank you, child."

Betty waved down Sue and asked for a check. Sue brought it out immediately. "How was everything? Do you need any change, sweetheart?"

"No, thank you, Sue. Everything was amazing as always. I'll see you again tomorrow."

"Looking forward to it, Betts."

Betty threw down some cash and got to her feet. She wobbled about for a moment before steadying herself on her chair. "You still have my keys?"

"Would you like me to drive you home?"

"I think that would be for the best."

I escorted Ms. Plumpkin back to her car and drove her home. She closed her eyes the whole way. Driving felt more natural the second time around, though I was still far from masterly. It helped that the watchful eyes of Betty weren't bearing down on me.

I parked on the street in the same spot outside Betty's house. I quickly unbuckled and made to hurry outside to open Betty's door, but she placed a hand on my arm to stop me. "Son," she started, opening her eyes and turning to me, "I'm sorry you got caught up in this. What comes next in your story is not going to be fun. You're doing just about the most dangerous thing you can do, and you're probably going to die doing it. I wish there was another way for both of us, but there just isn't.

With that being said, I've changed my mind about something. I want you to come see me again. Don't get me wrong, you're not going to stay with me, and I don't mean you can come to me when you get a little scared. You're going to be scared and you should be scared. I mean when you've found that group of rebels and are planning your attack against Frankie, come find me. I've always dreamed of defeating that evil man. Instead of doing it, I've done nothing but run as far away as I could. Well, I'm done running. I believe in you and when the time comes, I want to help. Just remember to come alone."

"Thanks, Betts. I believe in us too."

Chapter 13

I took my time walking along the creek. I would be making a home for myself there and it was good thinking to scope out a spot while my belly was full. The winter would be tough, and having shelter would be the difference between life and death. Already the nights dipped below freezing now and again. In the winter, there would be weeks that didn't get above it. It was ambitious enough to believe I would live to see those cold winter days, let alone survive them.

I found a cozy patch of land on a small tributary of the main waterway. It was in a part of town my family would never chance upon. There were thick pine trees surrounding the spot that wouldn't grow bare in the winter, perfect for staying hidden. The creek smelled of old socks. I would have to get used to it. Hopefully the smell would deter other people from wandering in.

I took note of every landmark I could find on my way back to the house and positioned fallen branches into X's along the way. I didn't want to forget where I had found my new spot. Its quality laid in its difficulty to be found and without leaving a trail of markers, it would be impossible to find again, especially in the middle of the night when I was to go back. It's often our most desirable qualities that isolate us.

The Autumn sun dipped low in the sky, giving ample room in the shadows to scurry in secret. A line of darkness stretched from the roof of my house to the bushes along the creek where I hid. I watched the yard for some time, hoping to see some sort of proof that I wouldn't be caught running across it. There was no use. No such proof existed. Waiting for certainty is foolhardy. I ran.

I made it to the wall and slid in the gap behind the hedge. My breathing was heavy and my belly scraped against the prickly twigs with every inhalation. Dad was no longer in the garage. If he were, he would have heard me. Fortune was on my side. I wasn't sure why no one was there to take notice of me, but I was grateful. It didn't matter why they weren't around. They could have been having a party celebrating how much they all hated me. All I cared about was sneaking back into the room unseen.

The window was still open. That was a good sign, I thought. Had anyone gone in to check on me, they would have closed it. Nothing was quicker to enrage my father than an open door or window to let the bugs in or the heat out.

Alas, there was a problem. It had been easy to get into the window from the inside with the help of a chair, but I had no chair on the outside and the ground was a full step lower than the floor of my room. I could barely get my elbows up to the windowsill. I clawed and pulled, but my plumpness anchored me. I needed higher ground.

I used my hands to build a platform of dirt. The soil was soft and easy to dig. Paulo once told me that to grow a bush you must first grow the soil in which it will grow. It pained me to undo his great work, but of all people, Paulo would understand the necessity.

I built the mound to the height I needed several times, but each time I stepped on it, the dirt compressed to a fraction of its peak. Finally, I decided to build the mound to the full height of the window. I had to climb atop the mound on all fours when it was complete, but it was a success. Even after compressing, I was able to stick my torso through the window. I was so excited I jumped and plunged onto the floor of my room, crashing into the chair I had left there. The chair toppled, hitting a lamp that teetered back and forth before shattering on the ground with a bang. There was a silence that followed in which I saw my whole life shatter to dust just like the lamp.

A roar came from within the house, followed by thunderous footsteps heading my way. My dad slammed the door open so hard it bent the hinges. He stood in the doorway, a terrible silhouette of raw power and rage. I averted my eyes only to see the broken glass on the floor. I would be in so many pieces soon. I looked down at my clothes. They were covered in dirt, as though he had already buried me in the backyard. This was the end, I thought.

Dad reached out his left hand to hold me in place while he raised the right to give the killing blow.

"Rodger, stop it." My mom's voice was thin and raspy but snapped like a whip. She had come to save me.

Dad was paralyzed with indecision. He still held me by the shirt, but there was a crack in his resolve. His hand trembled like he was trying to resist a force much greater than his own. It was Mom's. I always knew she was more powerful than Dad, but she never showed that power. It was just evident by Dad's complete subservience. Now I was seeing it first hand on display, and it was being used to protect me.

"But the mess," Dad pleaded. "The noise. For God's sake, Judy, this boy needs a beating."

"We have company, Rodger. There are reporters outside. You can't beat your kid with reporters in the kitchen."

"Can I beat him when they leave?"

"Fine. Humphry, clean up this mess and don't come out for dinner. You're filthy."

Dad released me and stepped back. Mom shook her head at both of us. I was wrong. She didn't come to save me; she came to make sure Dad waited for the reporters to leave. Mom had no love for me, and I would never again entertain the idea that she did.

They left me to clean, but I had no intention of doing so. Instead, when they were out of earshot, I snuck down to the basement. Jebediah wanted to go camping one year, and my parents bought him every piece of equipment he could think of. They were all still unopened and tucked away in the basement: a tent, sleeping bag, pocket knife, a pot, fire starter, stove, massaging chair and more.

It was more than I could carry in one trip, and that was before I packed all my clothes. I had planned on taking all of it over the course of the whole night, but I no longer had the time. The beating to end all beatings was looming. I had to be gone before the reporters were. If they were staying for dinner, that gave at least a couple of hours. I couldn't afford to assume they would stay any longer than that.

I took what I could up to my room and lowered it out my window. I stuffed all the clothes I could into a trash bag and tossed it outside too. In total I had a tent, sleeping bag, clothes, a trash bag full of canned food, a knife, lighter and a single pot.

I looked over my room one last time. There was nothing to miss but misery. I hopped out of my window and began moving my things over to the creek. Knowing everyone was in the dining room allowed me to move through the bushes with haste. They wouldn't hear me from there. It took three trips to get everything by the creek. From there, I had about an hour to move everything to my secret spot.

Two trips in and my legs ached. The bag of clothes I left for last felt heavy in my arms. I didn't want to continue. Night had come. I was cold, hungry and tired. I looked through the bushes at the house. My bed was only a few strides away. I wanted to sleep so bad.

"Humphry!" Dad's yell woke me up. "YOU ROTTEN LITTLE RAT!"

Dinner was over and Dad had seen I was gone. There was no going back now. I ran.

The way was ingrained in me now. The markers I left were needless and I kicked them as I passed to make sure no one else used them to find me. Dad's screams spurred me all the way to the hideout and didn't stop for hours afterwards. It must have been the loudest and longest anyone had ever yelled.

The tent was bigger and more complicated than I had expected. Somehow three giant sheets and fourteen metal rods created a tent. It took most of the night to realize I had no hope of assembling it in the dark.

The sleeping bag was much easier to understand. I unrolled it and climbed in. I closed my eyes and wished for sleep, but between the haunting echoes of my name and the rocky ground beneath my bottom, it was not yet in my power. I lay awake for hours more until at long last my exhaustion overcame my adrenaline.

...

The sun awoke me sometime around noon. I was late for church! It took me a moment to calm myself down. Church was nothing but an oddity of the past. This was the first day of a new life. I was no longer Humphry Bulgerdeen. I was an outcast, a free boy. The day was mine to live as I chose.

There was a brief time in that first afternoon alone that I felt a respite from all my troubles. There was no chance of getting yelled at or beaten. I had the fresh, sock-smelling air to breathe. It was clear why so many people lived by the creek. It felt like my natural habitat. The city was some strange form of captivity. In a different life, I believe I was a frog, and I believe I was much happier then.

But the respite was just that. The weight of my life returned with every bit of urgency it ever had. The doom of man is consciousness, and my stream was steep and full of rapids. It wasn't long before it flowed back to the encroaching doom. There was no time to spare on empty wishes of being a frog. I was a boy, and my city was under attack.

Chapter 14

The Alleymen lived across the tracks in a cross-shaped alley between the four poorest buildings in Bethlahoom. It was long believed that to be a man one must be able to get as close to the Alley as possible without running away. Trial by Alleymen, it was called. Enough boys had tried it without becoming a man that it was eventually recognized as a false promise. Courage was said to be an essential ingredient to manhood, but it was all too easily confused with recklessness. The Alley still held importance as a schoolyard threat, but aside from Deedris, no one had stepped foot in the Alley for years.

I came to a stop outside the southern entrance. There were four known entrances to the Alley, one at each end of the cross. I chose to stake out the southernmost point as it was closest to Deedris's house, and presumably the one that he had entered when he learned about Blane. I wished I had asked him more about his experience, but he was so traumatized it was probably for the best I didn't. Poor Deedris.

Blane was my only lead. I didn't know anything about him beyond his supposed role in delivering dark magic to the Alley. As one of the most magical places, I assumed whoever was supplying its magic would be a powerful wizard in his own right. It was for this reason I decided to learn as much as I could from the safety of the trash can across the street.

I watched the Alley all day but saw no one resembling a powerful wizard. It was foolish to believe I would on my first day out. It was unlikely I would see him on any particular day, but every day of the following week I skipped to that trash can with the full expectation of finding Blane. Every night I sulked back to the creek disappointed and hungry.

Rationing my food was taking a toll. Beans were my staple. I had lima beans, kidney beans, pinto beans and of course, the flavorful garbanzo. I thought I had brought enough for the winter, but in a slight miscalculation, with my best rationing, I was halfway through my beans in just one week. Running out of beans meant running out of time. Something had to change.

I brought an extra serving of beans with me to the trash can the following day. I would stay there for the night if I had to. I had assumed Blane worked regular hours, but wizards are not like other people. He could just as easily work in the evenings and possibly even overnight.

The day dragged on just as the others did. There were plenty of people walking around, but no wizards. Just hoards of regular folk going about their leisurely Monday. Why did so many people live by the Alley? As far as I could tell from within my trash can, it was by far the worst smelling part of town.

The crowds dispersed by sunset. The street lamps ignited just before the final light of the sun dimmed completely out of the sky. The entrance to the Alley was in the dark section between two street lamps. It wasn't long before it disappeared in the moonless night.

Hours crept by. I opened my last can of beans hoping it would help keep my eyelids up. If it helped, I couldn't tell. My blinks got longer and longer. Sleep was beckoning me like a siren. I had to do something. I had to stay awake. I put the fingers of my left hand over the edge of the trash can and with the right hand lifted the lid. How can someone be strong enough to lift a metal lid and not an eyelash? That was the question I asked myself while slamming my poor little fingers. The pain brought me the extra minutes I needed but at a heavy cost.

A shadow moved under a lamp down the street. I was just quick enough to notice it before it disappeared into the darkness. It appeared again moments later beneath the next street lamp. It was moving towards the Alley. The shadow walked under the final lamp before the entrance. The outline of a man was clearly visible now. It disappeared again into the darkness. I watched the light under the next street lamp and waited, but the shadow appeared no more. It had entered the Alley.

I tipped over the trash can and tumbled out. The crash of metal against concrete echoed around the empty neighborhood. I brushed off a banana peel resting on my shoulder and rushed to follow the shadow into the darkness.

It was like stepping into another world. The Alley smelled of cats and cheese. The air was thick and slowed my pace like I was trudging through mud. My eyes adjusted to the darkness. Alleymen were curled in blankets along the walls. Any one of them could eat me whole. What was I doing?

I panicked. I twisted all around, fearful that someone was sneaking up on me. This was too dangerous. I had to go back. But which was the way? In my panic, I lost it. I picked a direction and tiptoed as quickly as I could.

Nothing looked familiar. A dumpster on my left had a pair of men's underwear hanging from it, not a bag full of used needles like the one I saw earlier. I went the wrong way. I was deeper in the Alley than any kid had ever been. I had to go back. I turned. There was an Alleyman blocking the way. I couldn't go back. I had to go through.

I kept moving. I had to be nearing the heart of the Alley where all four paths converged. My heart was pounding in my throat. Then I saw it up ahead. It was the shadowman. He was standing in the heart of the Alley making an exchange with one of the Alleymen. I stood and watched. The Alleyman bowed and pleaded with the shadowman. He bent to his knees and tried kissing the Shadowman's feet. The Shadowman kicked him away like a stray dog. This was it. This Shadowman was the wizard Blane.

A hand fell on my shoulder. The Alleyman who was blocking the path earlier had been following me. I screamed. I shouldn't have done it. The other Alleymen stirred from their cardboard boxes and rags. I swatted the hand from my shoulder and ran towards the heart, towards the wizard Blane.

Blane noticed me coming. He must have also seen the swarm of Alleymen chasing me because he began running down one of the other paths. I followed. Blane was much faster than me, but with the added pressure of a horde of hungry Alleymen, I did surprisingly well at keeping it close. His shadow stayed just at the edge of my line of sight.

The light from the street glowed up ahead. The shadow of Blane passed through it. I was almost free. The Alley would take no victims tonight. I strained for every bit of strength at my command. I took one final leap towards the light.

A hand snatched my ankle, sending me face first on the filthy cobblestone. Half my body was on the sidewalk, the other half was still in the Alley being gnawed by Alleymen. I clawed at the ground, trying to pull myself free, but it was no use. "Blane!" I yelled. "Help me! Blane!" My grip on the cobblestone failed and I slid back into the Alley. All was lost.

The wizard Blane came rushing back. He kicked off two Alleymen with a single roundhouse. He swung a stick that sent another flying. The rest cowered back in the Alley. I looked up with the last bit of strength I had left. The wizard Blane stood triumphant, basking in the light of the streetlamps. My hero, I thought, before all went black.

Chapter 15

I awoke on a couch. It was daytime. I was in a small, dusty living room that was somehow also a dining room and a kitchen. And just to the right of the fridge appeared to be the front door. What kind of circus house was this?

A toilet flushed behind a second door. Out came a young man drying his hands on a cloth that he threw to the ground behind himself. "You're awake," he said. "You should drink some water." He pointed to a glass on a table in front of me. I took one sip that ignited a voracious thirst and chugged the rest. I looked around for more but was met with the end of a staff hanging inches from my face. "Why were you following me?" The man asked. His welcoming tone had vanished.

"Are you the wizard Blane? I have been searching for him. I was told he is a strong wizard who deals in magic."

A second man walked out of a bedroom. "Strong wizard, eh? What kind of nut did you bring here, Blane?" The new man talked like a leprechaun, a powerful magical being. Suspicious company to keep for anyone but a wizard.

"Shut up, Seamus. He's just a kid."

"Nuts come in all ages, you know." Seamus walked to the kitchenette and poured himself some coffee.

"Screw you," Blane muttered to himself, before refocusing his attention. "What do you want from me?"

"So you are Blane, the powerful wizard."

"Stop calling me a wizard."

"Whatever you say, Blane the Powerful."

Seamus snickered. "I think he wants to make love to you, Blane,"

Blane held his middle finger high. Seamus just laughed harder.

"Cut it out with that shit. My name's Blane. That's it. Now why were you looking for me?"

"I'm sorry for upsetting you. I came to you because..." I looked at the two young men. Neither could be trusted with the whole truth. Certainly not this new man, Seamus. "I want to work for you." That was as much as I could say.

Seamus slapped the counter. "I say we put him on the corner and see what he's worth. A lot of freaks and dandies be walking about these parts."

"We're not pimping out little boys, dude." Blane lowered his staff. His frustration of Seamus superseded his suspicion of me. "Look, kid, I don't need anyone working for me. Whatever you heard about me or this whole business isn't true. You don't want any part of it."

"But I must! Please, Blane. I'm desperate." I got to my knees and begged.

Seamus was delighted. "I swear, this kid would make a killing on the corner."

"You both need to shut up. You're not working for me and you're not a pimp."

"Alright, we won't put him on the corner, but you got to take advantage of this somehow. That's how you get ahead in life, you know. Get people to work for you." Seamus approached. He put a hand on Blane's shoulder and looked me over head to toe. "Jesus, this is the grossest kid I've ever seen. Where the hell did you find him?"

"He's been hanging around the Alley watching me. He lives in a trash can. He followed me on a sale last night and the Alleymen got him. I had to yank him free. Good thing they don't have teeth."

"A trash can, eh? I guess it makes sense. Who else would ask you for a job?" He laughed at his own question. "You gotta start somewhere, though. Homeless kids can work as well as anyone."

"I don't think this kid's homeless." Blane pointed his staff at my feet. "Look at those shoes."

"What about them? They look like he found them in a trash can."

"They're Jontleys. My Grandma used to wear them to help with her corns. They're expensive." Blane prodded me in the chest with his staff. "What's your name?"

"My name? It's... It's..." I couldn't say my real name, and I hadn't thought of a fake one to use. I racked my brain. What would Ms. Plumpkin want me to say? I found it, the perfect name. At once an homage to my adviser Betty Plumpkin and also a reminder of my purpose to find and take down Frankie. "My name is Frumpkin."

Blane dropped his staff and yanked at his hair with both hands.

"Blane and Frumpkin," Seamus said. "The unstoppable duo. I trust the home is safe with you two at the helm." He laughed and punched Blane's arm. "I'll see you lovebirds around. Good luck on the corner there, Frumpkin. " He finished his coffee and threw the mug in the sink on his way out.

Blane rubbed his temples. "Your name is Frumpkin?"

"Yes, sir."

"What kind of name is Frumpkin," He mumbled to himself. "Alright, listen. I know you have a place to go. Those shoes are too expensive for a kid who lives in a trash can. I don't know why you're following me, but it's got to end now. Go back home."

"But I can't go back!"

"Well, you can't stay here, either. Come on. Get up." He grabbed me by the shirt and dragged me outside. "Go home," he shouted and slammed the door shut. A pulse of air rocked me to my heels.

Where was I supposed to go? I didn't have a home. What I used to call a home was just a den of thieves, stealing every bit of joy I showed them. I couldn't go back even if it was a home. If my dad didn't kill me the moment he saw me, I would be a sitting duck for Frankie to come and kill us all. Blane was the only hope I had, and I wouldn't give up on it that easily.

I made my way back to the creek to eat some beans and rest. Now that I knew Blane was a wizard of the nighttime, I too would have to become nocturnal. It was tough going to sleep that morning, but I managed.

. . .

Sixteen hours of sleep does the body dirty. Sleeping that much triggered an ancient drive to hibernate. I felt the urge to wade through the creek and fill my belly with fish for the winter. I settled for a can of garbanzos instead.

The walk back to Blane's apartment was swift and easy. It was late in the afternoon. I found a trash can on the other side of the street. When no one was looking, I jumped in. There was a clear view of the front door to Blane's building. If he left that night, I would know about it.

Seamus came back around sunset. He must conduct his business in the daytime. It makes sense for a leprechaun, I thought. There are no rainbows at night.

Hours went by. Many strange things happened that night. A woman chased a man out of the apartment building while beating him with a magazine. A man with an urge to touch everything tried opening every door of every parked car along the street. A street performer showed off her balancing talents on enormous stilted shoes. Many people came by to stop and marvel at her act before a friend of hers picked her up to go home. It was a whole different world at night. A world of mystery and wonder.

Just as the night was coming fully alive, an evil wind swept down the road. The night-folk panicked and scattered back into the cracks and crevices from which they came. A beam of light, blinding to the eyes of those adjusted to the night, flared from the eyes of a prowling monster scanning the sidewalk for food. I closed the lid just as it passed over my trash can. The icy breath of the monster chilled me through the metal. I could feel the light hovering over me, waiting for me to move. My heart beat so heavily, I was afraid it would shake the can. It didn't and the light passed. I lifted the lid as soon as I dared to better glimpse the monster. It was a police car, the apex predator of the night, hunting for potential prisoners. I should have known.

The police car left a trail of darkness behind it. The night-folk were slow to creep back from their hiding places and when they did, they carried a weariness about them that soured the spirit to see. It was not just in the Alley where danger lurked. No place was ever safe from the cops' watchful eyes and jagged teeth.

Blane the wizard left his apartment sometime around midnight. Most of the night-folk rambled with a limp or wobble of some kind, but not Blane. He moved swiftly and with purpose. His quick strides caught me off guard and I tumbled out of the trash can trying to keep up. The crash made him turn. He looked straight at me, but I lay motionless on the ground, hopefully out of vision. He shook his head and redoubled his pace. I followed.

Blane stopped at the entrance to another building. He buzzed for one of the apartments. An older woman in a robe answered the door. She tried waving Blane inside, but Blane refused. The woman started pulling open her robe, but Blane stopped her again and began rifling through his backpack. The woman waited, crossing her arms and rocking herself like a baby. When Blane pulled out a small bag from his backpack, the woman again tried opening her robe and waving inside. Blane shook his head firmly and the woman relented. She pulled a wad of cash from her robe and exchanged it for Blane's baggy. Blane said a quick goodbye and scurried off. I followed.

Blane stopped at a dozen or so more buildings. Both men and women came down to see him. Every woman tried to get him to come inside, but he refused every one of them. Some of the men tried to as well. He refused them just the same. All of these interactions seemed to be centered around the exchange of small bags for cash.

It was all suspiciously ordinary. Blane never wielded a wand, nor chanted any spells that I could see. He wore no cape or tall-brimmed hat. There were no telltale signs of wizardry to be found at all. There was a teenie, tiny, itsy bitsy, barely audible, wisp of a voice inside me that questioned if he was truly the powerful sorcerer I believed him to be. A voice that was quickly drowned out by police sirens blasting from down the street.

Blane sprinted by me and away from the police car whipping towards us. I screamed and ran behind him. Blane turned down an alley too narrow for a car to drive through. It was not the Alley itself, but one of the many unnamed corridors defining the slums of Bethlahoom. These were smaller and more sparsely populated, though considerably dangerous in their own right. I followed but struggled to keep up.

The police car stopped and beamed its spotlight down the way. It seared my dilated pupils and I fell to the ground. I was unable to move. I had no strength left. There was nothing to do but lie and wait for the police to capture me. By some miracle they did not. They turned off their siren, directed their spotlight back to the street and kept driving. I was spared by nothing other than laziness.

With no chance of catching up to Blane, there was little point in rushing to get up, so I stayed for a while staring at the night sky. The glow of the city left it void of stars, but after a few minutes of watching, a few appeared. There were less than I could see in my old neighborhood and nothing compared to the skies in Totenbourough where my family used to go to camp. Those were the best times of my life. It was before Tabby became disgusted by everything I did and before Jebediah developed his insatiable thirst for domination. Mom was awake during the daytime and Dad was too angry at the firewood to be angry at me. I wished I could travel through time as easily as I could through the city. I would go back to those early summers when the skies were full and my family was happy.

I got up slowly. I decided to walk all the way through the alley. It wasn't a long one as far as I could tell, and I was worried the police car from earlier was still prowling the street from which I came.

Downtown Bethlahoom had no defining markers between the wealthy and poor neighborhoods. Unlike in the suburbs where a wide set of train tracks marked the clear delineation, the neighborhoods of downtown were saddled next to each other. The poorest and wealthiest inhabitants of Bethlahoom could live on opposite sides of the same block. The alley I walked through cut through one of these invisible gradients, from a boulevard of broken homes to a lane of luxury apartments. The street I came upon was newly paved and lined with fancy street lamps. It was always a wonder to me why the city spent more money on the neighborhoods that could already afford nice things.

This street wasn't as busy as the others. There didn't appear to be anyone living in the cracks in the buildings. The sidewalk was not covered in trash. It seemed like great effort was taken to ensure that someone could walk down this road and believe that the world had no problems at all. For a moment I was fooled myself. I thought about finding a good trash can, a dumpster even, and moving my beans here for the winter. Nothing could harm me on such a charming street, I thought.

A commotion down the road spoiled my dream. Three squabbling men were up ahead. I raced towards them and hid behind a car to watch. One man was on his knees while the other two took turns slapping him around. I recognized the two men as the ones from the summer. Sam and Mitch. My heart pounded. I wanted so desperately to intervene, but what was I to do? I kept watching. The man on his knees was slapped to the side. He lifted his head and looked straight at me. His face was covered in blood but I recognized him right away. It was Blane. I had to save him.

I was no match for either assailant in combat. I could use a trash can lid to go for their knees, but this was foolish. I would only get one of them before the other spotted me, and that was the best-case scenario. More likely they would smell me coming and kill me in an instant. I had to outwit them, but how? How does a dumb boy outwit a pair of wizards? The only thing I knew that was strong enough to scare the likes of these was the police.

I began mimicking a police siren. "Whawoo, whawoo." I started quietly like the police car was far away and got louder as though it were coming towards us. "Whawoo! Whawoo!" It worked! The two men stopped beating Blane and looked in my direction. They looked concerned. That's it, foolish wizards. The police are coming for you! I wailed as loud as I could. "Whawoo!"

Mitch, the larger of the two men, stepped towards me. "Who's your idiot friend, Blane?"

"Whawoo?" I was not as convincing as I thought.

The man plucked me up by the shirt and threw me to the ground beside Blane. "Is this your friend?"

Blane shook his bloodied head. "I told you to go home, Frumpkin."

"I'm here to save you from the bad guys. Did you hear the sirens? That was actually me."

Mitch grabbed my chin and pulled my face into the light. "I've seen you before. You've been spying on me? Trying to help little Blane here steal our business?"

"We saw him this summer," Sam said. "He's the kid who ratted us out."

"You don't say. It's about time I killed you. " Mitch raised his gun to my head.

"What are you stupid? We got to take him back and find out who he's working for. I might get a hell of a prize for information like that."

"You mean we'll get a prize."

"Don't forget who has the brains, here, Mitch. You might just forget how to breathe, too."

Sam and Mitch snarled at one another. For a pair of best friends, they were awfully contentious.

Mitch, backed down and kicked Blane in the chest. "What do we do with him?"

Sam pulled a gun from his coat pocket. "I'm afraid it's the end for our little pal Blane. Any last words, bucko?"

"Fuck you, Sam." Blane spit blood at his shoes.

Sam snorted and pointed his gun. His eyes narrowed. His teeth barred and his fist clenched.

Time slammed to a halt. The thin hairs on my arms raised like the quills of a porcupine. All the fibers of my muscles twitched alive. I felt a power I had never known.

Sam's finger pressed against the trigger. Anger coursed through me. I lunged at his legs. His instinct was to protect his groin, but I was aiming for his knees. His left leg buckled along the wrong axis. He dropped his gun and fell to the ground, screaming. Blane scrambled to the gun and ripped it away from Sam before he could recover. Mitch was too slow to do anything but watch and grunt.

A siren blared from down the road.

"Shut up, Frumpkin."

"It's not me this time."

The siren got louder and flashing blue lights sparkled in the reflections on mirrors and chrome bumpers. The police were coming.

"Run!" Blane sprinted down the street. I followed. My muscles were still tingling with power and I did a better job of following him than before. We ran down the first alley we could. Blane didn't stop. We ran all the way through and into another alley. I thought I was going to die trying to keep up. He didn't slow down until the third alley we came across. Once we were in, he pulled me behind a dumpster and pressed me against the wall. "What the fuck do you think you're doing?"

I clawed for breath. I tried answering but could only manage grumbling nonsense in between gasps for air.

Blane relaxed his grip on me, realizing my limitations. "You shouldn't be out here."

I gasped some more.

"Are you alright?" It was an odd thing to ask with a face caked in his own blood.

"I'm okay," I managed to spit out.

Blane looked me over. "Are you hurt at all?"

A sharp pain in my side throbbed with every breath, but I knew that was only from running. I was otherwise unharmed. There was one thing that had been bothering me for the last few days, however. I would not be seeing my pediatrician anytime soon, and Blane didn't specify the scope of his concern. "I have been having trouble cleaning this fingernail. There is some grimy stuff that keeps appearing under it. No matter how well I clean it, it's dirty the next time I look. What could it be?"

Blane threw up his arms and spun around in frustration. "What is wrong with this kid," he mumbled to himself before grabbing my hand and taking a look. "Have you ever eaten a banana by any chance?"

"How did you know?"

"This is Banungus, a banana-eating fungus. It starts in the nails and goes straight to the brain."

"Oh no! What do I do?"

"You should go home, Frumpkin. Be with your loved ones."

"But... I thought you were my loved one?"

"Oh, God." Blane dropped my hand and leaned his back against the wall beside me. He had a far-off look in his eyes that I assumed was from thinking about possible cures for Banungus. I checked my fingernail. I had been so worried about wizards and warlocks, but it was bananas that would take my life. Is anything safe?

Blane took a deep breath and launched himself off the wall. "Come on. You can stay with me tonight."

"You mean it?"

"Just for tonight."

"Thank you. And do you by chance have anything for my Banungus?"

"There's no such thing as Banungus. You're just a gross kid."

"You mean it? Oh, joyous day!"

"Thanks for saving my life," he said.

"That's what friends are for."

Blane cracked a smile that quickly faded back to a grimace.

Chapter 16

I awoke the following afternoon to see Seamus standing in the kitchenette reading a newspaper and drinking a beer. "Top of the after-morning to you, Frumpkin. Pleasure to see you and Blane worked things out. What does he have you doing for him anyway?"

"Oh, good after-morning. The only task so far is being his friend."

"Aye, friendship be the best path for lovers."

Blane trundled out of his room. "Fuck you, Seamus."

Seamus lifted his beer in salutation. His perpetual smile never faltered.

"Top of the after-morning to you," I said to Blane.

"Top of the what? Fucking freak." Blane opened a beer and collapsed on a recliner on the other side of the room with his eyes closed.

Seamus whipped his newspaper open with a snap. "Did you hear the good word? Some town wench is with the good lord's child. One Tabitha Jean Bulgerdeen. That good lord sure is a horndog, eh there Frumpkin?"

Hearing Tabby's name startled me. Did Seamus know who I was? How powerful were leprechauns? Were any of my secrets safe?

"What the hell are you even saying?" Blane spat. Your accent is ridiculous." Blane clearly didn't know who I was. That I could be certain about.

"See for yourself, Mr. Grumpikins."

Seamus pirouetted to the recliner and dropped the paper in Blane's lap. Blane glanced at it for a moment and tossed it aside. "People are crazy." He closed his eyes and continued drinking.

"What's gotten into the two of you? It's like I'm back in the old country. A bunch of sourpussies with nothing to do but scowl. Look out the window, boys. We've got the whole world. What more do you need to make you happy?"

"How about a fucking bullet in my head."

"Oh, Blane, Blane. Never has there been such a sourpussy. Tell me what makes a sourpussy so sour?"

Blane rolled his head back and sighed. "I got robbed. It's bad."

"You got mugged, eh? Well, you ain't getting mugged now. Plenty of folk have been mugged, you know. That's how we got the word for it."

"I didn't get mugged. I got fucked."

"Well, now I really don't know why you're complaining."

Blane threw up his hands in anger. His beer splashed on his shirt, however, extinguishing the brief spark of rage. He lowered his hands and shook his head in resignation instead. "I was running from the cops and I ran into Paltry Square. The guys who run it thought I was dealing there and now they're probably going to kill me. They took all my shit, so even if they don't kill me, I won't be able to pay back Ignacio, and Ignacio will kill me."

"I think he'd put you on the corner. Ignacio knows as well as I about the freaks and dandies."

"Or he could put me on the corner. Thanks, you fucking asshole."

"Just want to be clear about what we're up against."

"There's no 'we', man. This is my problem."

"And you think Frumpkin here is going to sit by while you're getting raped in the Alley? That's not the kind of lover I know Frumpkin to be."

"We're not lovers!"

A heavy silence followed. The three of us stared at one another. Seamus's smirk gave me tingles in my belly. There was something devious about him, but it was inspiring as much as it was worrisome. It may have been otherwise if he were not so convincing of our allyship in times of such desperation. Noble qualities seem less important then.

"These muggers, you know where they live?"

"I have a pretty good idea, yeah."

"Well then what's the problem? We go over there and straighten things out."

"These guys aren't the kind you go looking for."

"No need looking when you know where they are. No need waiting either. It's about time you stood up, Blane. You're not a clerk at the market. You're in the magic game. If someone takes your stash, you take their life."

Blane's face turned pale and cold. He picked at the label of his bottle. I understood his predicament. Our situations were remarkably similar. What Seamus suggested disturbed him just as it did me when I first heard it from Betty. Neither of us would come to such a conclusion on our own, though it was perfectly clear when seeing it from the outside that no other solution existed. Blane had to kill those two men like I had to kill Frankie. This was the way of the world of magic. Trepidation was foolish.

"Can guns kill wizards?" I asked. Blane's eyes shot up. He stopped picking the label.

"Aye, Frumpkin." Seamus sneered. "Guns will do."

A silence fell. No more words needed to express our circumstance.

• • •

The three of us marched down Salsbury Lane towards Paltry Square shortly after sunset armed to the teeth with weapons procured from Seamus's room. Blane had been surprised to find Seamus so well prepared. He asked Seamus about it, but Seamus blew off his questions and told him to grow up. "You're a bum-licking fool," he had said. I found the whole thing rather strange. I obviously needed a weapon, but why did a wizard and a leprechaun?

The pistol felt awkward to hold. I had to keep it out of sight while I walked, but also securely in my hand so I didn't have any accidents. My gait turned wobblier than normal as I tried to keep up my pace. The other guys didn't have this problem. They both wore coats with inner pockets to conceal their weapons. Blane walked as smoothly as ever. Seamus bounced up and down as he walked. The closer we got to Paltry Square, the more he bounced and the wider he smiled.

We crossed the invisible barrier between neighborhoods. My gun felt even more awkward surrounded by pretty buildings and light posts. Blane must have had the same reaction. He stopped walking. "I don't think they're going to let me into their apartment," he mumbled. "This is a dumb idea."

Seamus turned and stepped inches from Blane's face. "It's not for them to say, Blane. That gun you got in your pocket there, that'll take you wherever you want to go." He squeezed Blane's shoulder and waved us onward. His bounce grew into a full skip.

We stopped outside an apartment building and waited beside the stoop to the front entrance. There was a trash can there, but Blane told me I shouldn't hide in it. I informed him that as a regular boy, I was not able to turn invisible as wizards could. He gave me a strange look after that. I assumed he was bound by magical law to not divulge any information on the subject of invisibility. Out of respect, I did not press the issue.

We waited for quite some time before the door to the apartment building opened. Two men stepped onto the porch and walked down the steps to the sidewalk. It was Mitch and Sam. Seamus leapt out of the shadow of the stoop and into the path of the two men. Blane stayed in the shadows with me.

"Good evening, gentlemen. I hate to interrupt your romantic stroll, but I'm afraid it's not safe out here. Do you mind turning around and going back to your room?"

The two men looked at each other and laughed. "You hear that, Mitch? The streets aren't safe tonight." The two laughed some more before Sam got serious. "Get the fuck out of my way."

Seamus's laugh echoed around the whole neighborhood. He lifted a gun from his coat and stuck it hard into Sam's chest. "I'm afraid I can't do that for you. Now turn around like a gentleman and take us to your room."

Mitch reached into his pocket but froze when he saw Blane step out of the shadow with his gun drawn. Mitch and Sam didn't say a word. They looked as helpless as Blane did when I found him getting beaten up. It was the same look that I saw in Deedris when Anatoly would grab a hold of him. I couldn't help but have sympathy.

Blane nudged Mitch to get moving. "Come on. Don't drag this out."

The two men moped up the stairs with Seamus and Blane at their backs. I followed, but Blane stopped me at the door. "Wait here, Frumpkin. Keep watch. If the police come, yell for us and run away. Don't try to help. You're not part of this."

I opened my mouth to object, but he shook his head with an authority I couldn't break. The four men disappeared into the building. The stoop was cold and lonely.

I kept a lookout as Blane asked. Nothing happened on this street. It was lifeless. The dirty street by the Alley had interesting people walking all around, doing interesting things. They had a smell that took getting used to, but at least they were alive. Fancy light posts and polished cars don't do much of anything when it comes down to it. I preferred watching the weirdos.

Three shots shook the whole world.

BANG BANG BANG

There was a terrifying pause before two more shots rang out.

BANG BANG

Nothing I had ever heard was that loud and clear. It was like I had been hearing everything from another room my whole life, with my ear pressed against the wall, and those shots blew a hole in the barrier between me and the real world. I was awakened to the moment. I was alive.

Seamus skipped past and down the stairs. His shirt was speckled with red. "Come along now, Frumpkin. It's time we be moving."

Blane barged into my back. His eyes were wide and his panting heavy. "Run, Frumpkin."

. . .

Seamus whispered calming spells in Blane's ear all the way back to the apartment and sometime after we arrived. I didn't know much about leprechauns, but it seemed that the voice was their magical tool of choice.

Seamus unloaded three blocks of a powdery blue substance wrapped in plastic from his coat, along with several fistfuls of cash, all while chanting his spells. "It was either you or them, Blane. You did the right thing, and this is the reward. Those guys deserved what they got. Good people only get good things if they go out and take it from the bad ones. Those were the bad guys. They got what they deserved. We're the good guys, Blane. This is what we deserve."

Blane reached out for one of the piles of money. He rubbed it between his fingers and examined it closely before turning and nodding to Seamus. A little color returned to his pale face.

Seamus stopped chanting and nodded back before addressing me for the first time since we left Sam and Mitch's building. "And this is for you Frumpkin. Good work."

He handed me a roll of money. It was more than I had ever held. I could buy a million beans with that money! "But, what is this for?" I asked. I was not expecting payment.

"This is your cut, Frumpkin. You work for us now. That's what you wanted, right?"

"Yes. Yes, I did." I admired the cash.

"You should wash up, Frumpkin. We have company coming and you don't want to be smelling like trash when they get here."

Seamus showed me to the shower and gave me an extra pair of clothes to wear when I got out. I hadn't showered in nearly two weeks, and the feeling was transcendent. The relief was so strong that it seemed to wipe me clean of all my problems. I can really only feel one thing at a time. It's one of those things that makes feelings so tricky. Satisfying one need can make me forget about the rest. When I'm deprived of something for long enough, anyone who supplies it for me will feel heaven-sent, no matter what else they are inflicting upon me. Nothing is stronger than relief.

The shorts Seamus gave me fit perfectly as pants. The shirt fit more like a dress. Seamus was quick to point this out, and Blane, now several beers deep, found joy in it as well. I laughed along too, though more because I was happy to see Blane with a smile.

Seamus's friends arrived soon after. Sabrina, Jessica and the lovely Marlene. Seamus was a gracious host, but due to the lateness of the hour, thought it best that we go to bed. Seamus went with Sabrina to his room, Jessica with Blane, and the lovely Marlene stayed with me in the main room. She took a seat next to me once the others had left.

Marlene's smile was the nicest thing I had ever seen. There was nothing but sweetness and kindness to be found in the dimples of her rouged cheeks and the crinkles of her bright, brown eyes. I had only seen such an expression of warmth from the side, directed at someone else. It was paralyzing from the front.

"Are you just going to stare at me?" she asked playfully.

"I, I, I," I stuttered and turned away.

She giggled and put a hand on my shoulder. It seemed to meld into my skin. "You can stare at me if you want. I wasn't offended." Her voice was a melody so generous and caring.

"Oh, thank you."

"So, who are you anyways? How do you know Seamus?"

"Me? I'm Humph... I'm Frumpkin." I barely caught myself.

"Frumpkin?" Marlene giggled some more. "Are you nervous, Frumpkin? There's no need to be nervous."

I was nervous. I didn't know why, either. Of all the people I had come across along my brief journey, Marlene seemed to be the least threatening. Everyone I had ever known had the capacity and apparent will to hurt me, but Marlene was like an angel. It seemed like anything she did would be welcome and good. I guess I was nervous that I would ruin my one opportunity to be next to her.

I shook my head. "Nervous? Of course not." I squeaked an octave higher than usual. It was a lie. So far I had told the lovely Marlene nothing but lies. I was not actually Frumpkin, the magic dealer. I was Humphry, the disgusting, unlovable little boy. That's why I had to lie.

She giggled some more. It felt like she could see through me. "You're adorable," she said, leaning into me. What was she doing? She was getting close. I couldn't move. My heart pounded. She led with her cheek. It pressed into my chest and melted into me just as her hand had on my shoulder. It felt so good that I wanted to cry for all the time I had spent without her cheek upon me. Her own shoulder snuggled beneath my arm. Her legs wrapped around mine. Our bodies were one.

I couldn't speak. I could only utter gibberish. "Dooberonioni clapaclapa dingdong..." My body was whole, but my mind was broken.

"Relax, Frumpkin."

I obeyed.

Interlude 2

"And that is the story of how I met the lovely Marlene," Humphry finished. He sat cross-legged on the floor with his hands clasped in his lap and a vacant stare towards his feet.

Merideth sat to attention. "That's the end of the story? Are you kidding me?"

"You wanted to know how I met the lovely Marlene, didn't you?"

"Well, yeah, but that can't be the end of the story! What happened with Frankie? You just moved in with a couple of killers and that's that? What happened with your sister? Your poor sister..." She sat back and wondered how different her life could have been.

"I'd prefer not to continue," Humphry said. "Some things are better forgotten."

"Oh, don't be dramatic. Come on. You can't stop there. What happened next?"

Humphry hugged his knees. If Merideth weren't so eager to be entertained, she might have noticed the tremble in his voice and far off look in his eyes.

"Hello," she said impatiently.

"Fine," Humphry whispered. He laid flat on his back with his eyes fixed upon the ceiling. He took one deep breath and continued telling his story.

Chapter 17

An apple dropped from the sky and fell on my chest. "Lovely Marlene?" I asked. "Is that you?"

"No, little lad. I'm not as lovely as she." Seamus was finishing an apple of his own. "You and me are going shopping. You can't be working for Blane looking like a dangle."

"Is that what I look like? That's not why Marlene left, is it?"

"I can't tell you why she left, but you definitely look like a dangle. Now, let's get on with it, eh?"

Seamus took me to Sox Avenue in Paltry Square. It was a promenade that cut through the nicest section of downtown. I had been there before to see a movie at the theater, but I otherwise avoided it. It was the most beautiful part of town, with fountains and pretty flowers in the spring and summer that were replaced with colorful lights in the winter, but I never felt like I belonged there. It was Tabby's favorite place in the world. That was enough to keep me out.

Most of the stores were geared towards fancy women, but scattered amongst them were stores that sold vibrating chairs where men could sit and pretend they weren't out shopping. Women shopped like they were picking berries. They went through every bush of blouses and examined every single one. If they could, they would pick them all. Men were like hunters. They paced through the mall with their eyes peeled, tracking a single pair of pants. They struck with precision and speed. If the pants weren't the right size, they didn't bother looking for another pair. They head back home to conserve their energy for the next hunt.

The store to which Seamus led me sold suits and trench coats. It was the kind of store that had very few items on display. Instead of sifting through options, an attendant took measurements of the man's body and gave him a pair of well-fitting clothes at a later agreed upon date. I had never undergone this process before but found it impressive. We were only in the store for a few minutes. For the first time in my life, shopping was not unbearable torture.

Seamus bought us sandwiches that we ate together at a table on a patio in the middle of the promenade surrounded by a low-lying, ornate brick wall embedded with planters and dripping with strings of glass crystals and lights. It was shaded beneath trees that were trained to perfectly cover the entire patio. The trees were nearly bare, as was the patio itself. We were alone to speak freely.

"Tell me, Frumpkin, what do you think about working for Blane?"

"Well, I didn't realize I had started, to be honest. Is all work just walking around eating sandwiches?"

"Aye, it's a good deal. Walking here, walking there. But you should know something, it's not always just eating sandwiches. Sometimes it's pizza." Seamus winked.

"Oh. I don't quite understand what that accomplishes."

"You don't need to know what you're doing to do it. You just got to do it."

"I see." I didn't really see. This magic business all seemed too simple to be true. There had to be more to wizardry than walking around eating sandwiches. "Uh, Seamus?"

"Yes, lad?"

"I was wondering if you could tell me a bit more about magic. How does one become a wizard? I know that you, of course, are a leprechaun, and that leprechauns are not the same as wizards, but they are very powerful and knowledgeable as well. Do you have any advice for a prospective wizard like me?"

For the first time, Seamus's smile vanished. In its stead was an expression of complete confusion. He looked around, making sure no one was in earshot before leaning over the table. "You think I'm a leprechaun?"

"I didn't mean to offend you, I just assumed that's what you were. Blane is a wizard, of course, I know that. Dealing in magic is wizards' business, obviously. And Leprechauns'! Not that you are definitely a leprechaun, but that maybe you are. Are you a leprechaun?"

Seamus's gaping mouth slowly reverted back to a devious smile. "Aye, Frumpkin. You caught me. I'm a leprechaun, but don't go telling anybody else about it. Not even Blane. And don't go calling Blane a wizard, either. He doesn't like that, though he most certainly is one."

"I knew it."

"And I can show you some magic, but you gotta do what I say. No matter what it is."

"Of course! And just one more question. The lovely Marlene, I suspect that she is a pixie of some kind? I think she may have put a spell on me. Everything I once cared about seems to have been replaced by strange urges to be close to her."

"She got you good, eh? She's not an easy lass to wrangle, mind you, but she'll like you better working for me. I can assure you that."

"I would like that very much."

"Glad to hear it." Seamus seemed to be quite satisfied with the conclusion of our conversation.

Gangster Magic

We finished eating and made our way back to the apartment. Blane woke up shortly after we arrived, and Seamus explained to him what was to happen. Blane would teach me to do his job before moving over to Paltry Square to take over the new turf they had recently acquired. My clothes wouldn't be ready until the next day, so all this would have to wait until the following evening. This left quite a bit of time to lay around thinking about the realities of my new situation.

With a belly full of something other than beans, a roof over my head and the promise of wizardry in my near future, I began losing sight of why I started this journey. The Lovely Marlene may have had something to do with it. As far as I could tell, she sunk into my body, latched onto my soul and ripped off a piece before leaving. That piece may have contained the bit that cared about my previous life. Whatever it was that dimmed my concern for Tabby and Deedris and the whole town of Bethlahoom, it left space for a growing desire to experience the full power of the wizarding world. With a leprechaun and wizard teaching me the ways of magic, it would surely soon be mine.

. . .

Blane met me in the kitchenette where I was modeling my fancy new trench coat in the mossy reflection of the sink faucet. "What the fuck are you doing?" he asked.

"Did you see my new coat?"

"Yeah, it's the same as every other coat I've ever seen."

"And it's all mine."

I admired it one last time before Blane slammed a bag of blue powder on the counter beside the sink and stopped me mid-twirl to look at it.

"This is magic. We're the distributor for the blocks between 42nd and 48th street and Chadburry and Tattlewick. We get this from a guy named Ignacio, distribute it to the dealers, and the dealers sell to the freaks. Some of the dealers are freaks too, but they got the money to buy in bulk, so we sell to them too. Remember, Ignacio will kill me if you mess this up. So what are you not going to do?"

"Mess this up?"

"That's right. Do you have any questions so far?"

"Are you telling me that that stuff is magic?"

"How stupid are you? Yeah, this is magic."

"Wow." Pure magic. I never knew what it looked like. I always assumed it was some invisible force that magical beings could harness. Apparently it could be isolated and put into a crystallized form. "How do we use it?" I asked.

The force of Blane's hand across my cheek nearly spun my head all the way around. Blane's berating felt just as harsh. "Don't ask that again. I swear to God, if you start using, I'm dropping you in the Alley. Do you understand me?"

I cupped my cheek where the sting of his hand lingered. I understood pain well enough. If that's what I got for bringing up using magic, then I could see why I wouldn't want to use it. I nodded and stared at the floor.

Blane took a deep breath. His anger softened. "Look, I didn't mean to hit you. This is just really important. This stuff is dangerous. It rots out your brain and kills you. We get it. We drop it off. That's it. We don't use it. If you use it, you lose it. Do you understand?"

"I think so." I didn't need Blane to explain any further. This was magic. Only a wizard or similarly magical being could wield it safely. As a regular boy, it would kill me. I was just here to safeguard it and bring it to those privileged enough to use it safely.

"Alright, let's go."

The trench coat gave me a confidence I had never had before. It was like hiding in a trashcan but without the confinement and stench.

No one could see what I had beneath it, and that mystery was a power of its own. Though I currently had only my twiddling thumbs, the night folk did not look at me that way. They saw their greatest hopes and fears beneath my trench coat. It was not magic, per se, but an effective illusion.

Blane stopped at a familiar apartment building, the same one he had gone to on the night I was spying on him. "I'm going to do the talking," he said. "Just be quiet and watch. Okay?"

"Yes, Almighty Blane."

"What the hell is wrong with... Good."

Blane stepped up to the door and buzzed for ROOM 618(Ms. Kooklioni). We waited. Blane checked his watch. Finally the door creaked open. Ms. Kooklioni stuck her arm out of the door and did a seductive dance with her hand, tempting us to come inside. Blane was not amused. He spoke like a father to a young child. "Come on out, Ms. Kooklioni."

Ms. Kooklioni danced her way out the door. Her whole body never stopped moving. She was barely dressed in an untied pink robe. It looked just as it did a few nights earlier. There were, however, about a thousand wrinkles in her face and body that I didn't notice the other night. Her voice sounded halfway between a cough and a whisper. "I've waited all day for you, Blane." She moaned and creened.

"I'm just here to drop off the stuff and get my money."

"Why don't you come up to my room? I have a pie I want you to taste." Ms. Kooklioni dragged the top of her robe open while bleating like a sheep.

"Please, put those away, Ms. Kooklioni. Just give us the money and we'll be on our way."

"Oh, Blane. Who is this handsome gift you've brought me?"

"He's not a gift. This is Frumpkin. He works for me. You'll be buying from him going forward."

"Mhm. Frumpkin Pie, such a tasty treat. Why don't you come upstairs and give me a nibble."

"Hey, he's not going with you. Just give us the money and we'll be on our way."

"Oh, I love it when you tell me what to do, Blane. Have your way with me. Bahhhh" She bleated some more and opened her arms wide. Her robe fell open completely revealing a thousand more wrinkles, much larger than those on her arms and face. Two in particular sagged from sternum to hips.

"The money," Blane said firmly and stuck out his hand.

Ms. Kooklioni pouted and closed her robe. She reached into her pocket and pulled out a roll of cash. Blane handed her a bag of magic and wished her a good night.

"I'll be waiting, Frumpkin Pie!" She called out as we walked away.

Blane walked quickly. Once we turned the corner and were out of sight of the apartment building, he turned around to address me. "That's Ms. Kooklioni. The only thing you have to remember is never go up to her room. Just be firm. Demand the cash and be on your way."

"Demand the cash. Be on my way. Got it."

"Never go up to her Room," he said again, emphasizing every word.

"Never go up to her room. Never go up to her room. Got it."

Blane squeezed my shoulder and nodded his approval. We continued on his route. Each person had their own quirks that I was charged with remembering, but the solution to all of them was the same: demand the cash and be on my way.

With only one more apartment building left to visit, Blane started acting strangely. He breathed heavier and looked into every car window to adjust his hair and trench coat. When we finally did get to the last building he took a few moments on the street to collect himself before walking up to the door. He buzzed room 917(Ganglia). I thought I could hear his heartbeat in the following silence.

A young woman stuck her head out of the door so just the top half of her head and fingertips were visible. Her wavy brown hair calmly bounced up and down in juxtaposition to her wide eyes that appeared to belong to a wild animal watching for predators. Blane was stiff and didn't speak. The woman's eyes darted from him to me and back to him again. "Hello?" she said cautiously.

"Marie! Hi. Hello." Blane smiled and waved.

Marie furrowed her eyebrows and stuck out one of her hands. She opened the door a little more to do so. She wore a baggy blue sweatshirt that hid her much like my trench coat.

"Of course," Blane responded, taking out a bag of magic from his coat and putting it in Marie's hand. Marie swapped it for some cash and tried to disappear back into the building, but Blane grabbed the door and held it open against Marie's yanks of the handle. "Wait," Blane said. "This is going to be my last time delivering to you." Marie's grip of the door slackened and Blane managed it back open.

Marie raised her clenched fists as though she were ready to swing. "No," she said curtly. "You will keep coming."

Blane had a rare smile. "I'm sorry, Marie, but it's true. I'm moving to a new part of town and I won't be coming around anymore. Frumpkin will make the deliveries to you from now on, but I would love to go get coffee together one of these days if you'd like." Blane had a rare smile.

"He will still deliver to me?" She pointed to me.

"You mean Frumpkin? Yeah, he'll be taking over my route. Maybe you and I could get dinner instead?"

"Oh. Okay. Goodbye." Marie closed the door.

Blane clawed unsuccessfully at the doorknob. "You mean okay to dinner or Frumpkin?" he shouted at the closed door. There was no response. His smile sunk along with his shoulders and he moped down the steps to the street. I followed.

We had gone well beyond sight of Marie's door without him stopping to tell me about what I needed to remember about the last stop. Maybe he had just forgotten. I decided to remind him. "Hey, Blane. Is there anything I should know about Marie?" Blane didn't acknowledge my question. I tried speaking louder. "Blane? Do you want to tell me about Marie?" Blane kept walking. "Will she ask me up to her room like the others?"

Blane stopped and turned on a dime. I smashed into him and fell to the ground. "No. She won't speak at all, and don't bother trying to make her. Don't even try talking to her. Just give her the magic and take the money. Nothing more." He didn't wait for me to get up. He spun around and sped off in the direction of the Alley. The Alley!

I hurried behind him against the urges of my gut. It had not yet occurred to me that I would have to go into the Alley alone twice a week. I always had a healthy fear of the Alley, but after narrowly escaping my last and only visit, that fear had grown fat and malignant.

We passed through the darkened entrance. How did Blane move so surely in the dark? I had his blurry outline to follow, but he walked blind. I hoped he would teach me before I had to go alone.

The Alley appeared to brighten as we walked. Alleymen stuck to themselves along the wall. Some of them noticed us and held out cupped hands for charity. Blane passed them by without flinching. "Don't look at them and they won't bother you," he said. It was a difficult task. I wanted to look so badly, either to apologize for withholding my charity or to make sure they were not about to attack me, but Blane was right. The less I looked at them, the less interested they were in me. I could see them well enough in my periphery to anticipate any attack, and it was easier to keep my heart shut against sympathy. Shutting my heart was a new experience.

A cloaked man waited for us in a power stance at the center of the Alley. He and Blane embraced with a secret handshake that ended in a bumping of shoulders and patting on the back. It was well-choreographed and executed to perfection. I began practicing it on my own to help remember it. It would be difficult to perform with a partner with such a significant height disparity.

"Is that kid with you?" the man asked.

"Yeah. This is Frumpkin."

"Is he right in the head?"

Blane looked at me. I was still practicing the handshake. "Sometimes I wonder," he muttered. "Hey, Frumpkin! Pay attention. This is Jerry. Jerry, this is Frumpkin."

Jerry stuck out his arm in a manner between a handshake and slap. "What's good, little man?"

I mirrored his action as best I could. "What's good?" I wondered aloud. "The flowers in the spring, I suppose. Or a friendly kitten in the Fall! That would be more timely."

Blane buried his face in his hands while Jerry laughed and grabbed my hand, pulling me in for the same sort of shoulder-bumping hug he had with Blane. There was no messing it up. Jerry's overpowering strength directed me like he was leading me in a dance. "Nice to meet you. So, you're Boogie's brother?"

"He's not my brother," Blane interjected. "He's a new employee. He's taking over my route for me."

"And this is the best you could find?" Jerry pointed to me. "No offense, little boy."

I wasn't sure why I would be offended. It was a great honor knowing I was the best Blane could find.

"He's a weird kid, but it's an easy job and I can trust him."

My ego was thoroughly stroked.

"Welcome to the team, sunshine. I'm not calling you Frumpkin, though. Your name is Fruitloop." He jabbed my chest with his finger. I wasn't sure what to make of this development. Blane didn't seem to object, so I didn't either. Jerry turned back to Blane and spoke to him as though I wasn't there. "So, when's your last day?"

"It's actually today. This is it."

"Shit! You're leaving just like that?"

"I'll still be around. I'm just going over to Paltry Square."

"P-town? What happened to Sam?"

Blane looked around to make sure no one was listening, something strange to do in the middle of the Alley where no one would ever come to eavesdrop. "Sam's dead. Same with Mitch. That's why I'm taking it over. It's free territory and I got to pounce before it's taken again."

"Oof. How'd they die?"

Blane looked at me and shrugged his shoulders. "I— I don't know. I think it may have been a robbery or something."

Had he forgotten already? I wouldn't dare correct him in front of Jerry, but I made a note to remind him later.

"Well, shit. A reminder to be careful, huh?"

"Yeah."

"Hey, you ask out Marie? No way you'll stop seeing her."

Blane's blushing cheeks was the first bit of color I had seen since entering the Alley. "I tried, but I don't think it's going to work out."

"You lucked out, man. You're moving up. You'll be making more money. You got Fruitloop working for you now. This ain't the time to get saddled down. Your stock's just going up. Forget about her and keep on your grind. Pretty soon you'll be killing so hard, she'll beg you for it, and you won't even care anymore."

Blane scoffed. "Yeah, we'll see about that."

"Mark my words." Jerry stuck a roll of cash in Blane's chest and nodded encouragingly. "You got my bag?" Blane looked around once more before slipping Jerry a bag from his coat. Jerry lifted the bag up and down like his arm was a scale. "This feels a little light."

"Come on, man. It's the same ounce every time." Blane counted the cash.

"We'll see. We'll see."

"We gotta get going. I'll see you around, Jerry." Blane and Jerry performed an abbreviated version of their secret handshake and Blane walked away. I waved goodbye to Jerry and raced to catch up.

"See you soon, Fruitloop," Jerry called out.

Blane kept a swift pace until we were out of the Alley. He stopped me once we made it to the street. "That's Jerry. He'll try to get to know you. Don't tell him too much. He's just looking for secrets. And always count the money he gives you. He'll say he's not getting a full ounce, but he is. Don't listen to him. Be firm and demand the cash. Got it?"

"Be firm, demand the cash. Got it."

"Good. Any questions?"

"Can you show me that secret handshake again? I think I will need some practice before I can perform it correctly."

"You don't need to know the handshake. Just..." Blane exhaled audibly. He grabbed my shoulder and bent over to my level. "Are you sure you're ready for this?"

I looked into his eyes. I thought I saw a mix of fear, compassion and weariness there. I knew too little to recognize it as guilt. Guilt is the only feeling I've learned to trust. It is the specter of fate lashing its whip to steer us clear of selfishness. It only comes about while we are deviating from our moral compass. Regret comes along after our selfishness has been revealed. I've learned to mistrust regret most of all. It is self-pity masquerading as guilt. It is abominable, a sure sign of evil. Remorse has no validity after a man's reputation is besmirched. The sorrow is only for one's self and the desire is for absolution of responsibility. Guilt is all that counts in the measurement of the soul. A guilty man does not seek forgiveness. A guilty man seeks punishment.

"Yes, sir," I said with the confidence of a fool.

Chapter 18

Distributing magic to The Shank became second nature to me. 'Get the money and go' was the refrain by which I lived. Most of the money went to Blane, but I still kept more than I could spend. Comic books, a BB gun, roller skates, and everything else I always wanted was mine. I gave the rest of my money to the lovely Marlene.

I thought of her day and night, though she could only come over once or twice a week. My concerns of her pixie-nature were replaced by compassion. It became clear that she was not of this world, and that she was being drawn back to her natural realm at all times. Every time I saw her, she seemed to have faded away just a little more. The sadness in her sinking eyes grew in spite of her perpetual soft smile. Her skin was thinner, almost translucent, and pocked with ever more bruises and scars. The more she faded from the world, the more I clung to her. I wanted her to stay with me all the time. She couldn't drift away if I was holding her hand, I thought, no matter how many times I woke up alone.

My lavish lifestyle blinded me to the means by which it was procured. Taking down dark magic then would mean losing every joy I had ever known in the world. I'd like to say I did the right thing, but as the season turned, so too did I from truth and purpose. Winter was fully upon us and my heart turned cold.

...

January 13th

13th Murder in 13 days, by Rudolphus Slim

Not two weeks into the new year, and it has already been christened The Year of Death. Timothy McToot, suspected hooligan with prior convictions, was found bloodied and mangled like the soiled sheets of my incontinent grandmother. No word yet from the police as to the motive, but this reporter believes it is another case in the Dark Magic Murders.

Dark Magic: The Bane of Bethlahoom. Disgraced Officer Murphy Flannigan has this to say on the matter, "I'm sorry, I missed the question. Could you repeat that for me please?" Disgraceful. It is such incompetence that keeps this reporter shaking in his boots. No one is safe on the streets past mid-morning. Will the streets ever be safe again? Continued on A8...

I set the paper down on the couch and unfurled my legs from the coffee table in front of me. The paper haunted me with ghosts of my past. Tabby's baby, the spawn of the demon I summoned, was now widely heralded as the savior of the town. The murders I had once been so keen on stopping had only grown more frequent since I began my new life. The only omission from the paper was of the lost boy Humphry. The boy I once was. His disappearance was never reported. It was mentioned in one of the weekly interviews with the Bulgerdeen family that he had been taken out of school to avoid the potential obsessive questioning he might receive in the public eye. Lies. They were all lies.

That single mistruth, so well-proven false by my vantage, undermined my belief in everything the paper reported upon, even the events I knew were real, like the murders of Sam and Mitch, of

Jose 'The Jalapeno' Martinez, Gabriel 'The Gassy' Muttinberg, and so on. I knew those men and I knew they were killed, but seeing their names in the paper surrounded by lies made it seem unreal. The lines between truth and fantasy were blurred. The world was fragmented between what I saw and did and remembered, and the narratives that were popularized to describe it. Controlling the narrative was enticing. I found that I could do one thing and tell myself that I was doing something else. There was no need for those things to be the same. Nobody else seemed to think so. Seamus in particular.

Blane and Seamus moved to a bigger apartment in a nicer part of town, leaving me to take care of their old place which still operated as a storage facility. A small mountain of magic was locked up in Blane's old room, and weapons still lined Seamus's. In addition to distributing magic to the dealers in The Shank, I was in charge of protecting the apartment. Nobody was supposed to know where the apartment was. I was never to tell anyone of its location and had to make sure I wasn't being followed whenever I was coming back to it. Blane and the lovely Marlene were the only people to have come by for nearly two months, and they always came at night.

A knock on the door spooked me. I grabbed my putt putt club and stood on my tippy toes to look through the eyehole. A menacing green eye stared back at me. I yelped and fell backwards to the floor.

"You alright there, Frumpkin?" A familiar voice asked. I heard keys jangle from behind the door and the lock click and clank and unlatch. Seamus stepped inside and lifted me off the ground. "Took a tumble, eh? Well dust yourself off and take a seat. We need to talk."

"Is everything alright?"

"Splendid, I'd say. I suppose you heard about the lucky mishap with Tootin' Tim?"

"Are you talking about Timothy McToot? I just read in the paper that he was—"

"A fine man? Sure. God rest his soul. Coincidentally a big player in uptown distribution as well. It'd be all the more tragic to let his business parish along with him."

"What an unbelievable coincidence. That's got to be the twentieth time this month. You must be the luckiest person in the world." It was a string of luck that only made sense for a leprechaun.

"Luck is for anyone who dares take it. Like lightning, it comes seldom but strikes in bunches. There's a storm raging out there. The winds of change are blowing and our sails be tall and taught." Seamus's chest heaved like wind-whipped waves. His voice bounced around like a song. "The weak shall slip under the turning tides and those left will plunder their prized hides. But only with ties as strong as brides may the ride be survived. Are you following me, Frumpkin?" His eyes flared with the power of his ancient people.

"I don't know…" I had no idea what he was saying.

"I'm saying we need more people!" His voice cracked like thunder and his mood resolved in an instant. "Do you have any friends looking for work?" His voice was as casual as ever. "You need to find your replacement."

"You're replacing me?"

"You're replacing you. I'm promoting you."

"A promotion?" A promotion was frightening. I had only just mastered the job I had, and starting a new one would reopen the possibility of failure. And yet, the creep of stagnation was beginning to show in my life. The goal I once had, though no longer at the forefront of my mind, was nudging my soul to act. A growing restlessness within me spoiled the gifts I had been given. A change, though frightening, was welcome.

I thought for some time, but there was only one person I could trust to take my place and I thought of him immediately. I often thought about Deedris and wondered if he was thinking of me too. "I know a guy," I said at last.

"Excellent. You'll be needing for haste. You start working for me this weekend."

. . .

There were safer options than to corner Deedris at school. I could have gone to his house and waited for him in the morning before he got on the bus or in the afternoon when he got off. I could have left him a note in his mailbox or tapped on his window late at night. He would have been alone, under the cloak of darkness, and far from anyone who could recognize me. It was obvious to me, even then, that any of those options were better than the one I chose, but the mind relents to the will of the heart in matters of loneliness, and though the company of the lovely Marlene was intoxicating, I was a lonely boy.

I was concealed under a thick, white fur coat I had splurged on and a wide-brimmed hat that dipped over my forehead. Sunglasses covered an additional half of my face. Sparkling chains dangled around my neck. If someone were to recognize me, it would be by my hairless chin.

It was nearing lunchtime when I approached the school. I crept to the gap in the building and up to the chain link fence barring off the empty patio. A thin layer of snow tracked my steps. Everything was so calm and innocent. That fence kept out all the horrors of the world and I was on the wrong side. I yearned for the simple life I once knew.

The bell rang and a flood of yammering kids stormed out of every door. Deedris would be coming out of History class. I crouched low to stay unseen though it may well have been for nothing. Everyone was too consumed in their own lives to take notice of their surroundings. The flood of students slowed. It was unlike Deedris to be slow. The last trickle of students came out, and still no Deedris. Where was he? Had I missed him?

The door to the history room opened once more and Deedris snuck out. He looked terrified. He clung to the wall and scooted around the edge of the patio towards me, hiding behind some bushes just to my right. The stars were aligning.

I called out for him as loudly as I dared. "Pssst, Deedris!" He fell to his knees and clasped his head. What was going on with him? "Deeds! Look over here!" The roar of the other student's chattering afforded me room to project further.

It worked. Deedris saw me. He was hesitant to come my way, but I managed to coax him over with encouraging waves. He checked the patio again before crawling behind the bushes to the edge of the fence. "Who are you?" His voice was hollow and rushed.

"It's me!" I lifted my sunglasses.

"Hump!" Deedris slapped the fence with both hands.

"Shh! Don't call me that. My name is Frumpkin now."

"I've missed you so much, Humphry. Things have gotten so bad without you." There were tears in his eyes.

"What? What happened? And quit it with the name. It's Frumpkin."

"Oh, it's awful. Anatoly seized control of the whole class and gave all his power to Scrotumus. He rules with an iron shoe. Lunch is a hopeless game of hide and seek. His minions don't like him but still do as he commands. When he demands they find me, they pretend they haven't seen me. There is good in them, but it doesn't last. Scrotumus tells them to find me or smell his butt, and they always cave eventually. Every day I am held down and beaten with a shoe."

"I'm so sorry, Deeds." I couldn't believe what I was hearing. Poor Deedris. He always took the brunt of Anatoly's wrath, but it was never this bad. Barnaby would always keep things in check. "What happened to Barnaby?" There was something more going on.

Deedris looked at me like I was crazy. "You didn't hear?"

"Hear what?"

"Barnaby was killed by a wizard."

"What?" I exclaimed louder than I intended. Loud enough to be heard.

"It was last month. He was out with his family on the weekend buying gifts for the holidays. There was some sort of shootout and a stray bullet caught him in the head."

I was speechless. I stood watch for a shootout like that. His blood was on my hands. The guilt was unbearable. The mind plays tricks to avoid such an intense feeling. My conscious split. The guilt, the only feeling that could have swayed my ill-fated course, was sequestered to a far off-corner of my soul, too painful to touch.

"Barnaby was a good little boy," I said at last. "That's what happens to good little boys."

Deedris slumped.

"Listen, I didn't come here to talk about Barnaby. I need your help. Remember when I asked you for information about magic?"

"Of course, I almost got eaten by Alleymen."

"Well, I've learned a lot since then. I can't tell you everything here. Come meet me by the creek so I can get you caught up before lunch is over."

"I can't. They won't let us leave the patio for lunch anymore."

"Why not?"

"It's the end of days, Hump."

"Frumpkin!" I shook the fence for emphasis.

"Sorry. It's the end of days, Frumpkin. Principle Chewbooger instated new rules to keep us safe. We can't leave for recess or lunch and we have weekly interviews with him to tell him all our secrets. He says that he can tell if we are lying and that if we don't tell him everything, then at the end of the year, he will reveal all our secrets to everyone."

Things were worse than I thought. "Don't listen to him, Deeds. He might be magic, but he can't read minds. He couldn't read mine anyways. Don't tell him anything about our conversation."

"But he said–"

"He lied. Meet me after school on the corner of Hilkglen and Carnwick."

"But that's in The Shank. It's too dangerous."

"You'll be safe with me. I promise."

Deedris looked scared. He had every reason to be. I was lying to him as much as Chewbooger. I couldn't keep him safe. I was leading him straight into danger just as I had done before.

"Okay," he whimpered. "I'll meet you there. I should start moving. The more I move, the longer it takes Scrotumus to get a hold of me."

"Good luck, Deeds."

"Good luck, Frumpkin." Deedris trotted off just as his watery eyes began to drip. Poor Deedris.

I clung to the fence a while longer. I missed the simplicity of school. I missed knowing what was right and wrong. I mourned my old life.

At the height of my self-pity, I saw a head stick out from behind a tree. A bespectacled face framed with jet-black hair staring straight at me. Molly Mucasine had seen me. I couldn't move. Her eyes were so wide they seemed to consume me. Unlike Chewbooger, Molly was powerful enough to read my mind. It disturbed me to no end, and yet I had risked everything to experience it once more. Deedris knew me well enough, but Molly calved my spirit and gazed within. No motivation is more mysterious than that to be seen. Even a witch will do.

Her hands tightened on the bark and her mouth slipped open. For a moment I thought she would come to me, but she scurried away like the beautiful little rabbit she was. She read my mind and found it putrid. I had succumbed to the pleasures of deviancy and failed in my quest to stop dark magic. I could lie to myself, but there was no fooling her.

I detached from the fence. I should not have come to the school and stayed too long regardless. I snuck out of the gap in the building and checked the grounds for watchful eyes before racing away. The way was not as clear as it appeared. Mr. Smellington screamed behind me and leapt into chase. "Hey! Come back here! Who are you?" His jiggling body was not built for running. Though I was the slowest kid in class and weighed down by a thick fur coat and heavy gold chains, I easily outpaced the grossly out-of-shape gym teacher. My footprints in the snow were not as swift.

. . .

An easterly wind drew upon the yet unfrozen waters of Lake Bethlahoom, casting a thick layer of icy fog upon the city. In the wake of the 'magic murders', the streets emptied soon after sunset, which in the winter happened in what ought to have been the middle of the afternoon. The chill drove most of the street folk into hiding. Those unable or unwilling met their deaths on frigid nights like these.

Visibility was so poor, Deedris and I nearly collided. He was properly bundled in several layers of mismatched clothes along with a shabby blanket cloaked upon his back. It was easy to envision him as one of the street folk. They had a similar style.

"I'm glad you came," I said. "We've got a lot of work to do."

"Are you going to tell me what's going on now?"

I opened my coat, revealing a line of blue bags. "This right here is pure, concentrated magic."

"You're a wizard!"

"Shh! Not quite, but I work for one. Blane, the guy you told me about. I found him and started working for him."

"Why would you do that?"

I hesitated. I wasn't sure if that question was relevant anymore. My reasons to join were not my reasons to stay. The best answer, I decided, was not the truth, but the one that satisfied the person asking the question. "To become a man."

"You know how to become a man?"

"I'm already a man, or nearly so, anyways. And you will be too if you do as I say." The right words to manipulate came to me naturally. I had heard some version of them so many times before.

"I'll do anything."

"I know you will." Deedris trusted me so much. "First things first. You need a new name."

"What about Manlyman?"

"I was thinking of something more subtle. How about Abraham?"

"Abraham the manly man. I'll take it. What's next?"

Desperation is a boy's greatest teacher, and Abraham was its star pupil. I taught him everything I knew that night. He shadowed me just as I had with Blane. I pulled him aside after each drop and repeated that old, reliable refrain, 'get the money and go'. He took to it like a boy to beans. He defied the temptations of Ms. Kooklioni's floppy wonders and squashed the seductions of the temptress Marie. It was only the final stop of the night that gave him pause.

"You're telling me I have to go in there by myself at night?" Deedris pulled his blanket tight around his face.

"It will be okay. Look straight ahead and walk with purpose. They are more afraid of you than you are of them."

"I find that hard to believe." His breath was loud and quick.

There was no sense in trying to quell his fear. I could only push him through it. "Follow me if you want to be a man," I said before disappearing into The Alley. There was silence. No footsteps followed me in. I kept walking regardless. *You can do it, Deeds. You can do it.*

The center was just up ahead when the pattering of Deedris's feet sounded behind me. Desperation at work.

Jerry was waiting like always. "Fruitloop, my man, bring it in."

"Jerry!" Jerry and I embraced in a secret handshake of our own that I was thrilled Deedris bore witness to. "Jerry, this is Abraham. Abraham, this is Jerry."

"What it is, Ham-man?" Jerry corralled Deedris in his custom. Deedris had no response.

"Abraham is going to be replacing me soon."

"Shit. Already? I got Boogie for two years. You for three months. Ham-man's going to leave me next week."

"I'm sorry, Jerry. It's nothing personal, you know. I am just moving up like Blane did."

"What's he doing now anyway? It must be good, considering he hasn't been back to see me."

"I don't know exactly. Every time I see him we just talk about what I need to be doing. Whatever he's up to, it seems stressful."

"Tell him I got his back, whatever it is. If that son of bitch is climbing to the top, he's carrying my fat ass with him."

"I will relay your message, good sir."

"That goes for you too. If you ever find yourself in trouble, just let me know."

"Thank you."

"Now where's my shit?"

We left The Alley with a skip in our step. Abraham was well on his way to becoming a man and I was freed to continue my quest up the magical ladder. All seemed well in my twisted mind.

Chapter 19

The fog turned to heavy snow by the weekend. I would have liked to give Abraham a nicer night to go out on his own, but it was out of my control. Seamus was insistent that I join him and Blane that Saturday evening. They picked me up in the afternoon in Blane's new black speedster. It was the coolest car I had ever seen. The outside looked like it had just landed from somewhere across the galaxy. The interior was deep red suede with white leather trim, sophisticated, but lethal. He called it 'Betty'. The magic business had been good to Blane.

We drove past the edge of town, down Highway 17 along the edge of Lake Bethlahoom. The streets had not been plowed or salted since the morning, and snow began sticking to the pavement. Blane didn't slow down. "Betty can handle it," he said. "Can't you, Betty?" He patted the dashboard and hit the gas. He was right. It stuck to the road like a hot summer day.

"So, what's Ignacio like?" I asked. They had been frugal with their information about him. I knew he was powerful but was otherwise oblivious.

"He's a fine man," Seamus said. "True as a friend can be and ruthless to everyone else. You'll meet him soon enough. Just so, I'm afraid."

Blane gripped the steering wheel and hit the brakes before banking a sweeping turn down an unmarked country road. He reduced his speed and cut his headlights. The bumps in the road outmatched Betty's shocks. We continued bumping up and down for several minutes in silence.

The windows of a log cabin glowed through the falling snow and thick conifers. Blane and Seamus kept a keen eye for anyone lurking about in the snow, but there was nobody outside. Why would there be on a night like that?

We parked at the corner of the cabin in a blind spot of the glowing windows. Seamus addressed me like a mother before church. "You'll be on your best behavior, boy. As far as I know, it's just Ignacio in there. If that's the case, you'll stand by and watch. On the off chance he's got company, we'll need you for more than your eyes. You still got that gun in your coat?"

I padded my side. Cold steel pressed against my liver. "Yes, sir," I mumbled. Having the gun hidden in my coat made me feel powerful, but the thought of using it terrified me. I would only fire it if life was in jeopardy.

"You're a good boy, Frumpkin. Being a good boy is not the same as being a good man. A good boy is kind in the day and goes to bed early. A good man provides good boys like you the luxury of innocence. He shoulders the burden of reality and tells nobody about it. Nobody. Under the fiercest questioning, he's silent. What we're doing here, this is one of those burdens. If you make it through tonight without telling anyone what you see, you'll be well on your way to manhood by morning. If you tell a single soul, you'll be a dead little boy. Do you follow me, Frumpkin?"

I followed every word. In all my years of wondering, I never guessed what it took to be a man. Even upon hearing it, I was suspicious. Seamus was one of the biggest liars I had ever met, but in every good lie, there exists a kernel of truth. "I think I understand," I said.

"We'll make sure of that later. Let's go. Keep close and don't be a fool."

We snuck around to the front door. Seamus picked the lock as easily as though he had a key. From years of practice or Leprechaun magic, I could not tell. We followed him inside. The entrance led straight into the main living room. It was a beautiful hunting lodge with polished wood floors, crisply cleaned plush rugs, rich leather sofas and walls of freshly fell cedar logs adorned with the faces of friendly forest creatures. A bursting fire crackled along to swinging jazz playing from the other room. The coziness was made all the more appealing by the contrasting snowdrift climbing the walls outside.

A fat man, naked but for a long white apron, backed through a swinging door from the kitchen, picking at a plate of cheese while swaying and scatting with the music. "Skippity-doo-bop-a-dee-bop--." He froze mid-scat. A half-chewed cube of cheddar fell from his mouth back to the plate. It was the cube that broke that man's wrist. The plate slipped from his hand and crashed on the floor. He laughed nervously. "Silly me, I dropped my cheese."

"It's well past time for cheese, Ignacio," Seamus said, stepping forward with one hand tucked in his coat. "Best get us all a drink and take a seat."

The surprise faded from Ignacio's face, and resignation overcame him. "Of course. Drinks for my friends. Why don't you all wait here while I get those for you."

"I'll come along with you." Seamus jostled his cloaked hand. Ignacio grimaced and obliged. The two stepped into the kitchen alone. Blane gestured to a table in the corner of the room. We seated ourselves and waited.

Seamus and Ignacio returned soon after. Ignacio held a bottle of whiskey in one hand and a plate carrying four glasses in the other. Seamus walked behind him with one hand still resting in his coat. Ignacio passed the glasses around and filled them before taking a seat. He raised his trembling glass. "To long-lasting friendships built on not shooting each other."

I raised my own glass to toast. "Here, here," I said instinctively.

Blane gave me a stern look, but Seamus smiled. "Here, here, boys. Cheers to the good times ahead." He clinked glasses with Ignacio and me and gulped his whiskey. "Ah, tastes like the old country, don't it?"

Ignacio and Blane bumped glasses awkwardly and drank too. I took a sip of my own and nearly choked to death.

"You sourpussies never change, do you?" Seamus slapped Ignacio's bare back. "Lighten up my friend. I have a gift for you." Seamus whipped out his concealed hand. Ignacio recoiled and hid behind his raised arms. "Are you afraid of cigars, Ignacio?" Seamus popped open the box in his hand and passed a stogie to each of us.

Ignacio peaked between his fingers at the cigar resting on the table in front of him. Seamus slid a pack of matches along next to it after lighting his own. "Relax. We're here to celebrate. That's a genuine Cublon, right there." He puffed on his own and blew a ring across the table. He blew a smaller one that passed straight through the first. "Bullseye." He laughed at his magical prowess. A cackling laugh that coaxed Ignacio from his feeble shield.

"Does this mean you're not going to kill me?"

"For the love of St. Florence. I'm not here to kill you. We're here to celebrate."

Ignacio looked around. His fear of being murdered began subsiding. As it slipped away, new feelings were free to stir. "Well then why the hell did you break in and scare the shit out of me?"

Seamus cackled. "A good laugh, for one. Don't be sour. Tell me what I should have done. If you thought I was here to kill you, you would have shot me the moment you saw me coming." Ignacio blushed. His feelings were as close to the surface as any person I had ever seen. "These are strange times," Seamus continued. "I don't blame you for being paranoid. I'm a bit myself. That's why I came in here like I did. All my friends have killed each other because of that paranoia. I don't want that to happen to us." There was a quiver in his voice that fooled even me.

Ignacio placed a hand on Seamus's shoulder. "And it never will, my friend." He lit his cigar and took a couple puffs before sagging into his chair. "I can't believe what's been happening. You're the only ones left alive. Everyone else I sold to is dead. I keep thinking I'm next. There are a lot of people who want what I have. I think I'm cursed for having it."

Seamus calculated his next words and took a new angle. "The whole world can be explained by curses and luck if you don't look too closely. Simple explanations are like that. They aren't true; we believe them because we can understand them. The real world is nuanced and piss poor to be summed up in a phrase. We live at the confluence of human nature and circumstance, and both elude comprehension. The best we can do is see what didn't work for them, and try something different."

"I have to be honest with you, Seamus. I have no idea what you just said."

Seamus squashed his cigar between his tightened lips. "I'm saying we have to learn from their mistakes. They died for a reason, not a curse. It was isolation, competition and fear. They thought the others were out to kill them, and because they all thought that, they all were. Some ideas are like that, self-fulfilling, where believing it's possible is all the proof needed to know it's true. It never seems to be the good ideas. Just the ones that ruin everything."

Blane finished his fourth glass of whiskey and chimed in. "Who's the sourpussy now, Seamus?"

Seamus cackled. "My God, you've done it to me. You turned me out. Sour as a lemon, I am."

"I think it's going to be okay," Ignacio said. "Like you said, it was the isolation that did them in. The fear. I was afraid of you guys until a minute ago, but coming together like this solved the whole thing. I think what we need to do is get everyone together just like this. Have a party or something. Show everyone that we're on the same side."

"Do you know all their names? Where they all live?" Seamus's words struck like a snake.

Ignacio seemed to notice Seamus's unusual eagerness but was too committed to the plan to change course. "I have an idea, yes."

"Well then spit it out. Let's give them a call right now. Make a list. It'll be easier to keep track of everyone with a list."

"I can make a list if you think that's a good idea." A new sense of fear came over Ignacio, but it was unlike that of earlier. He didn't want to believe what he feared. He would rather believe that they really were planning a party. Desire and fear faced off to a draw, and social pressure held the tie-breaking vote. Seamus had seized command of his will.

"Just write down everyone you know. We'll figure out who to invite after that." Seamus pulled a notebook and pen from his coat and handed it over. Ignacio held the pen for a moment before jotting down a name. "Who's that you're putting?" Seamus asked.

"Well, I just put down 'Malto'. He's over in Seabrook."

"Best be thorough and write down his address and notable traits."

"Notable traits?"

"You know, for the party. Seating arrangements. You need to be thorough to make good seating arrangements."

"Of course. For the seating arrangements."

Ignacio added some extra details about Malto before starting a new line. He wrote down dozens more names while Seamus went on about how wonderful the party would be, occasionally asking Ignacio about his preferred color of streamers or pizza toppings, anything to keep him writing. I found myself imagining stepping out of Blane's speedster dawning a new black coat with the lovely Marlene at my arm. I couldn't wait.

Blane took the time to keep drinking. He tried to get me to drink along with him, but I couldn't manage more than a sip. The cigar gave me even more trouble. My first breath of smoke threw me into a coughing fit. Blane demonstrated how to stoke the cigar without filling my lungs, but even that wasn't pleasant. I felt a tingle in my skull and down the back of my spine. If there were no other feelings the cigar gave me, I would have loved it, but it was accompanied by an agonizing sickness that left me grasping the table in search of a position I could take that wouldn't make my insides feel twisted. I had yet to find one by the time Ignacio finished his list.

"Any more people you know?" Seamus asked. His voice felt like a needle dragged across my eardrum.

"I think that's the last of them."

"And this is all you know about them, eh?"

"That's pretty much it. I'm going to go to the bathroom if you don't mind." Ignacio slid his chair out and stood. "This is going to be a great party," he said weakly. Nobody answered him. Blane was too drunk, I was too sick and Seamus had already said everything he needed to say.

Ignacio gave a solemn nod and turned to the bathroom. Seamus rose from his seat like a wisp of smoke. Swift and silent, he pulled a gun from his coat and shot Ignacio once in the back of the head. The crack of the gun split my ears. The sound was so shocking, I couldn't process what I was looking at, Ignacio's blood and brain splattered on the wall.

"What's happening?" I muttered. "What's happening?" I couldn't take my eyes off of Ignacio's limp, naked body.

Blane, drunk though he was, had the sentience to lift me from my stupefied state and drag me from the room. My eyes tracked the body all the way out. Blane propped me against a tree outside. I was somehow still looking at the body. Seamus stood over it in the snow with a smoking gun and a list of more people to kill. Everywhere I turned, the image followed.

The real Seamus beelined out of the house and straight towards us. "Oy, Frumpkin. You remember what I told you about being a man?"

I couldn't remember anything but Seamus and the gun and the body and the list.

"I'm asking you a question, you little shit!" Seamus's voice lashed like a whip. He grabbed my throat and pressed me against the tree. The image of the gun and body played in the blackness of his snarling eyes.

His fist appeared as a streaking comet, growing until it smothered my whole vision. My nose burst with pain and the foregone murderous scene finally faded away. Seamus's fists followed me to the ground and beat me into the snow. "If you tell anyone, I'll fucking kill you and all your fucking friends you worthless piece of shit." Each swing knocked me farther from control. My mind held nothing but the power of Seamus's scolding voice and the sting of his restless fists. "I'll kill you! I'll fucking kill you!"

"He gets it! He gets it." Blane pulled Seamus back and stood between us. "He gets it," he said again and again.

Seamus pointed at me over Blane's shoulder. "You get it, Frumpkin? If you tell anyone what happened here, I'll come for you."

I got it. I couldn't say so or nod or do anything except clutch my bleeding face and hope to keep it from falling apart, but I got it. Apparently that was enough for Seamus. He took a few deep breaths and patted Blane's shoulder. "You did good, boys. Let's get you all home and happy."

. . .

Seamus drove us back the way we came. Somewhere along the way, the searing pain in my face lessened to a dull throb. I found myself thanking Seamus for ending the beating when he did. Relief knows no context.

"You took it well," he said. "It's good for you, too, you know. Keeps your head on straight. Too many little shit kids can't take a punch these days. I'm proud of you, Frumpkin." The compliment found a part of me I never knew was aching. It was a very small weight mounted immovably through a lifetime of forbearance. It took no effort on Seamus's part to lift and toss aside. These are the gifts of people like Seamus. They see our weakest, most neglected point and take a single pebble from our load. Relief is the sharpest tool a person can wield.

They dropped me off two blocks from the apartment building in case we were being followed. Seamus handed me a roll of cash through his window that was several times larger than the ones I was used to. *How many beans does a man need?* "Thank you," I said.

"You're one of us now, Frumpkin. If you need anything, let me know. I'll be doing the same for you."

"Okay. Thank you."

Seamus whipped the car around and sang out his farewells as he sped off in the opposite direction. I waved them off. Blane held out a hand from the passenger window. There was not much else he had the will left to do.

Charlie D. Weisman

Chapter 20

The snow was halfway to my knees. Walking the two blocks took as long as it normally did to walk five or six, long enough for the cold to sink through my coat and the many layers of wool beneath. Who would walk the streets on a night like this? They would have to be a real dummy, I thought. A real booger-brain.

"Deedris!" I yelped upon reaching the stoop of the apartment building. He was bundled in every scrap of fabric he owned, looking like a tumbleweed of cloth. He tried waving, but his arms were kept down to waist-level by all the layers of frozen blankets.

"Hi, Hump. Are we using our real names again?"

"What? No! Get inside." I looked around to make sure no one was there to hear my mistake before opening the door for Abraham. I had to be more careful, especially with the new secrets I held.

Abraham waddled into the building and I followed behind. Once we were in the apartment, I turned on him. "Did you make all the deliveries and get the cash?" In my effort to be cautious, I was stern.

"Sure did. Every one of them." He peeled off several layers of tattered blankets and dug out a pile of cash.

I snatched it from his hands. I don't know where my aggression was coming from. I just had to make sure that Abraham was doing his job. That's all he was there for. Nothing else seemed important. I counted the money. It was all there. There was never a need to be curt after all. "Good work, Abraham." I counted out his cut and passed it back.

"What's this for?"

"That's you're cut. You work for me now. This is your payment."

"Wow. Can you imagine the gumballs this could get me?" His frozen lips were tinted blue and his wind-lashed cheeks bright red, but he smiled the same boyish grin I'd known my whole life. That was Deedris I was looking at.

I had a single moment of clarity, another chance amongst many to assume responsibility. I had ensnared my best friend in the same trap I had fallen for myself. The evil I set out to stop had adopted me as an instrument of its will. Everything I believed was right and wrong had been tossed aside for the prospect of beans. In a single moment I saw all of this and felt the now familiar stab of guilt. It was obvious in that moment that embracing the truth was a direct path to freedom from it all, a clean and protected path leading straight to wherever I was supposed to go.

Then the moment was gone. That clear path was lost in the endless forest of lies. From the trees, the path looks like the most dangerous place of all. Anyone can see you. There is no place to hide, and when you know what's in the forest, hiding feels like the only option. Guilt is the barrier that holds the dangerous creatures in the forest and keeps the path free and safe. But I ran from guilt and so into lies. This was Abraham, and I was Frumpkin. I embraced the lie once more.

"I can get you all the gumballs you can chew," I said. Abraham's eyes flashed with submission. He was mine. If I was going to make it in the forest, I had to act accordingly.

There was a familiar knock at the door. Its rhythm was distinctly sweet and melancholy. The Lovely Marlene had come once more. I flushed bright red and squealed. I may have been a big fish to Abraham, but I was but a tadpole next to the behemoth toad that was the Lovely Marlene.

The tender knocks drew me to the door. I opened it. The Lovely Marlene smiled with closed lips and weary eyes. She was bundled in a thick fur coat and tall, fur-lined boots. Still, she shivered in the doorway. "Come in!" I said. "You must be so cold." I took her hand and ushered her inside.

"I'm alright, sweetie," she said with her soft, faded voice. "Who's your friend?"

"How could I forget! Lovely Marlene, this is Abraham. He is working for me now. Abraham, this is the Lovely Marlene."

"This is your girlfriend?" Abraham gazed in wonder. I held my head high. I felt something I had never felt before. It was pride, the forest-dwelling farce that masquerades as noble truth. The cloak of fools. A fresh coat of paint on rotten wood.

"It's nice to meet you, Abraham. Are you going to be joining us tonight?"

Abraham mumbled incoherently and looked to me for an answer.

"He'll be staying in Seamus's old room." I pulled Abraham's arm in the right direction. "It's the one over there. Just watch out for all the guns." I slapped his bottom on his way out. He looked back in awe once more before leaving us alone.

The Lovely Marlene shed her thick coat, revealing a short silver dress underneath. Doing so reduced her size by more than half. She was deceptively dainty, even thinner than the last time I had seen her, just one week earlier. How much more she could fade before disappearing was a grave question I dared not ponder. "Can I get you some beans?" I asked instead.

"No, thank you."

"Are you sure?"

She didn't answer, but stepped towards me and guided me to the couch with one hand tucked behind my ear. I clunked on my back. She followed, floating down like a feather, resting one hand on my shoulder and her head on my chest. It was ever more amazing how perfectly she fit next to me. A fallen star in my arms. Though her light was dimming, her warmth remained. If anything, as she shrunk, her warmth became more accessible as it smoldered closer to the surface. *Accessible and extinguishable.* I grabbed my blanket from under me and threw it over us as best I could. I would give my life to keep her warm.

"How are you holding up? Seamus told me you had a rough night. That's why I came over, to make sure you're okay." She looked over the bruises on my face.

"Seamus told you that?" Anger bubbled inside of me. *After everything he said about keeping quiet?* "What else did he tell you?" I had never spoken to her with such an attitude.

"He didn't tell me anything. He just said that you wanted to see me. I can go if you want me to." She unlatched, leaving a hole in my heart where she had just lain. I reached out to bring her back.

"Please don't go. I didn't mean to ask you like that. I just had a rough night is all. Like he said." Marlene lowered back onto me, but the connection between us was changed, as though in the brief moment of exposure, my wounded heart had calloused. Those never fade. The bruises on my face would last for a few days, but the scarring of my heart would last forever. Had I known that, I may have been more reluctant to reveal more to Marlene. As it was that I didn't, I scoured myself for anything on which Marlene could cling. The heart is blind and yearns only for connection.

"What happened?"

"Well, it's a long story." How much could I reveal? I couldn't say anything without revealing everything. The only things I wanted to say to Marlene were the things I had sworn to secrecy, but those secrets were burning a hole in me that hurt worse than Seamus's punches. I was again shown the path of truth. Again it looked obvious that I walk towards it, through the guilt and into the light. Again, my fear held me back. Fear feels like it is the only thing that keeps me alive. If I were to get rid of it, I would only have more reason to be afraid. There is no escape from the cycle of reinforcement.

"You can talk to me as much as you want, you know. I like to listen."

"A lot of it is a secret."

Marlene reached her soft lips to my cheek and kissed me. The warmth spread across my face and down my neck. My body relaxed completely and tingled with the most pleasant of all feelings. "I can keep your secrets," she whispered into my ear. She spoke hardly above a breath, but the words reverberated like a music hall housing a full chorus. They were magic. She kissed my lips. She may as well have consumed my soul. I would keep nothing from her.

"My real name is Humphry Bulgerdeen," I said, stepping onto the path.

She kissed my cheek again. "Tell me everything, Humphry."

I did.

Chapter 21

I awoke the following morning to an empty couch. Marlene had disappeared sometime in the night like she always did. I checked my coat. She took all the cash I had. I didn't mind. I had no use for it. Besides, an evening with the Lovely Marlene was worth everything I had, including my secrets. Those were the foundation of my life, and I had given them as willingly as a quarter. As it happened, I gave them to a great and unexpected end. Upon sharing my secrets, my life became clearer. The truth, shrouded for so long by lies, shone once again as a beacon to follow. I was Humphry, not Frumpkin, and I came into this world on a mission to end the spread of dark magic.

A fresh paper awaited me outside. The Sunday edition ran weekly updates of Tabby's baby. Some truths are harder to accept than others but only because of how easy it is to pretend that the truth is something different. It was easy for me to imagine that God really did come to Tabby. That's the lie I had been telling myself since that first night with Marlene. Now that I had stricken such lies from my mind, acceptance came without any effort at all. That baby was conceived through dark magic and I was its father. I was responsible.

This week's edition covered Tabby's new diet. The paper had a column called "The Voice of the People" dedicated to community members' opinions about daily life. The paper did not reveal individuals' names, and so the writing was earnest in a way that would otherwise be deemed impolite. Since Tabby's announcement, this section had been saturated with thoughts on the baby. Many of the thoughts were about Tabby's unworthiness, and most of their reasoning revolved around her diet. Today's article was surely in response to that. I cared very little about the number of rutabagas in Tabby's daily stew, but the idea of using the paper to anonymously communicate was intriguing.

Officer Murphy Flannigan made regular appearances in the paper, offering dissent to the popular idea that the strings of murders in Bethlahoom were chaotic and unrelated. His words were often cut short and ridiculed, but from my vantage, it was obvious that he alone was the paper's voice of reason. If I could somehow lend authority to his assertions, or better yet, enhance his understanding of events, then he may be able to more effectively use the power of the police to track Frankie Fourfeet. I could no longer imagine taking on dark magic alone. I needed his help.

Worried about the identifiability of my penmanship, I decided to write my submission for the paper in a collage of letters I cut out of various magazines and newspapers. The more varied the selection, the harder it would be to trace. It took much longer that way, but I was proud of the final result. I could say everything I wanted and stay completely anonymous.

Dear Bethlahoom,

Your people are not safe. The Grand Wizard Frankie Fourfeet is still at large, killing en masse with dark magic. All the additional murders of late have been by the leprechaun Seamus. The leprechaun Seamus is confirmed to be distributing magic through the subjugation and manipulation of good boys who are just trying their hardest to be kind and true. How this particular magic relates to the aforementioned dark magic is still uncertain. More information to come.

Yours truly,
Mystery Boy of Bethlahoom

It looked perfect, unassailable in every way. I folded my letter and put it in an envelope marked 'The Voice of the People' and addressed it to the news headquarters as directed by the paper. I sealed it with a stamp and was about to drop it off in the mailbox before Deedris came tumbling out of Seamus's room rubbing his neck and looking generally unsettled. "Good morning, Deeds," I said. "You feeling alright?"

"Hey Hump. I'm alright. Just hard sleeping on a bed full of guns. What's that you got in your hand?"

I mumbled incoherently while internally debating whether I should tell him. He already knew so much, and my streak of telling the truth had been nothing but prosperous. "It's a letter to the paper. I don't want anyone knowing it's me who's sending it though, so you got to keep quiet about it."

"Oh. A secret letter. I don't mean to pry, but they'll probably know it's you on account of your name and return address on the envelope there."

"Shoot!" He was right. I could always count on Deedris to have keen eyes and a good heart. Another gift brought by the truth.

"If you really want to be sneaky, you should use a drop box across town. Don't even use a return address. My cousin used to pull pranks on people like that all the time. Never got caught once."

"You're a genius, Deeds. You want to go with me to drop it off?"

"Can I get something to eat first?"

"Of course."

I made us both bacon and egg sandwiches that put my usual can of cold beans to shame. We ate in record time and left the apartment around noon. The sun was out in force, reflecting off the blanket of fresh snow from the day before. We agreed a pair of new sunglasses were worth an extra stop along the way. Deedris looked strange wearing fancy shades and tattered sheets for clothes, so we stopped at a shop to get him fitted for a new suit as well, the same one Seamus had taken me to in Paltry Square. The store clerk told us he could have it ready in a few hours given how slow business was at that time of year. January in Bethlahoom had few admirers.

I was counted amongst the admirers. My body shape was not suited for many things, but retaining heat was one of them. It felt great knowing that I had been blessed with an ability that others lacked. It was not that I felt better than other people, but that in acknowledging one gift I had been given, I was able to open my eyes to all the others I had not recognized before. I was given the town of Bethlahoom. We all were, and though it had many faults: murderers, evil wizards and cannibalistic Alleymen, it was a beautiful place worth saving. No single person could have built it. No group of people, even. The trees and lakes and rivers were beyond the creation of man. The world was a gift worth more than any of us could ever hope to repay. My warm, hefty bottom taught me that.

Deedris had no heft to teach him that lesson, but he seemed to have gotten it in another way. No matter what happened to Deedris, he always made it back to a hopeful disposition. I had never asked him how he did it. "Hey Deeds, why are you always so happy?"

"Me? I'm not always happy. I get sad and scared, confused. I would like to be happy all the time, though. Why do you ask?"

"It's just something I've noticed about you. Maybe you're not always happy, but you always seem to take a positive spin on things. It's something I want to do more myself."

"I always thought that about you. Every time something crazy happens, like Anatoly makes me eat a booger in front of the girls, you always cheer me up. I don't think I could have handled it without you."

"Thanks, Deeds." Like the rotundness of my rump, Deed's kind words opened my eyes to the kinder aspects of the world. I've always wanted to make people feel better. I've cleaned up after them and cooked for them, I have been their servant, and it never seemed to make a difference. With Deed's, I just had to exist. I had an unconscious quality that satisfied my most elusive desire. Maybe those are the ones most quintessential to a person. What we are before our minds start convoluting things is all we ever need to be. In stillness, we are our most beautiful.

"So are you going to tell me about that letter, or what?"

The envelope crinkled in my clenched fist. "It's a note to the newspaper telling them everything I know about magic. It's time we put an end to all of this."

"But what about the gumballs!" Deeds had only just gotten a taste of the high life. I had to remember how alluring it was for me. To experience luxury after years of deprivation is intoxicating.

"This is what it's all about. It's not the beans or gumballs or the women. It's about finding the truth and saving the town. I know it seems like a good life, selling magic in the Shank, but it's not. It sucks you in and then chews you up. Believe me, Deeds. It happened to me."

Deeds threw up his arms in objection, but slowly lowered them as he took notice again of the cuts and bruises on my face. My words weren't entirely figurative, and the proof couldn't be ignored. "I was really hoping this was going to be the start of a new life for me. The gumballs, the freedom, it was all too good to be true, wasn't it?"

"We'll get you those gumballs. And things will be okay. I promise."

"I'm not going back."

"What do you mean?"

"I'm not going back to school. Not with Scrotumus the way he is. Maybe selling magic isn't the best way out, but it's a start."

It's hard to tell the difference between wanting what is best for someone and wanting them to stay the same. I wanted Deeds to go right back to school because even if he was miserable, that was how I knew him to be. I knew he would be safe in the mortal sense and that he'd continue to need me. It was selfish. "We'll figure something out. Something tells me I won't be going back either. I've already been gone for half a school year and nobody noticed."

"I noticed."

"Thanks, Deeds."

"Molly noticed, too."

"What are you talking about?" I hoped my bruises hid my blushing cheeks.

"She asked me about you. Twice. Once when you first left and then again after you came to the school. I think she may have seen you."

"Well, she doesn't count. I think she's a witch. She sees everything."

"Really? Thank God she was always nice to me. Could you imagine having a witch in your class that didn't like you?"

"Pshh. She would probably use dark magic to get my sister pregnant with my demon baby."

"Yeah, that sounds about right."

I wished it were something different. *I wish it was Molly that came to me at night instead of the Lovely Marlene.* I shook the thought from my head. The Lovely Marlene deserved better, and Molly was a witch trying to destroy my life. *Maybe if I tried talking to her things would be different.* No. Even if she was a real girl not plotting my exceedingly elaborate demise, I was with the Lovely Marlene, and I owed her the respect to not think of another in such marital terms.

We made our way back to the clothing store right about the time Deedris's new suit was due to be ready. It was as simple as exchanging cash with one hand and receiving the goods with the other. It took a grand total of 8 seconds: the way shopping should be.

"Hey," Deeds started on the way back to the apartment, holding the suit up to his body for me to see. "Do you think Miss Kooklioni would like this?"

"Miss Kooklioni? Why would you care about that?"

"Oh, it's nothing. She just offered me something and I've been thinking a lot about it. I know you said never to go upstairs with her, of course."

"Deeds! What did she offer?"

"She said she would make me a man. I don't know what she meant by it all, but I think it's worth a try."

"Blane told me never to go up there. He said it was the number one rule. Never go up to Miss Kooklioni's room. And that's coming from the guy who told us it's fine walking into the Alley!"

"I know. I know. I'll just keep looking for another way I guess."

The sunset lasted the whole walk home. The thin clouds and fresh coat of snow acted like parallel mirrors, reflecting the light back and forth so we saw the colors of a thousand sunsets in one. That night was a dream come true. We ordered pizza and stayed up late on a school night. What could spoil a night like that?

. . .

The following morning started with all the splendor of the previous night. Pancakes and sausage filled our bellies and reruns of cartoons filled our hearts. The height of humanity was reached, the pinnacle of civilization achieved. For a brief and unstable moment, Deedris and I had solved the great puzzle of life. A point of perfect calm and tranquility at the center of chaos.

An unexpected knock came from the door. I leapt to my feet. On such a morning as this, there is never a worried thought to be found. "I'll get it," I sang and pranced to the door. "Remember you're still Abraham! And I am... Frumpkin. That's it. I almost forgot!" Another knock came on harder than the first. I spared no more time opening the door.

Seamus towered in the hallway, draped in his deep green coat and cap. His usual sneer had turned to a stern furrow and frown. He stepped inside without a word.

"Hello, Seamus. It's me, Frumpkin, and this is my friend Abraham." Deedris waved nervously from the couch.

"Mornin' to you both and fine meeting you, Abraham. I've heard good things about you."

"You have?" Deedris looked on in wonder. I had a feeling nobody ever told him that before, and he probably felt a great sense of relief upon hearing it.

"Aye, but I'm not here to say anything good." He put both hands on my shoulders and glared into me with his sharp green eyes. "Marlene's dead."

All the joy of the morning sank past my feet and vanished through the floorboards. Dread came pouring in from the ceiling. "What are you talking about?"

"Said it simple enough. Marlene's dead. It was a matter of time with that one. Magic, of course. It's dangerous stuff when you have too much."

"How did she get too much magic?" A haunting notion came to me. There was only one source of magic I knew about in Bethlahoom.

"I don't mean to insinuate, but I assume you gave her a little more than you usually do on Sunday? I knew Marlene well. Everything you gave her went to one place. That's how all this works, you know."

"It was me? She died because of me?" I ran through our last night together. *What did I give her? What did it mean that everything went to one place? Everything went to Seamus. I gave her all my secrets on Sunday and Seamus killed her to punish us.* I don't know which felt worse, the grief or the guilt. They worked in tandem, one freezing me brittle and the other smashing me to a million pieces, priming me for the onslaught of fear that would soon melt me down to soup.

"Best not to think of it now. I'm sorry for your loss, Frumpkin. I'm giving you the next few days off to clear your head, but I'll need you fresh and ready on Sunday. We have a busy week ahead of us."

I couldn't speak. I wasn't sure if I could even stand without Seamus gripping my shoulders.

"I'll leave you two alone. Just rest up and don't be too hard on yourself. And remember, keep your mouth shut. I'll come by Sunday afternoon. Wear your finest coat."

He squeezed my shoulders and patted my head. It was all the affection that a man like Seamus could pretend to give. Just enough to convince me he cared. He didn't care. He was a murderous leprechaun, a fierce user of dark magic hell-bent on taking over Bethlahoom, possibly even the world. Yet, in a twisted sense, he spared my life. He could have killed me as he had Marlene and now he was forgiving me for my transgressions against him. Melted by fear and guilt and grief, my mind could be cast to any shape Seamus desired. I was only a boy after all.

Interlude 3

Humphry stopped speaking and lay in a tight ball on the floor. Merideth grabbed a fireplace poker from behind the couch and prodded him in the back. "More please," she said.

"No more," Humphry groaned.

"Come on."

"No," Humphry whimpered.

Merideth kept poking him. "More, please," she repeated between pokes. "More, please."

Humphry swatted at the stick unsuccessfully several times before submitting.

Chapter 22

He left us to our cartoons. I wobbled to the couch and collapsed. There was so much to think about and too many feelings to think at all. Deedris was unequipped to help. He started to speak a couple dozen times but cut himself short halfway through the first word. I didn't think anything less of him for it. There was nothing anyone could have said to make me feel better.

Deedris did much more than speak over the next couple of days. He cooked for me as best he could. It was cereal three meals a day. He cleaned around the apartment. He used the same dirty rag on every surface, but at least it made the filth consistent. He picked some flowers for me as well. Or as best he could in the dead of winter. Pine needles make a lovely bouquet.

In my head, the war between truth and fiction raged. It was one that I had been fighting for some time. My previous victory was short-lived and came with dire consequences. I thought I had eradicated every lie I lived by, but there were so many hiding in plain sight. Marlene was not the confidant I believed her to be. She told Seamus everything I told her. *Or did she?* I told her things Seamus would not forgive so easily—Seamus seemed like he never forgave anything—yet it was clear that she had told him enough to have her killed. Maybe it was haste to punish me that kept her from revealing the whole truth. I couldn't be sure.

In those damned days, I recognized a fuller extent of my lies. Many were meant with good intentions. It was not a fight between good and evil; it was a fight between truth and fantasy. My lies to Seamus were as dishonest as those to myself. They also had greater stakes to navigate. There was no simple way to shed them. If I came clean, he would kill me. I would have no more lies then. It would win the war in principle but at the cost of all my good intentions. *Were my intentions lies as well?* I could not yet tell. Self-deception is the most elusive foe.

The death of Marlene was its own war. That war was lost. I had been cheering on the sidelines, hoping to offer whatever help I could, but I was powerless. Her death, though unexpected in cause, was a certainty in time. She had been fading since I met her. Every time I saw her was worse. It would not have been long before her condition took her had Seamus not intervened. Had I not lived my life of lies.

Grief was no less heavy for her drawn-out demise, but I was made better prepared to bear it. It was an unconscious process. I had been thinking about her death for months, and all those thoughts were unnecessary to repeat. The worst part of a sudden death is the months' worth of thoughts that steamroll through in a single wave. It makes me wonder if we should always be mourning each other. Everyone we meet will die, and we know that from the beginning, but we hold off thinking about it for as long as we can. Maybe we hold out hope that we will die first. The first to die needs never live with death. It's a subtle omission of truth with which we all gamble.

After days of dwelling in my thoughts and contemplating the nature of life, I came to the following conclusion: the obvious consequences of lies are experienced when the truth is revealed, and they grow for the entirety of their concealment. We begin with the hope that the truth is never revealed, but that hope sours into desperation as the disparity between the truth and our lies widens, tearing our souls apart. We find ourselves in immeasurable pain with the only solution appearing to be more painful still: social doom. In the presence of some people, that meant worse things than with others. I did not want to reveal my secrets in such a burst that would see me killed, but the quicker I could do so, the lesser my consequences would be. If coming clean now meant death, then it would only mean a more grisly death in the future if I kept hold of my lies to Seamus. I did not want to live a life of lies anymore. So it was that I decided I would tell him everything.

. . .

Sunday morning came with an eerie calm. My mind had gone quiet now that my decision to tell the truth was made. The weather was nice for the middle of January. The Sun shone in a cloudless sky, and in the heated apartment, I was free to imagine the temperature outside to be as warm as I liked. The townspeople would be getting ready for church. All the little boys and girls were getting yelled at and shushed at the same time. It was the only time of the week when I knew what everyone was doing. Sometimes I knew what everyone my age was doing, but on Sunday mornings I knew the whereabouts of nearly the whole town. If fear comes from not knowing, then I can't help but think that this little bit of certainty made Sunday mornings a touch more peaceful than the others.

But not everyone went to church. I found that out when I stopped going myself. Once I didn't go, it seemed everyone I came in contact with didn't either, like there were two groups of people walking around that just happened to never cross paths, and I had been transferred to the other group. It meant anything could happen on a Sunday. That small bit of peace was lost.

An urgent knock came at the door followed by the rattling of the lock. Before I could ask who was there, Blane stormed through the door. He slammed it shut behind him and came at me with a newspaper in his hand. He pressed it against my chest and pushed me back onto the couch. "What is this?"

"What do you mean?" I was too stunned to process what was happening.

"Tell me what it is." Blane pointed to my chest where the newspaper still clung. His eyes were wide with adrenaline.

"A newspaper?" I didn't understand.

"The story! Look at the front page." Blane grabbed his hair as he often did when he was overwhelmed.

I peeled the newspaper off my chest and looked at the cover. I gasped. My letter was on the front page with the title, 'Deranged Serial Killer Taunts The Town'.

"What were you thinking?"

"I just sent a letter to the 'Voice of the People' section. It was supposed to be anonymous."

Blane pulled a tuft of hair from his head. "Fuck. Fuck. Fuck…"

"Wait a second. How did you know it was me?"

"How did I know? You called Seamus a leprechaun! You used his name. Dude, when he sees this, he's going to kill you. What were you thinking, man?"

"I just wanted to be honest and help. I was going to tell Seamus to his face when he comes by today. I think what we're doing is wrong and we should stop. If he kills me, then that is for the best. I can't live a life of lies anymore."

Blane slapped me across the face. The sting derailed my whole train of thought. "You have to leave before Seamus sees this. I took our copy, but he'll see another eventually. Whatever your idea was, it was dumb. You're a kid and you're in over your head. Just run and never come back."

"But I have to stop dark magic. Someone has to. It's killing everyone and I've already come so far. If we can just find Frankie Fourfeet. That's what this is all about."

"You think you're going to stop Frankie? Dude, he's an old man on an island somewhere. Nobody's touching Frankie."

"But you're a wizard. Surely you can help!" My words had struck him dumb. As a wizard he surely must have felt some responsibility for the world of magic. I could see it in his eyes. It was regret and guilt. I was finally able to recognize it. He had failed to follow his moral compass and was now lost like I was. "We can work together on this. Seamus too, if you think he would be up for it. We just have to find Frankie and maybe we wouldn't even have to hurt him. Maybe all we have to do is show him the light and he will make his own way towards it! What do you say? Will you join me?"

Blane's eyes grew glassy as he contemplated my words. There was such a struggle in them to do what was right. *Do the right thing, Blane. Do the right thing!*

He slapped me as hard as he could. "There is no such thing as magic." His words hit me harder than his palm. "We are drug dealers. Magic is a drug. Dark magic is just magic cut with paint chips. Seamus is not a leprechaun. He's been messing with your head to get you to do whatever he wants. What he told you is a lie. He's a murderer and he's going to kill you. Grab whatever you can carry and get the fuck out."

"But-"

"NOW!"

Deedris stumbled out of Seamus's old room rubbing his eyes and yawning. "What's going on?"

"Is this your girlfriend?" Blane asked, confused.

"Of course not. This is Deedris. I mean Abraham! This is Abraham!" I waved my arms in a feeble attempt to emphasize that he was, in fact, only called 'Abraham'.

"Deedris Slinksy?" Blane's head slagged to the side as though he no longer cared enough to hold it up straight.

"How did you? No! This is Abraham."

Blane nearly went bald yanking at his hair. "Frumpkin, I'm going to tell you one last time." Blane struggled to keep his voice level and measured. "You and your friend need to leave before Seamus finds you. Run as far as you can and don't look back. Your whole life's ahead of you and whatever you think is going on here is not real. It's not worth dying over. Please leave."

Blane stared at me. Tears were forming at the corner of his eyes but never fell. I could see his chest rising and falling under his heavy coat. *He was serious.* When the truth is finally revealed, there is no unseeing it. It was not the magic of wizards and leprechauns that I had been peddling, but a derivative of the Pukapuka plant, harvested in Squatamala, refined in Splatistan and combined with an assortment of household detergents in the high desert of Rimplock. Chemical name: syphiloxicide. Street names: Magic, Bumnuggets, Sphincters' Delight, the list goes on. The lavish life I was corrupted by was built on nothing more than the crippling addictiveness of a rectally administered street drug. The truth in all its glory.

The wind was lost from my sails, but the waters were still choppy. Though I may not have been dealing true magic, there was still evil to face. "Okay," I said at long last. "We'll go, but I'm not running away. Say what you will about this not being real magic, that doesn't mean it's not evil. I know what I've seen. All this death and destruction has to stop. My town is in danger and it's my responsibility to stop it."

A tear finally broke free from Blane's eye and a steady stream rolled down his cheek. He turned away and wiped it off discreetly.

"Good," he said curtly. "Be quick about it." He took one more look at us before leaving the apartment, a tattered man.

"What was that all about?" Deedris asked, stretching like a cat while moseying to the fridge for some milk.

"That was Blane coming to tell me that Seamus is on his way to kill us both."

Deedris sprayed milk all over the kitchen table. "Are you serious?"

"Yep. And I'm starting to think we should leave."

The panic in Deedris cemented the notion that this was indeed a good idea. I had failed once again to consider the danger I had gotten Deedris into. The consequences of my actions were not for him to bear.

"Where should we go? He said my name. He knows who I am. I can't go home."

Deedris made an excellent point. *How did Blane know Deedris? And would Seamus know him too?* It took me a minute to think of what to do. "I know a spot," I said. "Fill up your coat with everything you can carry. We'll only have time for one trip."

Chapter 23

The tent by the creek was buried in several feet of compacted snow that hardened into something much like an igloo. It was fortunate that my parents had given Jebediah all the love they would have otherwise given me, for they had purchased for him a tent that could handle several feet of snow. Had they given me just one or two additional hugs during my childhood, maybe they would not have had enough love left over to provide Jebediah with such a lavish gift on the slightest of whims.

There was not much to carry from the apartment besides guns and magic. It was not safe to sell the magic with Seamus running the streets, so we just took the guns. Dozens of them wrapped in blankets. It was fortunate that we made the walk on a Sunday while everyone was at church. Two boys carrying dozens of guns in blankets across town would surely rouse suspicion on a Tuesday.

Deedris was uneasy about the transition. Apartment to igloo was an unwelcome change for a boy of his slender stature. But there was something more troubling him. I could see it in the way he rocked back and forth with his eyes as wide as the full moon. "Are you alright?" I asked. "I know this is not what we're used to, but I think once I get some beans working it will feel just like home."

"It's not that, Hump. I'm worried for my family. Blane knew my name. If they can't get to us, I think they might go after them."

What could I have said? A lie would have been so convenient. *Your family is going to be alright. There is nothing to worry about.* I couldn't say that. If I learned anything from my journey thus far it was the danger of lying. I wouldn't make that mistake again.

"I'm sorry, Deeds, but you're right. They might as well already be dead. Is there anything else bothering you?"

Deeds shivered and shook. I opened a can of beans and brought a spoonful to his lips. "Beans?" I asked. He shook his head 'no' so I took the bite for him and rested an arm around his shoulder. "We just have to be strong," I continued. "Seamus is only a leprechaun. I think if we really focus and give it our all, we can piece together a plan to stop him. It might be too late for your parents. I don't know. But if we start now, I think we can save your second or third cousins."

Deedris nodded. He was a strong boy. Not physically or mentally, but spiritually, and if there was ever a chance of success, no matter how small, he would persevere through anything. It was his greatest quality.

"There's something else I've been thinking about," he said.

"What is it?"

"Last night, when I was out doing my deliveries, Ms. Kooklioni offered me something in her room."

"Don't tell me you went up there? Deedris, there was one rule."

"She said she would make me a man."

"Why Deedris? Why?"

"I thought if I were a man I could help you more. You were so sad."

"What did she do?"

"She touched my dangles, Hump. She touched my dangles and I touched hers."

"Oh Deedris!" I tried my best to console him, but there was nothing to be done.

"It's okay, Hump. Truth is I think it may have worked. I feel different, like all that boyish wonder I used to have has died and been replaced by a stern and forceful bit of shame. Maybe that's what it takes to be a man."

"Maybe," I said. Touching dangly bits made as much sense as any other theory I had heard about becoming a man. "If so, then I'm happy for you." The truth was that I too felt such a feeling with Marlene. If there was a time to say it, it would have been then, but I kept my mouth shut for some ungodly reason. Even in the midst of embracing honesty, I could not reveal the secret relationship I had with her. It felt like such a tenuous connection that it could not be spoken of without being destroyed. Even now that there was no hope of ever getting it back, I dared not speak of it. Those secret feelings will haunt me for the rest of my life.

"Thank you," Deedris said. Confiding in me seemed to have lightened his load. If only I could have done the same. "So what's the plan?"

"First things first. Think of a plan."

"Good idea."

We sat for hours in the igloo saying anything that came to mind: We could run and hide; we could dress as Alleymen and live as the Alleymen do; we could build a tank and run over Seamus; etcetera. The ideas were solid, but none inspired great hope, and as the afternoon wore on, the gaps between them grew. Long stretches of silence filled the igloo.

Amidst the longest silence yet, I reached for the paper we took from the apartment. In the rush to leave, I did not get the chance to look it over as I usually did in the morning. My letter took up most of the front page. Though I clearly stated otherwise, the story beneath it claimed that all the murders of the previous months were the singular work of The Mystery Boy of Bethlahoom.

My attempt at anonymity, using cut-out letters from magazines, was misconstrued as the quirk of a psychotic killer. *Communication is tricky business.* The article continued to assume this killer had a myriad of evil traits typical of deranged lunatics. I may not have been perfect, but I don't believe anyone thought of me as aggressive and fond of hurting animals. I once spent an entire week trying to save a bee that stung me. It died after the first day, so I tied it to a battery in hopes of restarting its heart. Once all its insides were eaten by ants, I gave up hope.

The article continued on another page with a list of precautions that people should take with a serial killer on the loose. Keep your doors locked. Walk only in groups at night. Don't be a prostitute. The list when on.

In unusual fashion, the story continued to a third page where Officer Murphy Flannigan gave his opinion on the subject. I clutched the paper tight. This was the only part of the paper that mattered. I read as slowly and carefully as I could.

> Disgraced police officer Murphy Flannigan had this to say:
> "It appears that an insider is trying to anonymously communicate important information regarding the inner workings of Frankie Fourfeet's cartel. I would encourage this Mystery Boy to keep writing and be unafraid of contacting the police in a more direct manner. A trusted inside man is just the thing we need to make headway on the case. There are obvious complications for a person in his position, but we do offer immunity for informants in many, if not most, circumstances. As for the community, I believe we are safer than our imaginations may lead us to believe and it would be best to take this moment of fear to reconnect with our families and friends and spread love as best we can. Thank you."

Once again, complete and utter nonsense from disgraced officer Murphy Flannigan. How much more can he embarrass himself?

I couldn't believe my eyes. It worked! My plan had worked. I established communication with the most manly man I knew, and he wanted me to keep writing! "Deedris! Check this out!"

"What is it?"

"The paper! Read the paper!" I was too excited to say more. The words would have jumbled in my mouth.

Deedris grabbed the paper skeptically and began to read. I watched him, bouncing up and down with joy. He did not share my enthusiasm. The more he read the more somber he became. His rosy cheeks turned pale and then a light shade of green.

"Uh, Deeds? What are you reading there?"

"There is a whole section on us. They interviewed my mom. It says she was crying and just wants to know I'm safe."

"There is?"

"You didn't see it?"

Unbeknownst to me, some stories started on the second page of the newspaper. I had always skipped ahead to finish the stories that started on the front. I wondered what else I had missed. "Wait a second. Did you say it was about *us*?" *How did that involve me?*

"Yeah, it mentions you too. It says you've been missing for months and that my mom talks to your mom every day about it."

"Our moms know each other? WHAT?" I grabbed the paper from Deedris. *How does my mom know his mom? She never left her room!* I was so caught off guard that I didn't realize what else that meant. It took Deedris spelling it out for me.

"You've been reported missing too, Hump."

I looked at the page. He must have read it wrong. No. There it was. I had been reported missing and apparently, my mom had been troubled by it. Who would have guessed? It didn't change anything, though. The important thing was that we made contact with Officer

Murphy Flannigan. I threw the paper back at Deedris to read Officer Flannigan's words. Deedris was not thrilled.

"He says he needs someone on the inside. We're on the outside again." He gestured to the igloo. He had a point.

"Are you saying we should go back to Seamus?"

"No! I'm saying I don't know what we should do."

Our position was puzzling. There was no clear path to take. We could write another letter and wait, but as Deedris said, we did not have the value that Flannigan hoped we did. It would be at least a week before we could hear back anyways. We couldn't afford to wait that long for bad news.

Life as Humphry was complicated. Living in the truth meant accepting that I didn't know what I was doing. Frumpkin knew what he was doing. He was selling magic and moving up the ranks. He didn't care about the questions he didn't know, he just haphazardly assigned answers and treated them as solved. Frumpkin wouldn't be worried at all. Frumpkin, Frumpkin...

"Plumpkin!" I yelped.

Deedris shot to attention. "What?"

"Betty Plumpkin! She is the wise woman of Cornblower Lane. We will go to her tomorrow at exactly noon."

"Why exactly noon?"

"Because I know she will be there. When desperate, you do what you know will work. We're desperate, Deeds. We need Betty Plumpkin."

Chapter 24

The sun did its best to warm us on the frigid morning. Lake Bethlahoom finally froze over, shutting off the torrents of snowstorms flowing from its banks. The temperatures remained well below freezing, but something about the dryness of the air kept it from sapping our heat like it did in the early winter and late fall. The long stretch of winter was not as bad as the transition into it.

Deedris and I entered through Betty's white picket gate. The path to her front door was pristinely plowed and salted. I wondered if it was the work of Paulo. I hoped it was.

We came to the door as close to noon as we could guess. I rang the doorbell. Soft chimes tinkled. Thunderous steps clamored from inside. Betty unlatched her door and peaked at us through the crack before swinging it open and ushering us inside.

"About time you came!" She scolded us as though we should have come sooner. "Get inside and shut the door. You too, skinny buns," she said to Deedris. "Goodness gracious, look at those skinny buns." She turned her attention back to me. "I've been worried sick about you. Now take off your shoes and grab Betts her cocktail in the kitchen. We'll meet you on the couch."

Gangster Magic

Betty grabbed Deedris and used him as a cane to walk over to a living room on the left side of the house. I took a moment to look around before spotting the kitchen straight ahead. I found Betty's cocktail and met them back in the living room.

Every available space in Betty's house had flowers or a picture of flowers or a figurine that was painted in such a way as to remind you of flowers. As bleak as our lives were, the small charms of Betty's house were effectively uplifting. The outside world could be as harsh as it wants if you have a warm home to hide within. An igloo by the creek was no such dwelling.

"Bring it here, boy and don't be shy about getting one yourself." I handed Betty her drink and took a seat next to Deedris on an embroidered couch. Betty took a sip from an extra large rocking chair and set the nearly empty glass on a side table. She rocked forward and gave us both accusing stares. "So I take it you boys didn't kill Frankie?"

"No, mam," we responded in unison.

"You boys were supposed to kill Frankie for me. I'm looking mostly at you, son." She directed her eyes at me.

"I'm sorry Ms. Plumpkin. I did my best, but I'm afraid moving up the ranks of a criminal organization was beyond my capabilities. At least it was in such a short time. We are still trying. We want to stop Frankie, but there is someone else we need to take care of first. His name is Seamus. We were following him on his way to the top, but he seems to be every bit as evil as Frankie Fourfeet himself."

"You said his name is Seamus? I guess he's some hotshot upstart, huh? Is he the one killing off all my people?"

"He is the one behind all the murders, yes. It took me a regrettably long time to discover his treachery, but now that I have I can no longer let him continue unhindered. I would have gone and talked to him about it, but upon discovering we are not loyal to him, he is going to kill us. My good friend Blane told me that"

"No shit, sweetheart. You can't negotiate with a killer. It's kill or be killed."

"I see. Well, as you may have figured out, we do not know what to do. You told me to come to you if we had nowhere else to turn, and here we are. Can you help us?"

Betty drank the second half of her drink and handed the empty glass to Deedris. "You know how to make a gin and tonic?"

Deedris took the glass and shook his head 'no'.

"It's gin and it's tonic, son. Go ahead into the kitchen and figure it out."

Deedris nodded silently and left to the kitchen.

"Something tells me that's going to buy us some time to talk alone. It shouldn't, but something tells me it will. Look, you're in the thick of things right now. Sometimes we go in thinking we're doing one thing and life tells us we're really doing something else. It doesn't mean we were wrong to go do it, it's just that we never know exactly what we're doing.

Now, you started this whole thing because you thought Frankie Fourfeet was after you. Maybe he is and maybe he isn't. The more I've thought about it, the more I think he wasn't. Sometimes these low-level gangsters will use a name like that to make it seem like they're tougher than they really are. Whoever it was that threatened you to begin with is probably dead by now. Is that right?"

I nodded slowly. They were dead. They had been dead for months and since then nothing else suggested that Frankie Fourfeet was still looking for me. I hadn't considered that they lied to me about it, but after learning of the prevalence of deceit amongst those in the magic game, it fit perfectly.

"I thought as much," Betty continued. "Damn near every dealer in town's been killed. But I don't think that's the real reason you got into all this. I think finding this Seamus character is the real reason you're here. You say he's an evil man. I bet he's got some evil plans that you know about. Is that right?"

"It is! How did you know?"

"I just had a feeling you'd be able to find that out. You got that quality in you that makes people talk. You trust too easy. People see all that trust and they feel like they can trust you back. People are funny like that. Anyway, this Seamus, what's he planning?" Betty's rocker creaked another inch towards me. Her plump visage took up my entire field of vision.

"He's going to throw a party. He's convinced magic dealers from other towns that the discord in Bethlahoom came from a lack of communication between everyone, and that the only way for the conflicts to stop is to get everyone together and look each other in the eyes. I think he plans to kill them all. There was a man. Ignacio..." The image of his blood sprayed on the wall played to the side of Betty's unmoving gaze.

"You saw Seamus kill Ignacio?"

The image disappeared. It was just Betty staring at me like an all-knowing toad. "Yes. And I think he means to do the same to the rest."

Betty rocked back. The chair creaked like a falling redwood. The full strength of timber was tested. A toad thinks how a toad thinks. There is no knowing how it is unless you're a toad. The same was true for Betty. Her mind worked in ways that I could never imagine. It's true for all people. We never have access to any thoughts but our own, but some people do and say things that would be impossible for ourselves, and in them we have no guess of what is ticking.

"We'll have to take care of this Seamus character then. Do you have any idea of when this party will happen?"

"No. I was soon to find out I'm sure, but no. Seamus never told me anything ahead of time, and even when it was time he was vague and outright lied on occasion."

"Yeah, he's a real piece of shit it sounds like."

"Yes, mam."

"I'll tell you what, I'm going to do some investigating of my own. Make some phone calls and such. Don't worry about it. I'll find out when this meeting is happening and when I do, you'll get your little team together and shut it down. Does that sound like a plan?"

"You can do that?"

"Don't worry about it. When you're my age you just know a lot of people. Come by this time next week and I'll tell you when and where it's going down. No need to come inside. I'll have Paulo leave a note in the mailbox. And don't go telling people we met. This is your business. I'm just a whisper on the wind. You got it?"

"I believe I do. Thank you, Ms. Plumpkin."

Deedris came inching back into the room trying desperately to keep the glass, bulging over the top with the resistance of surface tension, from spilling. He lifted it towards Betty whose bemused stare softened when she saw he managed the whole journey without spilling. She extended out her lips and slurped off the top layer like a toad catching a fly. "Perfect," she said with a smile.

Chapter 25

Betty Plumpkin left us much to decide for ourselves. She did not tell us how to stop Seamus or who to enlist if need required it. There was a part of me that wished she gave us more, but it does not do one well to dwell on what is not, and though I often had trouble identifying truth from fiction, I had no qualms about which, in the general case, to favor.

Deedris was less principled. He went on about how much he wanted to go back home to see his family. I couldn't blame him for wanting to go back but continuing to talk about impossibilities ground down my patience.

"Look, Deeds, it's impossible! Seamus knows where you live. He might already be there waiting for us to show up."

"Please, let's just go and see. We don't even have to go in. I just want to look. Please."

As ridiculous of an idea as it was, I couldn't say no any longer. Deedris was in pain, and though it was not I who wounded him, the pressure I applied caused him more pain. Maybe I was afraid he would blame me for all his pain instead of the wound.

"Alright, we'll go and look, but nothing more. And if anyone sees us we have to run. Okay?"

Deedris wiped a mess of tears and snot from his face. "Thank you."

We marched across town. A bitter chill gripped my neck as we neared The Shank. We narrowly steered clear of the neighborhood. If only Deedris had lived in the suburbs like me.

We approached Deedris's block. He lived on a cul-de-sac like me, though his was lined with rusty chain link fences and barren yards. A single tree would have done so much for the atmosphere, but for whatever reason, no one bothered to plant any.

I insisted we stay on the far side of the street. Deedris agreed. I think he was beginning to feel the danger we were in. This part of Bethlahoom had a special way of making people feel fear.

Deedris's house was a perfect rectangle that stretched away from the street like all the others in the middle of the block. A window looked into the living room. If it was lit well enough, you could see all the way into the kitchen, which was separated from the living room by a counter. The bedrooms were behind the kitchen and hidden from view.

Deedris and I crept behind a car on the other side of the street and peered over the top into the window. Two shadows occupied the room. The reflections on the window made it difficult to make them out. Deedris grew concerned and slipped out from behind the car.

"Deedris! No!" I yelled with a voice more like my dad's than my own. I stumbled out and grabbed his hand before he could make it to the fence.

The shadows raced to the window, still blurred by the obtrusive sunlight. They heard my yell.

Deedris snapped back to reality. "I'm sorry, Hump."

"Just run!" I screamed

The shadows moved to the front door.

Deedris sprinted ahead of me. I had forgotten how fast he was. I glanced back at the shadows. One had run to the car across the street and the other had gone back inside. I ran harder. I called out to Deedris to head for the creek. Even Deedris couldn't outrun a car.

We barely managed to hide under a bridge before the car caught up to us and drove past. It was the type of narrow escape that can make a bad decision feel empowering, like destiny was on our side. It's so easy to misinterpret events like that. I could see Deedris alight with confidence. The risk enthralled him while I was shaking in my boots. The same event can yield such divergent outcomes. Like two raindrops falling an inch apart on a mountain peak. One side leads back to the ocean where it belongs. The other side leads to a desert basin where rivers run dry before reaching the bottom. At the time I thought it was my drop that landed on the right side of the mountain, but the fear I felt in that moment never fully resolved, and I've grown to understand that a brief delusion is needed to buy time for someone's mind to prepare for the heaviest blows of life. It is only when the delusions stick around that they become problems.

Deedris's excitement fell quick and hard. By the time we made it back to the igloo, he could barely stand with the torrents of emotion raging through him. I kept telling him that we couldn't be sure who was chasing us, but with only two possibilities, his parents or the people who killed them, it was tough to console him in this way.

His condition cascaded down. I don't think he could hear me talk anymore. He just whimpered to himself, pleading with God to help him. When hope is needed most, that is the only source.

I began wondering where my hope lay. I was counting on myself to solve my problems, but in me, I had no hope. My problems were too big and out of my control. While watching Deedris weep in the corner of the frozen tent by the creek, I saw how hopeless I was in protecting him. Under my tutelage he was maimed, molested and his family was murdered. Poor Deedris.

I should have known I couldn't protect him, but I was entombed by walls of delusion. I thought they had been crushed several times already, but there were deeper layers that had yet to fall. Each one kept me from seeing some uncomfortable truth. Each one I had mistaken for my last. How many more needed to collapse before I could be at peace?

...

I left Deedris alone in the igloo the following morning. There isn't much that can be done for a boy in his state. The best I could do was save myself. We had plenty of drug money to spend, and a warm breakfast was just what I needed.

Ol' Gilly's Pancake Saloon was a bit of a walk away, but it was worth it. Situated off the main highway just before town, Ol' Gilly's was a staple for outlaws. Nobody knew anyone's name and nobody asked. If you did, you were asked to leave. At least that's what the commercials said. My family went there after church on occasion, and all the waitresses wore name tags that my Dad used at the objection of the rest of my family. I was always worried we would be asked to leave. The rest of my family was more concerned about him acting like a doofus.

I arrived around noon. The midweek crowd in winter was much lighter than the Sunday crowd in the middle of summer. Only two tables were occupied out of a possible 25 or so. A single waitress was working who was busy taking the order of a trucker across the restaurant. She waved at me to acknowledge she would get to me in a moment.

I picked up the daily paper while I waited. It was a hollow shell of the Sunday paper. Weekday issues usually contained national articles that the paper bought to fill space. Not enough happened in

Bethlahoom to justify a daily paper driven by local events. At least not usually. Stories can break any day of the week and a random Tuesday's paper might be worthwhile to read.

The waitress approached before I had time to delve into the paper, so I stashed it under my arm and waved with the other. "Table for one, please."

"Right this way, sweetie." Her voice was hoarse from decades of smoking. Her name tag said 'Jean', which I dared not speak aloud.

I followed Jean to a booth in the corner with a tall window facing the parking lot. A light snow fell, but the clouds were thin enough to keep it bright outside.

"Anything to drink for you, dear?"

"Do you have hot cocoa?"

"Sure thing. And you need time with the menu?"

"I'll take pancakes if you have them."

"I'll get that right out for you." She smiled. Her gray skin folded into clumps around her eyes, reminding me of Ms. Kooklioni and in turn, Deedris. Poor Deedris.

I sat back with the paper. The squishy booth was welcome after two nights on frozen ground. Jean returned soon after with the cocoa. It was sweet and warm and perfect. I looked out the window. The clouds were darker towards town. A bolt of lightning streaked across the sky there. I couldn't believe it. Lightning in winter came only in the harshest of blizzards. It must have been an isolated storm that just missed me and hit the town. *Maybe I should have asked Deedris if he wanted to come too.* I pushed the thought from my mind. No sense worrying about it now.

I took another sip and looked at the paper. The main headline was about the war. It always was, but the war was all the way in the South. Nobody really cared in Bethlahoom. At least I didn't. The real stories were the ones about my town and the people I cared for.

There was a local article in the bottom right corner of the front page. 'Disgraced Officer Murphy Flannigan Demoted and Shamed.' I had to reread it. That couldn't be right.

Disgraced Officer Murphy Flannigan Demoted and Shamed

Officer Murphy Flannigan, previously demoted to a beat-cop after fumbling the notorious 'Frankie Fourfeet Case', a string of solvable murders that he falsely attributed to a single person, has once again been demoted after flummoxing us all by supporting the psychotic killer, The Mystery Boy of Bethlahoom. Former Officer Murphy Flannigan is Bethlahoom's newest meter maid. Watch out ladies and Gentlemen, Murphy Flannigan has the authority to write you a harshly worded warning! Good luck, Mr. Meter Maid.

What on Earth is wrong with people? The only man in Bethlahoom with any sense at all was being laughed out of his job. The paper was often unkind to Officer Flannigan, but this had gone too far. I had only met him briefly, but it couldn't have been more obvious that he was a good and trustworthy man.

"Here are those pancakes for you, dear," Jean said. I was too absorbed in the paper to notice her coming. "Didn't mean to startle you."

"Oh, thank you. I was reading the paper."

"I can see that. Can you believe that Flannigan? I'll tell you, it's no wonder we got serial killers all over town with police like that. You ask me, I say he's working with the Mystery Boy himself."

"If only he was," I said more curtly than intended. "Then maybe the Mystery Boy wouldn't be so upset." I grabbed the pancakes from Jean's hands.

"You know him or something?"

I blushed. "Officer Flannigan is a good man."

"Well, I'm sorry I said anything. Do you need anything else?"

I sat for a moment, my fists pressed into the table clutching my fork and knife. "Maybe just a little respect for my friend. And some extra syrup if you have any."

"Syrup's on the table. I'm all out of respect." Jean walked back to the kitchen, presumably to talk to the cooks about my bad attitude.

I shouldn't have said anything about Flannigan. I just wanted to restore his good name so badly. Talking to waitresses was clearly not the path. *Maybe there was nothing I could do.* It was just like Deedris. I wanted to protect Deedris, but it was beyond my control. Officer Flannigan would have to find his own way back to the public's good graces. All I could do was wish him the best and offer to help if he asked for it.

But he did ask for it! That's why he was demoted! He wanted my help so much, he was willing to risk his job for it. He had asked for an insider, which I no longer was, but I still held information that could prove useful. I needed to write to the paper again as the Mystery Boy of Bethlahoom. Or better yet, I could find him myself. The paper said he was a meter maid now. They only patrolled the streets with timed parking, which was just a few blocks downtown. I could hang out there until he showed up.

My spirits lightened with the formation of a plan. I dove into my fluffy pancakes, reapplying liberal plops of syrup after every few bites. I needed the nutrition. The storm over the city looked even worse than before. Traveling back to the igloo could be rough. Hopefully Deedris was alright. Poor Deedris.

I closed my tab with Jean and asked if she had any spare magazines I could take with me. She looked weary when I told her I needed it for a letter but pointed to a stack by the door. I thanked her and took one on my way out.

Charlie D. Weisman

Chapter 26

The blizzard made walking the streets impossible. The snowfall itself was not such a great issue, generally being of a similar intensity to the local storms coming off the lake, but the relentless wind blurred visibility to nothing. I scurried along the creek bed instead, where thick trees shielded me from the battering wind. If the storm lasted long enough, even this option would cease, as the wind eventually crushes the trees burdened by the weight of snow-laden branches. The creek then becomes the most dangerous place of all. A winter storm of this strength would not be over soon. Summer thunderstorms came and went well within an hour. Winter storms stretched across the continent and lasted days. This was the strongest I had ever seen. *Almost supernatural.* I could not guess how long it would last.

The tent was barely visible beneath the growing snow drift. I dusted off the entrance and dove inside. It was quiet in the igloo. The thick walls of snow were perfect insulators. Deedris sat facing the opposite wall with his back to me. A lantern in the middle of the tent projected his shadow across the back wall. He did not move.

"Deedris? How are you holding up?" I asked delicately.

His voice came back low and hollow. "I have gone through the gates of hell and returned with a treasure."

"Uh, Deedris? What are you talking about?"

"I have summoned the storm. It will cleanse the world of filth."

Deedris twisted his head to face me. His pupils swallowed all the color in his sunken eyes. Trails of salt carved his cheeks like the dried river beds of badlands. My friend, Deedris, had been taken.

I approached as softly as I could. "Maybe we should crack open a can of beans and talk this over?"

"I CURSE THEE BEANS!" Deedris turned back to the wall and rocked back and forth.

A good boy like Deedris did not curse beans. Something foul had consumed him. The battering of life had weakened him and left him vulnerable to possession by a supernatural force. *Supernatural.* This really was a magical storm and Deedris was controlling it! Deedris, be it as a puppet or not, wielded magic of extraordinary strength. Harnessed correctly, his powers could swiftly bring Seamus and his contrived magic to his knees. There would be no need to find Officer Flannigan or follow Betty Plumpkin's breadcrumbs to certain death. A new option presented itself. I just needed to convince Deedris.

"Deedris," I whispered, "it's me, Humphry, your friend. Remember me?"

Deedris grumbled.

"I want you to remember who you're fighting. It's Seamus. Remember him?"

Deedris grumbled even more and began shaking. It was working. He was directing his anger towards Seamus.

"Everything is Seamus's fault. I am your friend. Seamus is the enemy. Kill Seamus. Kill Seamus."

"AHHH!" Deedris yelled and punched the igloo. A clamoring of thunder broke through the insulating walls. He punched again and again. The thunder reverberated around the sky. He punched one last time, as hard as he could, and collapsed to the floor out of breath. The thunder dissipated and the silence returned.

I checked outside to see if it was still storming. The blizzard was indeed ongoing. I decided this was a sign that Seamus was still at large. Of course he was. We had to get closer for Deedris to strike him down. Until then, the storm would rage. It would be our cloak. Our compass. Our sword.

When Deedris caught his breath and returned to his senses, I told him of our new plan.

"You mean it?" he said. "I was just being dramatic when I said I was causing the storm. You mean to tell me I actually did?"

"Yes. And it's just the break we've been waiting for."

Deedris smiled. Wielding magic had been a dream of his, as it was for every boy. It may have been the only thing that could have lifted him from grief. If it were anyone else, I would have been jealous. Instead, I was happy for my friend and willing to do anything to help.

Though an impressive start, we quickly found Deedris needed more practice. When he tried summoning the lightning again, nothing happened. It seemed to stem from the fact that he wasn't as angry as he was before. I tried slapping him, but it didn't work. I insulted him every which way I could. I gave him wedgies and made him smell my shoes. Nothing was working, but we kept trying. I would not give up on my friend.

For days I beat him and called him names. I plucked his eyebrows one hair at a time. I smeared beans on his face and rode him like a donkey around the creekbed. I tried everything I could think of to rouse his anger, but he was so excited at the prospect of being magical that nothing fazed him.

We were running out of time. It was already Saturday, and Deedris had only grown more docile from the constant beating and humiliation. We needed a fallback option in case Deedris's powers did not mature in time. Officer Flannigan would have to do.

Parking was free on the weekends, so waiting for him on the block was not an option. We had to contact him through the paper as I had done before. I pulled out the magazine from Ol' Gilly's and got to work drafting a new letter.

Dear Bethlahoom,

Firstly, my apologies for the storm. It has been summoned by vengeance and won't stop until the streets have been cleansed of evil.

Secondly, it grieves me to see Officer Flannigan disrespected. He is the only man in Bethlahoom that I count as an ally in my mission, and I would like to cordially invite him to join my cause.

Thank you,
The Mystery Boy of Bethlahoom

"Sounds good," Deedris said after I read the letter aloud to him. "But it won't be delivered by tomorrow morning. The mail doesn't come on Sundays, and even then it usually takes two days for local mail."

He was right. Mail would be too slow. "We'll have to deliver it ourselves then."

"To the news station? But it's at the top of Mount Bethlahoom!"

The news station used its post atop the highest peak in town to keep watch of the whole city as well as pay lower property taxes. The top of the hill was technically only in the county.

"We don't have any other options."

Deedris balled his fists and grumbled.

"Hey! Your anger is coming back!"

Deedris looked at his fists in wonder. "You're right. Maybe we should go!"

We left for the hill wearing every layer of clothing we had. Deedris grew joyful at the prospect of wielding magic again, and to temper this joy, we decided it was best that I mount him like a donkey and ride him the rest of the way.

It appeared to work. The storm grew stronger the farther we went up the hill. In the blinding snow, gravity was our only valued sense. Up. Always up. Against the plea of every fiber in Deedris's muscles, we continued up. For miles and miles, we scaled the fabled peak: a weary wanderer and his trusted stead.

The snow was up to Deedris's chin and the bitter wind pushed us deeper still. Deedris strained to breathe under my bulky frame and ground to a halt. "Andale!" I spat and prodded him onward.

At long last the path crested. Gates sprung forth from the clouds of blowing snow. A mailbox glimmered in the distance. I spurred my steed with the heel of my boot. "I see it!" I yelled. "Make haste, my mule! Make haste!"

I hopped off Deedris's back to place the letter in the mailbox. Deedris was slow to rise. His teeth were bared, but his eyes were shut with fatigue. I called upon him to wield his power once more, to smite Seamus from atop the hill. He cried out a boyish call that would evoke terror in no one. It was thin and feeble. He sputtered and collapsed. I barely caught him before he reached the ground.

"I can't do it," he whimpered. "I'm not strong enough."

"It's okay, Deedris," I said to him, cradling his wobbling head in my arms. "I never thought you were."

I hoisted him over my shoulder and began the long walk home. "I'm going to walk on the road if you don't mind," I said. The roads were neatly plowed and salted, much easier to walk on than the sidewalk piled high with snow. I had walked only a few feet before the wind died down and the clouds broke. The sun snuck through and a friendly hare popped out from its burrow to say hello. "Look Deedris! It was just a regular storm after all! Everything is nice again!"

There was no response from Deedris. I shook him a couple of times, but still nothing. I checked his face. His eyes were closed and from his nose blew gentle snores. He was most certainly not a powerful wielder of magic. All my abuses had therefore been for nothing. Poor Deedris. Maybe in his dreams things were different.

Charlie D. Weisman

Chapter 27

I snuck out of the tent the following morning while Deedris slept in. The sun had fully returned and the city glimmered in its fresh coat of white. I walked freely knowing that everyone was at church, or at least that all the people who weren't, which was a surprising many, would be too embarrassed to reveal themselves.

The closest newspaper box was downtown near The Shank, but I opted to stroll through Paltry Square instead, where there were more newsboxes and less obtrusive odors. It dazzled as it always did. Strings of lights sparkled against the fresh snow and made it glow like twilight. The sun was weak enough at that time of the year for streetlights to add meaningful brightness in the middle of the day.

The paper was two quarters and worth every cent. I grabbed a copy from the first box I saw and raced to a picnic table to start reading. My letter was printed across the first page with the title 'Psychotic Killer Infiltrates Police Department'. *What in Bethlahoom?*

Psychotic Killer Infiltrates Police Department, By Rudolphus Slim

The psychotic killer self-identified as The Mystery Boy of Bethlahoom has once again turned to taunting the community. But now he has a new ally. Disgraced former detective Murphy Flannigan has been singled out by The Mystery Boy as a co-

conspirator. We have been warning the public of Flannigan's ineptitude for years, but even we have been taken by surprise. It appears that he is not only inept, but also aiding the most notorious serial killer in Bethlahoom's history.

Disgraced former officer Flannigan was fired in shame late last night after we alerted the police of the new letter. We do not yet have an official announcement from the police department but can reasonably assume it will go something like this:

"Murphy Flannigan is a murderous buffoon who we at the police department are ashamed to have harbored as long as we have. We would like to thank The Bethlahoom Times, and specifically Rudolphus Slim, whose exceptional talent for reporting is the bedrock upon which Bethlahoom thrives. We hereby award Rudolphus Slim with the title of 'Sir' and the key to the city." *Continued on A8.*

I set the paper down and buried my face in my folded arms. Why did they have to assume the worst? I was just trying to help a friend, and instead, I got him fired. Could it be that I wasn't so good after all? Everything I did seemed to spawn the problems I hoped they'd stem. I felt such a strong conviction I was doing the right thing, but all my actions hurt the people I loved. Was it my intention? Was I secretly a bad person, holding the truth from myself so I may lie with ease?

"Yo, Fruitloop," a deep voice called from down the way.

I fell out of my seat attempting to run, right into a pile of snow. The man fast approached.

"Yo, Fruitloop, take it easy. I'm not here for trouble."

I lifted my head from the snow. "Jerry? What are you doing here? Why aren't you in church?"

"Church? I'm a Reformed Betswalli. We don't go to church. We smoke grass and play drums. What happened to you? Blane told me you're on the run."

"You talked to Blane about me?" I shimmied to my feet and dusted off the snow. "You didn't also talk to Seamus, did you?"

"Naw, I don't talk to Seamus. He gives me the creeps. Blane came last night. I was expecting your weird skinny friend, the one who's banging Ms Kooklioni. Instead, Blane shows up and tells me you both skipped town. So what's the truth? Why's everyone playing games with me?" Jerry opened his arms as though the answer would be tossed to him in a big fluffy bag.

He looked different outside The Alley: soft, almost bashful. I would have never known or even guessed. So much of a person, it seemed, is a reflection of their immediate environment. We are as mutable as our circumstances. It was a troubling observation. What does that mean for the soul? Are there any enduring qualities that stay with us no matter where we are? Could I be the psychotic killer the paper claims if only put into a particular happenstance?

"Speak to me, Fruitloop."

"Sorry. I was thinking about something else. I did run away. I have displeased Seamus and now he's looking for me. Please don't tell him you saw me."

"Fuck Seamus. He's a fucking douche. If he weren't Blane's boy, I'd pop his ass."

"You say he is Blane's boy?"

"They're second cousins or something. I don't know, but I'm not ratting you out. I got you." He seemed to mean what he said.

"Thank you."

"What's your plan anyways? If you're running from Seamus, this isn't really the best place to hide."

I wondered for a moment how much I should say, weighing my need for covertness and assistance. It came down to the fact that if I couldn't trust Jerry, then I couldn't trust anyone, and I needed help. "My plan is to kill Seamus before he kills me."

"Damn son!" Jerry looked around making sure no one heard. "You serious?" He leaned in and whispered. He seemed to have gained a new respect for me, or at least a heightened curiosity. "That fool's got that old country game. I don't fuck with that. I played with toy cars as a kid. He grew up slaughtering pigs, or whatever they do over there. He's fucked up. You better watch out."

"I noticed. I would run away for good if I could, but he knows who I am and I'm afraid he'll come after my family. I think he already killed Deedris's parents."

"Who's Deedris?"

"You know him by Abraham. His real name is Deedris. He's a friend from school."

"The skinny kid banging Ms. Kooklioni?"

"That's the one."

"God damn. This scene really went to hell. Man, fuck Seamus. I want him gone too. What do you need from me?"

It was music to my ears. With Deedris's magic disappearing, the question of how to kill Seamus was again opened. Jerry was just the seasoned veteran of the streets I needed to help answer that. "Meet me here in two days' time. I will have more information for you. We'll discuss our options then."

"I'll be here." He nodded sternly and went in for one of our special secret handshakes. It changed subtly for just that moment. Through some form of telepathy, we needed not communicate the change. It was something between a high five and a handshake that fit both the brotherly bond we shared and the seriousness of the stakes at hand. We each nodded to each other, silently acknowledging how cool it was.

Jerry began walking away but quickly turned back. "Hey, you wouldn't happen to know a 'Humphry', would you?"

I turned a ghostly white. "Humphry? I know a Humphry. Why do you ask?"

"There's some lady looking for him. They say she's a wild woman. She's going to everyone making threats and offering rewards. You know anything about that? Who's this Humphry anyways?"

The question was the same one I was asking myself before Jerry's arrival. Who was Humphry? A good boy caught in a bad storm? An evil fool seeking to destroy under the guise of toxic lies? Just a feather in the wind, blown hither and thither without hope of a sail. There were many potential answers, but only one worth placing my coin.

"I am Humphry," I said. *Whatever he may be.*

Chapter 28

Deedris slept the entire Sunday, restoring his energy and spirits in time to go to Betty's house the following morning. With a voracious appetite beyond satiation by beans, Deedris insisted we stop for breakfast along the way. The pancake house was too far in the opposite direction, so we stopped at a cafe, sure to disguise ourselves as much as possible to remain anonymous. The barista, however, paid such little attention to us beyond taking our orders, that I doubt covering Deedris's face in underwear was even necessary.

We ate our biscuits and scones on the road. Betty said to come by at the same time as last week, but it was hard to judge time without a watch. We did our best to keep from getting there too early, but the excitement of getting the letter prompted us to walk more briskly than usual. Deedris especially so. He was like a racehorse being led to the starting gate. The anticipation drove him to skip and prance around me as we walked.

My concerns were unfounded. An unmarked letter awaited us, and something told me it had been there the entire morning, possibly the evening as well. Considering there was no mail service on Sundays, it may have been there for even longer. I wouldn't put it past Betty Plumpkin to have planned this to ensure our paths would not cross that morning. There was more to Betty Plumpkin than met the eye, and there was a lot of Betty Plumpkin that met the eye.

"Open it!" Deedris exclaimed. "Open it!" The starting gun had been shot, and Deedris was in full gallop.

"Not until we get to the creek." Some things are so secretive that they may not even be whispered on a desolate street.

"Then hurry up!" Deedris trotted ahead and disappeared down the nearest clearing to the frozen creekbed. I picked up my pace and followed him down.

I had never been to this section of the creek before. It was next to a bridge with a double-wide road overhead. A tapestry of metal sheets and wood scraps covered the side of the bridge, making an enclosure underneath. Wisps of smoke poured from a vent near the top. Distracted by the unusual construction, I bumped into Deedris's back who stood stiff as a board, also captivated by the strange sight.

"Hump!" he shouted and pointed to a small opening in the bridge fort surrounding the creekbed. "There! I saw someone. It was a woman. She looked like a wild animal."

My heart pounded. "A wild woman?" I recalled Jerry's warning. It hadn't concerned me much at the time. I had so much else on my mind. Now it was real. "Deedris, we need to run away."

"What about the letter?"

A spindly pair of arms emerged from the opening. The scowling head of a crone followed beneath mats of crazed dreads. *She's real!*

"No time!" I yelled. "Run!" I started back up to the street. Deedris took one look at the wild woman and followed, passing me almost instantly.

Deedris ran so far ahead I could barely see him. Only by his footprints could I tell he was running towards the igloo. *Footprints.*

"DEEDS!" I yelled with the power of my father. It was even louder than the week before at Deedris's house. I stopped to marvel at my abilities for a moment before racing to catch up to Deedris.

Deeds had stopped. He waited for me with his mouth agape. "How did you do that? I felt that all the way in my butt cheeks."

"I don't know, but there's no time to talk about it now. We have to go somewhere else. Towards the city where the sidewalks are clear of snow. The wild woman can track our footprints if we go straight home." *Home? Is that what the igloo was to me now?*

Deedris saw his trail and understood. We found an indoor mall about ten blocks down. We entered and exited on the other side to ensure we couldn't be tracked.

We slowed our pace and walked side by side for a few more blocks until Deedris barred his arm in front of me and stopped us both. "I can't wait any longer. What does the letter say?"

"But the creek is safer."

"There is no such thing as safe. We read it now."

I looked around. We were as alone as we would be in the creek, and the pained look on Deedris's face was impossible to refuse. I had to remember it was his parents who were killed. He had every bit of motivation as I did to stop Seamus, and looking at the letter was the next step in accomplishing that. The only next step.

Maybe I was afraid to look because it meant being that much closer to the final moment of truth when the nature of my life would be revealed. If I didn't stop Seamus, my only enduring actions would have been helping him succeed. Every step of my life was towards glory or ultimate failure and I wouldn't know which it was until my boot hit ground for the last time.

But that face. Poor Deedris. Publicly shamed, beaten, molested, his parents murdered. When I looked at him I didn't care about my own outcome. I thought only of helping him. If my march shall lead to doom, may I lead the way so that others will see my fall and not follow suit.

I pulled the letter out from my coat and handed it to Deedris. "Open it," I said.

Deedris didn't hesitate. He ripped it open and read it silently, his expression unchanging. "This Saturday. Warehouse B8 on Dunghollow Road."

He handed the letter back to me. I read it to confirm the details before folding it and putting it back in my coat. "We have less than a week," I said. The news scared me.

"The sooner the better." The promise of finality seemed alluring to Deedris. His soul was burdened by grief, not guilt, so the end was something to revel instead of fear. I was not so lucky.

"We need help. I still don't know how we're going to stop him and I'm running out of ideas."

"What about Flannigan? I thought you were getting him to help?"

"According to the paper, I ended up getting him fired instead. I would have told you, but you slept the whole day."

"Well, let's just find him and talk to him. Who needs hidden messages?"

Deedris was not the brightest boy in Bethlahoom, but sometimes that allowed him to find obvious solutions when I was too busy looking for complicated answers.

"Just find him and talk to him?" I asked, perplexed by the simplicity.

"Yeah. Be direct. If you need help, ask for it. That's what I was always taught. You're only too dumb if you're too dumb to ask for help."

"That's interesting. My sister used to say if you're dumb enough to need help, you're too dumb to be helped. I like your version better."

"How's Tabby doing anyways? Is she having God's baby? When I asked my dad, he said she was probably just a loose goose, whatever that means."

I flushed. Deedris had brushed upon the secret source of all my shame. "It's my baby," I finally said. "I got her pregnant and I don't even know how. It was through magic. I know that. Jebediah told me, and ever since I've been trying to make things right. That's sort of how all this got started."

Deedris put a hand on my shoulder to comfort me. "That's disgusting," he said.

I nodded in agreement.

"But you're my friend no matter what," he continued. "Now let's go find Flannigan so we can kill Seamus."

There was a phone booth just a couple blocks away. We found seventeen Murphy Flannigans in the tattered phone book hanging inside. I tried committing all their addresses to memory before Deedris ripped out the page and yanked me from the booth. "Let's go," he demanded.

We knocked on sixteen Murphy Flannigans' doors, but it was either the wrong Murphy Flannigan who answered or no answer at all. By the time we reached the seventeenth, neither Deedris nor I had any remaining confidence that we would find him that day.

The last house was the farthest from the city center, on a quiet, dead-end road. Each plot had a single-story tract house with a backyard that stretched directly into the forest. It was idyllic for anyone seeking seclusion. Nobody would chance upon you all the way out there.

"Is this the right address?" I asked upon seeing Flannigan's squalorous hovel. It did not look like the kind of place an honorable man would live. The mailbox was stuffed full of letters, and old furniture was strewn across the unkempt yard. The windows were shuttered tight and the even layer of snow across everything suggested no one had come or gone in days.

"This is it," Deedris confirmed while marching towards the front door on what could only be guessed was a walkway beneath the snow. I followed without any hope at all.

Deedris pressed the doorbell. It was hard to tell if it made a sound. We waited for a polite amount of time before Deedris pressed it again. My hopelessness was starting to turn to fear. There was nobody who would chance upon you out here, but also nobody to protect you if someone did. These people policed themselves. Whoever lived in that house did not want to be disturbed and it was completely up to them how they punished those who broke that law.

Deedris grew frustrated and slammed on the door. He pressed the bell over and over again before holding it down for good.

"We shouldn't be here, Deeds. Whoever's in there doesn't want to be disturbed."

"Tough shit for them," he said. "FLANNIGAN!" he yelled. "WE'RE NOT LEAVING UNTIL YOU COME OUT!" He went back to banging on the door. If you don't fear death, you don't fear anything.

The lock of the door clanked and the handle rattled. Deedris stopped banging and stumbled back. The door slipped open just wide enough for the grizzly head of a man to poke through. He had an overgrown beard and mop of hair that hid everything but his oily nose and drooping red eyes. "Who goes there?" He mumbled. His whiskey-soaked breath was strong enough to get me drunk.

I regained my confidence and stepped forward. "We are travelers from Bethlahoom in need of help from Officer Murphy Flannigan. Does he live here?"

"Officer Flannigan is dead." He spat on the ground in front of us. "Anything else?"

"What?" I refused to believe it. "You're lying! He must be alive!"

"Dead and gone. Now get off my porch." He tried shutting the door, but Deedris pushed it back open, revealing more of the man. He donned a dirty meter maid outfit that appeared to have not been cleaned in many days. His belt had a holster filled with a pad and pen.

"It's you," I said. That tangled beard could only conceal him for so long. Those eyes, saddened as they had become, were still the same from the station all those months ago. "You're Officer Murphy Flannigan."

"Not anymore."

Deedris slackened his position on the door for a moment and Flannigan took the opportunity to slam it in our faces. The lock clanked swiftly behind it followed by the distinct sound of a large piece of furniture being dragged across a wood floor and lodged against the door. "DEAD!" He yelled once more, followed by silence.

Deedris and I looked at each other, neither knowing what to say. Deedris looked angry. The entire afternoon had been spent looking for this man, and Deedris seemed to blame all the inconvenience on him. I was more concerned with Flannigan's well-being. I couldn't help but feel that I may have contributed to his demise. Another heave of guilt was tossed upon my shoulders.

Deedris lunged off the dusty stoop and stormed off toward town. I took one more moment to whisper my apologies to the house and chased him down.

Charlie D. Weisman

Chapter 29

What purpose does a foul mood serve? It didn't help me that Deedris fumed the whole night. Flannigan felt no grudge from miles away in his hovel. Deedris himself was completely incapacitated by it. His anger stole his mind and left me alone to think about what to do next, an action proving to be one of my greatest weaknesses. All I could think about was Deedris's simmering rage melting the igloo's walls. A foul mood's purpose seems only to distract us from recognizing how ridiculous it is to believe we are both right and wronged, that we are simultaneously the most important person in the world and the most disrespected. Without a giant heap of rage distracting from the truth, who could ever admit to such contradictions?

Deedris stopped steaming by the following morning, but resentment crusted over him like a forgotten pot of salted water whose contents boiled off. He may have stopped steaming, but he had not cooled and was all the more dangerous for it.

"We should leave soon," I said as softly as I could. "Paltry Square is an hour away, at least."

"What are you talking about?" He snapped.

"We're going to see Jerry." I forgot I hadn't told him yet. There was never a good time between his days-long nap and the chaos of the day before.

"So that's your grand plan, huh? Make new friends?" His words slashed at my heart.

"Come on, Deeds. You know it's not like that. I ran into him a couple of days ago and he said he would help us. It slipped my mind until now." I did my best to remind myself it was not me he was mad at.

"Paltry Square you say?" Deedris sighed and began sifting through our sack of belongings.

"Yes," I said, grateful for his acquiescence.

Deedris pulled out a shimmering handgun. He cocked it back and pointed it at the wall. "Alright, let's go." He secured the safety and stuffed the gun into his pants. I stared at him, eyes wide. Deedris noticed my alarm. "What are you looking at?"

"You're bringing a gun?" I squeaked. "Jerry's a friend. We don't need any guns."

"Why don't you quit being a tootin' Timmy and grow up. I'm bringing the gun and you should too." He bumped my shoulder on the way out of the igloo. I fell back, my butt and spirits hit the ground hard. Deedris had never spoken to me like that before.

I got up quickly and caught up to Deedris. We walked uneasily beside each other, each locked in our own misguided worlds interpreting each other's follies with a sense of certainty beyond our true capabilities. That seems to be the way of the world. After proving beyond a shadow of a doubt that we are incapable of understanding our own lives, we vainly attempt to seize control of another.

Lost though we were, fortune held solutions to our friendship that we would never have otherwise considered effective. Walking was all we needed. Laughter may be the best medicine for the soul, but walking is the premier treatment for a murky mind. Something about the motion separates truth from insanity. It clarified our true attitudes towards each other like words never could.

"You were right to bring the gun," I said half an hour into our walk. "I've been childish for avoiding it. I'm just so desperate to make everything right again that I want to believe it already is."

Deedris didn't even acknowledge my apology but blurted out one of his own. "I'm sorry I was short with you earlier. I'm not angry at you. I'm just angry."

Nothing had to be said to prompt our admissions, just walking and thinking. Words are such a poor medium for communication. They cause most of our problems. When they fail, only silence mends. Recognizing this, we walked the rest of the way in silence. By the time we got to Paltry Square, we were again of like minds, our bond only tempered from the heat of our quarrel. Maybe that is the purpose of a foul mood.

Jerry awaited us at the bench. He stood to perform our secret handshake. It was as natural and cool as the last time. I felt so much pride knowing Deedris saw it. There weren't many opportunities in my life where I could be looked at with respect.

"Ham-man," he called out upon seeing Deedris. "What's happening, brother?" Deedris slid into the most natural handshake I had ever seen. It was both more elaborate and performed with far greater precision and grace than the one in which I had just placed all my pride. This couldn't have been more than the third time they've done it, and it was already cooler than anything I could ever hope to be a part of. So much for pride.

Deedris was cooled by the encounter. Far from jovial, but no longer scolding. "Hey, Jerry. Sorry for dipping out on you last week. Some stuff came up."

Jerry placed a protective arm around Deedris. "I heard what happened. You know I always got your back." His words were more soothing than any I could speak. An honorable man's voice is like a warm blanket. "Hey," he continued, jabbing a finger in Deedris's chest, "I heard you're banging Ms. Kooklioni. Good for you."

Deedris blushed. "You heard about that?"

"Kooks and I go way back. She tells me everything." Jerry shrugged and then turned to me, tapping my arm and raising his head questioningly "So what's this news you got for me?"

I gave him a full rundown of the previous day, from Betty's note to the disappointing encounter with Officer Flannigan. Jerry was not surprised by any of it, or at least he did not show it. Surprise is a symptom of inexperience and shortsightedness, weaknesses self-aware men try to hide.

He took a moment to think after I finished and nodded to himself as though everything was just as he had predicted.

"Nothing you can do about the wild woman," he started, his voice sure yet contemplative. "It happens when you get money. Some chick will just come up to you and start acting like you've been married twenty years. When you get your money from slinging dope, she's probably going to be missing teeth and living in a tent. It's all the same though. She won't hurt you. I wouldn't go back to her tent or nothing, but she doesn't mean you any harm. She's just desperate for her kids or something." Jerry pulled a cigar from his coat and puffed it aflame. The smoke clouded around us.

"Nothing you can do about that," he continued. "As for Flannigan, he lost his manhood. Every man lives to justify his existence. This guy, he becomes a detective, fights crime, sacrifices himself every day to serve his town. That's how he justified being alive. Without the job, he feels unworthy of life and he's going to kill himself. It happens all the time." Jerry shrugged his shoulders and took a seat on the bench to think some more.

This was illuminating, but not particularly helpful. Deedris, blunted as he had become, was quick to point this out. "So what are we supposed to do about it?" He spat.

Jerry coughed on his cigar. Even a man like Jerry couldn't help but be surprised by Deedris's newfound gall. "What to do about Flannigan?"

"What else?" Deedris folded his arms and sat angrily on the bench beside Jerry. Deedris's emotional swings could hit a ball to the moon.

Jerry raised his eyebrows at Deedris before relaxing and taking another puff off the cigar. His voice flowed from his mouth as wistfully as the fresh billow of smoke. "You got to find his woman."

"His woman?"

"Yeah. Everything a man does, he does for a woman."

"They do?" I asked in wonder. Details about the necessities of manhood were precious to me. Deedris, too, leaned in with an inquisitive ear.

"Well, some guys, they start doing everything to serve themselves, treating themselves like they're the woman. Psychos are what they really are. Not good. Flannigan is not a Psycho. Seamus, that's a psycho."

Deedris and I shared a look of wonder. *This is so cool,* our eyes communicated.

"There are other chumps who have no hope of ever finding a woman. It's usually just in their heads. They don't realize how desperate some women are to have a man. But whatever the case may be, they don't even try to find one. You see them living in dumpsters most likely."

He took another draw from the cigar. "Yep. That's where your boy Flannigan is headed. Tough as it is, men need women to pat them on the head and tell them they're worth something. We're like dogs. Flannigan, losing his job, he's sitting there thinking no woman is ever going to pat him on the head. That's his problem. That's your solution too. You find his woman, she butters him up, then you tell him how to be the hero. Easy." He stoked the cigar in rapid succession, disappearing behind a wall of thick smoke.

Find his woman? It seemed like a more convoluted task than the one I needed his help to solve in the first place. "How do I find his woman?" I shouted, growing frustrated with my growing list of things I didn't know how to do.

The smoke cleared, revealing Jerry shrugging his shoulders and looking wholly unconcerned. "I thought he was your friend. He never mentioned a lady in his life?"

I regretted showing my frustration. I may have been misleading about the nature of my relationship with Flannigan. I had spoken to him once, at the station. He walked me out of my cell and gave me my first piece of guidance on becoming a man. Despite being ridiculed by his peers, he stood true to his belief. He said doing so was essential to manhood. *He said that to a woman.* "There is a woman!"

"Well, then what are you fussing about?"

I leapt off the bench and paced back and forth, trying my darnedest to remember who that woman was. *Jezebel? Henrietta? Rubertastein? No, no, no! It was something else. Something with a B. B...B...B...* "*BABS!*" I jumped around to face my friends. "Her name is Babs!" She was the woman who came to his aide when he needed it. She had given him strength when faced with hardship. Babs was his woman.

"Great," Jerry said with a shrug. "Where does she live?"

"I have no idea." My heart sank. "All I know is that she works at the police station."

"Hey, cheer up," Jerry said. "That's a good start. We'll roll around there around five o'clock for the shift change and follow her home. It'll be easy."

Deedris looked scared. "Go to the police station?" he stuttered. The plan rang of the same hollow hopes of going to Deedris's house or the top of Mount Bethlahoom.

"Yeah. Why not? You guys got priors or something? You can hide in the back if you want, but I don't think you'll have to worry. They don't patrol that block like they do in The Shank. There's no need. No one's crazy enough to rob a police station. You know what I mean?" Jerry checked his progress on the cigar. It had burned down to the band at the bottom. He slipped off the paper ring and slowly ripped through the last smokable segment. It looked disgusting, but Jerry seemed to enjoy the last puff the most. He tossed the smoldering butt into the snow where it sizzled and sank out of sight.

Chapter 30

We parked across from the station as the final gleam of twilight left the sky. The days were so short in January that most people left for work or school in the darkness before sunrise, only to come home an hour past sunset. It was easy to miss entire days. If you missed enough in a row, your mind would mistake the darkness for death.

A heavy stink of cigar seeped from every surface of Jerry's car. The smell was pleasant at a distance, but nauseating in high concentrations. The window begged to be opened, but the frigid air outside kept it shut. Instead, heated recycled air flowed repeatedly over smoke-stained vents in the car, drawing ever more acridity into the dank tin box. Smell, however, was not a great enough deterrent for any of us. We would keep watch for however long we had to.

Many officers came and went from the station, but none were Babs. By 6 PM, the flow of people had stopped. It had been 10 minutes since the last person left the station. "Maybe she isn't working today," Deedris said. It was an obvious possibility, and one tempting to believe after an hour and a half of sitting in such a stinky car.

"We'll wait just a little longer," I said. It would be most unfortunate to leave right before she appeared.

"I think I might be getting sick from the cigars," Deedris snapped back. "How does anyone stand it?"

Jerry took a deep breath and sighed. "Is it that bad?"

"It feels like we're in an ashtray." Deedris cracked the door open and took a breath of fresh air.

"I've been meaning to quit, you know. It's tough."

Jerry looked helpless. The longer I looked at him, the less impressive he became. It dawned on me that I had only seen him in the Alley and the street. I had never seen him with anyone but Blane, the Alleymen and Deedris. "Hey Jerry," I started to ask, "what kind of man are you?" I had no malice in my voice, though the words themselves were sharp.

Jerry looked defenseless. "What do you mean what kind of man am I? I'm Jerry. You've known me for months."

"When you were talking about men needing a woman, you mentioned that some don't think they could ever be loved. You said I could find them in dumpsters. I only ask because I've spent my fair share of time in dumpsters, and your car smells much like those dumpsters. And by the looks of the pile of blankets in the backseat, you live in this car. Is that true, Jerry?"

"What's it to you, huh? You want me to tell you I'm old and fat and live in a car? Why do you make me say it? It's not enough for it to be obvious?"

"I didn't mean to offend you. I was just curious. You're such a cool guy. I assumed you lived a lavish life. Don't you make money from selling magic? Where does it all go?"

"Selling magic to the Alleymen doesn't pay as well as you might think." Jerry gave a halfhearted laugh and looked out the window. "Truth is, I used to have that life you're talking about. I had a wife and kids. Things were nice. She patted my head every once in a while and told me I was a good man. But I wanted more, so I started betting on squirrel races down in the Alley. There's no bigger rush than seeing your squirrel nibble its way to victory. They're high-stakes games, you know. I bet my whole life savings away. The wife didn't like that. She gave me a few more chances, but I used them all up on the races.

"Chances to do what?"

"Chances to be a better man. I failed. She kicked me out and took the kids. Found herself a new man to pat on the head. Good for her, I guess. I still can't manage to save for a month without betting it all on those beautiful little squirrels. It's the only time I feel alive." Jerry laughed to himself. "Life. What a shit deal. Most people say it's short but act like it lasts forever. I think it's long and we each get many lives to live. In each one, we get a little older, a little slower and a little closer to the end. What kind of man am I? I've been every kind of man. Now I'm just waiting for it to all be over." He turned back to me. The lines of his face held decades of anguish. "So, can you just let me smoke in peace?"

I squirmed in my seat. Living one life felt impossible. Knowing I had many more lives to ruin was too much for me to process. "Yes, sir," I said, not knowing what else I could say to cheer up the fat, old man. Maybe there really was nothing.

Jerry's attention was drawn to something out of the corner of the windshield. "Is that her?"

I squinted in the darkness. The lights did not fully illuminate the way, and the form of a woman paced in and out of shadow. She stopped at a car in the parking lot directly under a light and looked around like she was paranoid of being followed. The moment she looked in my direction, I recognized her. "It is! That's her."

She got in the car and whipped out of the parking lot, down the road like she was running for her life. Jerry could barely trail her in his beat-up dumpster car. We followed her across town to a house in a picturesque neighborhood near where Betty Plumpkin lived. Her house was on a plot a quarter of the size of the other properties in the neighborhood. It was the same width as Deedris's house, though it looked smaller sandwiched between two mansions. Small as it was, it had more charm than the other two houses combined. The fence was pink and the house was bright yellow. In the dark of night, it glowed like the moon.

Babs parked in the driveway. We slowed to a stop a half block away and watched her get out. She looked nervously in our direction before racing into the house.

We got out of the car. The clean air was a welcome change, though it was so cold I thought it might freeze my nostrils shut. The three of us walked up to the house. I rang the doorbell, which was shaped like a sunflower. The bell sounded like a bluebird singing in the springtime. It faded, and there was silence. I rang it again. A series of locks unclanked, and the door drifted open. The nozzle of a pistol stuck out of the pitch-black house.

"Who are you?" Babs yelled. Her voice, even at full volume, was breathy and soft.

Jerry threw his hands in the air and froze, too nervous to speak. Babs held the gun directly at him. I raised my hand to speak. Babs yelped when she noticed me. Deedris and I must not have been visible through the peephole.

"Who are you?" She repeated but with more confusion than before.

"My name is Humphry Bulgerdeen. We come in peace."

Babs looked like she might relax, but jabbed the gun in our direction a couple of times to remind us we were not yet done answering questions. "And who are you two?"

Jerry stuttered. "I'm, I'm Jerry. I'm just here to help. This is ah... this is ah... Deedris. He's banging Miss Kooklioni."

"You're the one banging Miss Kooklioni?" Babs relaxed her wrists. The gun tilted downward.

Deedris blushed a dark shade of purple. "How does everyone know that?"

"She tells me everything. What a sweet lady." Babs lowered her arms completely and smiled for a moment.

"Everything?" Deedris whimpered.

Babs nodded politely for a moment before recalling her suspicions of us. She was such a trusting person that to sustain suspicion for longer than a minute was an impossible task. "Why are you here?" The gun didn't rise but shook in her hand to let us know it was still there.

"We are here to talk to you about Officer Flannigan," I said. "We think he needs your help."

She studied me. "How do I know you?"

"We met a few months ago. I was questioned at the station and I walked past you on my way out."

"Oh my God. You're that boy who went missing. You both are. Murph didn't make you run away did he?" She started looking nervous again, but no longer the kind that comes from immediate danger. It was the kind of nervousness you feel for someone else who is too far away to help. "What in heavens did he do? Is he okay? Whatever it was, I know he meant well. He just does things I don't understand. I tried to tell him that Frankie Fourfeet wasn't real, but anatomy is just not his strong suit. He doesn't understand that people only have two feet. Anyone can make that mistake. Anyone!"

"Man," Deedris started, "this lady is crazy."

I scowled at him. "Be nice," I snapped. I turned to Babs. She was sniffling and wiping her nose with the gun. "He didn't make us run away," I assured her. "And Frankie Fourfeet is real."

"Why would you say that?"

"Because it's true. Frankie Fourfeet is the most powerful wizard in the world. He controls nearly all the magic on Earth. Officer Flannigan is the only person in Bethlahoom who figured it out. Unfortunately, he's too powerful to stop."

"Frankie Fourfeet is real? Murph was right along?" Babs hugged the gun close to her chest and twisted about like it was a baby. "I mean of course he was! I always believed in Murph. He's such a good man." A tear rolled down her cheek.

"Great," Deedris said. "Now go tell Officer Fanny that so he can quit being a baby."

Babs snapped her fists to her sides and scowled. "Don't you go calling him that. It's Flannigan and you know it."

I stepped in between Deedris and Babs. "I apologize on behalf of my friend. He's had a rough week. His parents died and then I rode him like a donkey to the top of Mount Bethlahoom."

"Be that as it may, Murph deserves your respect. He deserves everyone's respect."

Babs needed no further convincing. She only asked to powder her nose before we left. Powdering her nose meant showering, putting on makeup, picking out a new wardrobe and plucking every stray hair off her entire body. It took four hours, but by the end of it, she looked like a princess in a picture book.

I wanted to ask her why women got rid of body hair when it was the main source of power for men, but I was too intimidated by her prettiness to do so.

We arrived at Flannigan's house sometime after midnight. The moon was our only light. In the darkness we prodded. Babs was dressed in a short dress and heels, yet was the only one not showing signs of the cold. How do women do it? How do they walk around half-naked on a frigid night yet freeze inside with the heater on and all the blankets in the house wrapped around themselves?

A faint glow snuck out of the shuttered windows. Flannigan was awake. We rang the doorbell and waited. He did not answer. We rang it again.

"Go away!" came a shout from inside.

"Murph!" Babs called back. "It's me! Let me inside!"

There was a pause. Babs breathed heavily. Then came the rustling of things being thrown hastily about inside, followed by steps to the door and the unlatching of locks. Flannigan opened the door wide and stood tall in the doorway. His beard was grizzly and wet. His eyes were wild. He wore a stained white tank top that showed off his muscular arms and bushy chest hair. It rose and fell with each of his massive breaths.

"Babs," he said, his voice burly but gentle. "What are you doing out here? You should be home, not here. There is nothing for you here."

"You are all there is," she whispered and lunged forward, her hands outstretched to touch his heaving chest.

He grabbed her wrists just before they landed and held them firmly in the air. Her strength was nothing to him. He could pull her in close or toss her aside and she could do nothing about it. He took his time choosing which to do, holding her steady, looking her over from her stocking-laced legs to her red pouting lips. He stopped at her eyes and gazed intently. In one motion he pulled her tightly to his body. One hand caught her on the lower back, keeping her from bouncing away. The other clawed around her ear with fingers wrapped behind her head. Her hands finally found his chest.

"Kiss me," she pleaded. "Please, kiss me."

He gripped her hair and tilted her head back. For a moment we all thought he would kiss her, but he resisted. "No," he said defiantly.

"Why are you doing this to me, Murph? Why?"

"I'm not good enough for you." His grip slackened and Babs shimmied out of his arms. She held herself instead. The cold seemed to have finally found her. She shivered and looked ready to cry.

"Aren't you at least going to let us inside?" Babs had a manufactured bite in her voice to cover up her tears.

Murphy looked alarmed at the prospect of letting us in. "You want to come inside?" He glanced back at the house and began scratching his stained belly nervously. "Just give me a minute." He flew inside and slammed the door.

A chorus of jingling cans roared to life. There was the occasional flush of a toilet and clamoring of dishes. I looked to Jerry for reassurance. He was nonplussed as usual. "This is all part of the process," he said, noticing my concern.

At long last, Murphy opened the front door once more. His breath was heavy and his posture slouched so it was no longer his muscular chest heaving from his tank top, but his protruding belly. "Would you like to come inside?" he asked.

Babs brushed by him without a word. The rest of us followed more graciously. The door led directly into the living room. Piles of cans were swept into the corners along with pizza boxes and used paper towels. Two couches were covered in crumbs and the only source of light, a lamp sitting on the floor, had a dirty pair of underwear as a lampshade.

Flannigan ushered us into the kitchen which was slightly less obtrusive if only because the beer cans and pizza boxes lining the walls were a more thematic choice for a kitchen.

"Sorry about the mess. I was just about to clean up before you got here."

"It beats Jerry's house," Deedris said. "He lives in a car full of trash."

"Oh?" Flannigan looked curiously at Jerry who blushed and turned to his feet.

Babs stomped her heel. "Enough of this small talk. Humphry, tell Murph what you told me."

"Humphry?" Murph said. "Why does that name sound familiar? Wait a minute. You're that boy from the station, the one Cheech tried framing for murder. You've been missing for months. What's going on here? Who are you?"

I took a deep breath. It was the same question I asked myself every day. I could hold off answering no longer. "I will tell you! I was that boy, Humphry Bulgerdeen, and I did go missing—even I don't know where I went. I became Frumpkin, an aimless cretin of the night, a boy more animal than man. I am ashamed of what I became. But I am here now with a new name. A name that only you have given a chance. It bears grave tidings and the slimmest of hopes. I am the Mystery Boy of Bethlahoom."

Babs squealed and ran to Flannigan's arms. Officer Flannigan took her in without breaking eye contact with me. He scowled with the clear intention of fighting to the death. His powers were so far beyond mine that I could only wait and hope it was not I to be fought.

"Where's Seamus?" he growled. We found our champion.

Chapter 31

We spent the next few days cleaning and celebrating our presumed victory over Seamus. It was like we had already won. Nobody left the house and nobody wanted to. It had become a home. We ate together, laughed and carried on like a family.

While initially cautious about forming new familial bonds after the death of his real parents, Deedris soon embraced Murphy and Babs as his new caregivers and Jerry as an uncle. Murphy and Babs agreed to adopt Deedris and start a family together. I was welcome to join, they said, but it was clear to me that such a designation was meant for Deedris alone. I was the best friend, not the brother.

It was the happiest I ever saw anyone. Murphy and Babs got along best of all. They slept in the same room, though it didn't sound like sleeping. It sounded more like screaming for dear life. The lack of sleep did not wear on their moods, however. Their cheerfulness was the hearth that kept our new home warm.

Jerry was grateful for the place to sleep and food to eat. He had not had a home in so long. He was the first up in the morning ready to clean or cook and the last to bed each night, squeezing out every bit of conversation he could on the couches by the fire.

I enjoyed those days too, as much as I could, but by this point in life, I had learned to mistrust my feelings. There was still work to be done. Doom hung over our heads, waiting for the right moment to fall. Outside our home, Bethlahoom was in peril. Flannigan was a pariah. Deedris's family had been murdered. I was being hunted by a ravenous leprechaun. Trouble was all around us.

Saturday came suddenly. There was a change in the air from the previous night. Everyone but Deedris could sense it. Deedris stuffed his gullet with ham and eggs as freely as the lasagna we ate the night before. Nobody else picked off more than a couple bites. Our eyes darted around, trying not to land on the truth lying in front of us. The unease continued to build until I could take no more. I cleared my throat. "I think we should talk about tonight," I said. "We're running out of time to make a plan."

Deedris stopped shoveling and spit out the food from his mouth. "Why do you have to bring that up?" He was not ready to face the truth.

"Settle down, son," Murphy commanded, resting a hand on Deedris's hot head. Deedris cooled immediately. The power in Murphy's hands was encouraging. He was every bit as strong as I hoped.

Babs reached out to Murphy's other hand and gave an approving nod. Murphy nodded back and continued. "Your new mother and I have been talking, and we are going to go to the warehouse alone. She'll be on call with the department. I will sneak in, get the proof I need, and Bab's will call in backup from there. The two of you will stay here with Uncle Jerry."

"But you don't know what you're getting into!" I protested. Murphy was strong, and the police department was stronger, but something in me knew that it wouldn't be enough. The police didn't listen to him when he was on the force. Why would they start after he was kicked off in disgrace? Why trust a broken rope when his life depended on it? I didn't have the clarity of mind to communicate this reasoning, or even understand it myself. I could only see the conclusion to the logic: the plan would fail. I told him such to no avail. "It won't work!"

"That's enough," he said. "You boys have done everything you can. The police will take it from here."

I wanted to protest further, but I couldn't make a sound. No one would listen even if I could. Deedris had blind faith in his new father. However tragic the circumstances leading to his irrational attachment to his new parents, he found his peace. I could not fault him for it, and would never want to take it away.

Jerry was solemn, though accepting. I knew he had little faith in the police, but he was weary of disrupting the status quo now that it had finally come around to serve him. He was well acquainted with the impermanence of life's luxuries, and I could neither fault him for his silence.

Murphy himself was stoic. It was his duty to protect his new family. His life was in jeopardy as much or more than any of ours, but for him, the stakes were a matter of honor. He had already succeeded by taking responsibility.

The chill in the air did not linger. Everyone was so certain that things were going to be alright, that I slowly accepted it myself. By sunset, we were again happy and smiling and carrying on.

"It's time, sweetheart," Babs whispered, tugging on Murphy's sleeve.

Murphy checked his watch and took a deep breath. "We're going now, boys. Don't worry about a thing. We'll be back late. I don't want any of you still up when we get home. You hear?"

"Yes, sir," we responded together.

Babs hugged us all and Murphy gave each of us a stern handshake before leaving. The door shut behind them with a thud.

"You want to play vengeance and sadism?" Jerry asked.

"What's that?" I had never heard of it.

"It was my grandma's favorite card game. I'll teach it to you."

Jerry dealt out the cards. Each of us was given a pile with the top card revealed along with a hand of five cards that could be replenished at the start of each turn. The first person to get rid of their pile wins the game. The game was long. Deedris and I spent the first half learning the rules and fell well behind Jerry in the process. It was a very long game, however. The longer it went, the greater the chance Deedris and I had at making a comeback.

Jerry was not a good card player. He started getting nervous and making foolish moves. If we played a thousand more games, this would be the only one he had the chance to win. He knew that better than anyone. He started muttering insults at us. Some of them were wildly inappropriate, but neither Deedris nor I took offense. Jerry was nearly crying as he said them. I almost wanted him to win. Deedris had no such intention. He took the game's name to heart and attacked the moment he saw weakness.

It was late into the night and Deedris and Jerry were both down to their final cards. Either could win on any turn. Deedris drew an eight from the deck. Worthless. He growled as he set it on his discard pile. Jerry was hyperventilating. Sweat dripped down his cheek. He muttered incoherent curses. He pulled a card of his own. A two. The card he had been waiting for! He set it down right away, followed by a three and a four, a five and six, and finally a seven. But wait, he only used the cards from his hand, forgetting to play the final card from his pile, the one he needed to play to win the game, the six that had been staring at us all for half an hour. When he noticed his mistake, he screamed. He screamed as long as one could on a single breath.

In the uncomfortable silence that followed, the telephone rang. It was an ominous omen. A call this late was never for good news. "Should we answer it?" I asked the table. I only got shrugs for a response. No one had called the entire time we were there, and the etiquette of answering another man's phone was not clear to us. The phone stopped ringing.

"Who do you suppose that was?" Deedris asked. "Maybe someone's calling to confirm the new world record for biggest loser of all time?" Deedris pointed at Jerry and cackled.

"Deedris!" I exclaimed.

Jerry cried out in agony once more. As he trailed off we noticed the phone ringing again.

"I'm going to pick it up," I decided. "It might be Flannigan."

I answered the phone. "Hello?" I barely got the word out before shouting on the other end interrupted me.

"They're going to kill him! They're going to kill him!"

"What? Who's killing who?"

"Murph! They are going to kill my Murph!"

"Babs, is that you? What happened?"

"It's so awful. He went in alone like we planned. I was going to call for backup, but he said half the station is already there. They're all in on it. Murph is gonna try to arrest them all himself. They'll kill him. Oh my god. Oh my god." She started crying.

The phone slipped from my ear. I knew this plan would fail, but I never would have guessed it to be because members of the police department were working with Seamus. How could anyone hope to stop him now?

Jerry and Deedris must have seen the dread on my face. They stood and waited for an explanation. Babs kept crying on the other end of the line. It was time to act. Nobody was coming to save us. There were no more heroes to seek, or hidden powers to cultivate. It was me and a couple of raggedy rejects up against the untold might of all the magic I knew of in the world.

I hoisted the phone back to my ear. "Wait there, Babs. We're coming to get you." I hung up the phone and repeated it to my troops. "They need our help. We're going to the warehouse. I'll tell you more on the way."

Neither needed convincing. Deedris was more resourceful than I expected. He revealed a stash of guns he brought to the house beneath his coat. Jerry and I marveled at the weapons. Jerry grabbed a sawed-off shotgun and I reached for a familiar pistol. Deedris shoveled the rest back into his coat. All except an automatic rifle half his size. He slammed in a cartridge of bullets the size of my forearm and cocked it into place.

"Where did you get that thing?" I asked in wonder.

"It was in my room at the apartment. It makes for a good back scratcher. I was going to bring the rocket launcher too, but it wouldn't fit in my coat."

"There was a rocket launcher at the apartment?" I didn't like the sound of that. If it was at the apartment, it might now be at the warehouse.

"There were rockets, grenades, about 500 pounds of TNT. There was pretty much everything you need."

We left in Jerry's car. The roads were empty and dark. The moonless sky was sprayed with stars. Grim, gray streaks of light flashed across it, waving and shimmering. Northern Lights, some people called them. They were signs of intense magic. Under normal circumstances they were harmless and beautiful. These were not normal circumstances. Sure enough, they grew more intense as we got closer to the warehouse. They lit up the land with green light as bright as a full moon.

We pulled up a short walk away from the warehouse and went the rest of the way by foot. We saw Babs shivering outside her car. She clutched a gun at her chest with both hands.

"Psst," I called out on our approach. "Babs, we're here."

Babs jolted towards us with the gun drawn but lowered it when she saw us. She was shaking. Trails of frozen tears on her cheeks sparkled green in the haunting light. Deedris ran to her side. He looked upon her with the same desperation I did when my mother wept inconsolably. I would sit by her with every good intention in the world and no way to act on any of them. It felt like looking through a peephole you were also being squeezed through. I hated it. Seeing Deedris in that situation let me know we are not all the same. He had the same look of empathy and motivation, but he didn't see his limitations as clearly as I did. He believed he could actually help her.

"They're going to kill him," she repeated feebly. It was all she seemed to be able to say.

Deedris whipped his rifle out from his coat and rested it on his shoulder. "I'm doing the killing today. Don't you worry about a thing." Those words were as haunted as the lights in the sky.

Babs sniffled a little longer, but Deedris's rousing speech had found its mark. She took a few calming deep breaths and nodded. "There's scaffolding on the back that leads to a skylight," she started. "That's where Murph got in. We can get in there too."

"I'll lead the way," Deedris said.

We followed Deedris to the back. His confidence was infectious, a deadly disease. He looked like he had nothing to fear, but fear keeps us safe. Without it, we leap to our deaths and often drag others along with us. My fear was too strong for such a swift demise. I did my best to appear to match his enthusiasm, but it was an act. I was terrified. Jerry and Babs seemed to be somewhere in between.

The warehouse was a three-story relic of past ages when Bethlahoom served as a mining town. Parts had rusted away through the years. Inside were empty containers and outdated machines the size of houses. Hardly any living person recalled the days when Bethlahoom bustled with commerce. The empty buildings downtown were a constant reminder of the city's past glory. The warehouses were a reminder of the city's death.

The scaffolding had a ladder to the top. Half was buried in a snowdrift, and the rest was slick with ice. Deedris slung his rifle about his shoulder and climbed. Babs and Jerry followed. I stood paralyzed at the bottom, having been distracted by the ever-strengthening green lights tearing apart the sky.

"Hurry up, Hump!" Deedris called out near the top of the ladder.

"I'm coming," I said.

I only made it a couple steps before Deedris slipped on an icy rung in his haste. He fell past Babs, screaming. Jerry reached out to grab him, but could only slow his descent. I couldn't even do that much for him. He fell flat on his back and sunk into the snowdrift, disappearing into the hole he made. His screams disappeared along with him.

I raced to his body. "Deedris!" I yelled into the hole where his head should have been. "Are you alright?"

He groaned. That was a good start. I dug him out as fast as I could. "Are you alright?" I asked again.

"I'm fine," he said feebly. He wriggled his body free from the snow and sat up, groaning with every motion. He looked up at the ladder. "That was a force field," he said, his confidence returning with a vengeance.

"Maybe," I said, careful not to bruise his ego any further. "That or you just slipped on the ice."

"No," he said defiantly. "That was a force field for sure, but don't worry about it. I disabled it with my screams. We should be able to get through now." It occurred to me then that Deedris had lost his mind. "It's okay you guys," he shouted up to Babs and Jerry. "Just a force field. I disabled it with my screams."

He rose and dusted off the snow, ready to climb again. I looked around one last time before following. The snowy landscape glowed an eerie green from the ever-strengthening aurora. I glanced back the way we came. Someone was coming towards us. Someone crazed and urgent and wild. A woman's scream echoed from every direction. It came from the person trudging through the deep snow. She made a good pace. The next scream was clearer. "Humphry!"

I raced up the ladder, faster even than Deedris could. I tumbled next to him.

"Who is that?" he asked.

"The wild woman," I said, panting. "We have to keep moving."

We raced to the open skylight, following the fresh trail of Flannigan's footprints. There was a rope ladder tied to a post that dangled down into a small room that appeared to have once been an office. Jerry climbed down first. If it was strong enough to support him, it would have no trouble holding the rest of us.

Jerry made it down without a problem, followed by Babs. Deedris was clumsy in his haste and fell halfway down. Jerry broke his fall. Both made more noise than I would have liked, but neither seemed to be injured. It gave me an idea.

"Hey, Jerry," I whispered, "I'm going to pull off the ladder and jump down. Can you catch me?"

"Why would you do that?" He rubbed his chest where Deedris had just fallen and grimaced. If Deedris was a BB, I would be a cannonball.

"I don't want the wild woman using the ladder."

"She's just got the hots for you. Let her join us."

"Come on, Jerry. She's a witch!"

"Fine."

I unleashed the rope. The ladder floated down and curled into a neat mound with a soft thud. I closed my eyes and envisioned landing as softly as the rope. My prayers were not answered. I fell with all the grace of a sack of potatoes.

"You alright, Jerry?" I asked.

Jerry took the full weight of my fall and lay flat on his back with his arms splayed wide. He groaned in response.

Deedris jabbed me with the butt of his rifle. "He'll be fine," he said. "Leave him."

He was right, of course. We had to keep moving. "Thank you, Jerry," I said, before lifting myself off his belly. "When the wild woman comes, tell her I'm not around."

Jerry managed a nod and I knew I could trust him to do as I asked. He deserved the biggest pat on the head a man could receive. It's a shame how sacrifice is punished.

Babs, Deedris and I snuck out of the office onto a grated balcony overlooking the entire warehouse. The second floor consisted only of a thin line of offices on one side of the building. The bottom floor had one room and it was the biggest I had ever seen before or since, a mass grave of rusty drills and giant drums bathed in grim, green light dripping from holes in the snow-covered ceiling. In the center was a clearing where a fire raged. Flames licked high above the decomposing machinery. Around the fire, shadows of demons danced and cackled. We found our enemy.

Chapter 32

The three of us hugged the balcony railing and watched. One voice rang clear above the rest. "Gentlemen," Seamus sang, his voice always a dance, "such a pleasure we're having together."

A single dissenting voice called out, "You'll never win!" It was Flannigan. He was still alive and being held captive.

Babs rose to her fullest height and yelled back. "Murph! I'm coming, Murph!"

I grabbed her and covered her mouth to keep her from shouting again, but it was too late. The cheers stopped and one of the ghostly figures approached the fire. He gazed in our general direction. The intense light of the fire must have made us invisible to him. He tilted his head side to side, trying to get a better angle to see us. The flaring fire illuminated his face as he did. It was Seamus.

"I'll kill you, Seamus!" Deedris yelled upon seeing his face.

"No, Deeds!" I squealed.

Seamus bared his teeth and motioned to the other shadows. He drew a gun and sprayed bullets across the wall behind us. They all missed.

"Get down!" I yelled and motioned to a stairwell at the end of the balcony that led to the bottom floor. Dozens more shooters opened fire. We had to get downstairs before we were trapped.

We crawled down the stairs. "This way," I said, pointing along the side of the warehouse. Our only hope was to run around the room and surprise them from behind. I communicated this through hand gestures to Babs and Deedris. Deedris motioned with his gun that he could fight them all straight up. Babs communicated that he couldn't by smacking him in the head.

We were not yet to the far side of the room when the gunmen reached the bottom of the stairs. They would have seen us if their vision weren't still hindered from the fire. How long would that advantage last? Not long, I guessed.

We reached the far wall and glanced back at the gunmen's progress. A few walked up the stairs with guns drawn. Jerry was still up there. Deedris took a step back towards the stairs. "Uncle Jerry," he said.

I stopped him. "There's nothing we can do for him," I whispered. "He has a gun, too. Keep moving."

"But—" he began to protest but was stopped short by the renewed clamor of gunfire, this time from atop the stairs. I pushed him onward. There was no time to see who was shooting and who was being shot.

We snaked along through the graveyard of machinery back towards the fire in the center. Cast among the machines were little black boxes with flashing blue lights. I couldn't stop to investigate them, though I could assume they were evil. We were in Hell, after all, and every step took us deeper. At the end was the devil Seamus, ready to reap our souls.

We approached the clearing from behind and mounted the skeleton of a bulldozer that stood between us and the straggling demons still circling the flames. We watched and waited for the right time to strike.

The demons were clearer from close up. Most of the men I didn't recognize. All were cloaked with weapons drawn. Nearly as many women clung to their sides, each of a beauty beyond anything that should be possible. A couple I recognized as Seamus's friends. They reminded me of the lovely Marlene. Somehow the thought of her crushed me more than that of my imminent death.

Babs pointed to a man on his knees on the other side of the fire. It was Flannigan. A few men stood guard with guns drawn to his head. I recognized them too. They were the police officers who arrested me. "What are they doing here?" I whispered to Babs. She shook her head without an answer. Seeing them stripped her of the tenuous confidence she had minutes before on the balcony. I bumped her shoulder, looking for an answer, but she gave only a vacant stare.

The longer I looked, the more people I recognized. Each was more shocking than the last. There were more police officers from the station. The police chief and mayor stood side by side. Were they in on the dark magic trade too? Is that why they discredited Flannigan? Surely if they were here, they must have known Frankie Fourfeet was real. I pointed them out to Babs to get her opinion, but she was petrified. Useless.

There was a man who looked like Rudolphus Slim from the newspaper. The press was in on it too. A grand conspiracy laid before our eyes, and the man Bethlahoom entrusted to report such crimes was an accomplice.

Sandwiched between two half-naked women was Father O'Flacity. My mouth dropped. What was a man of the lord doing in the den of the Devil? Of all the people I knew, he was the last I'd guess was involved in dark magic. Did this have something to do with Tabby's baby? Was he the one who magically made me get Tabby pregnant in an effort to promote his congregation? It was such a dark thought, and yet this was dark magic we were dealing with.

Deedris growled and pointed to two more men who should not have been there: Principal Chewbooger and Mr. Smellington.

"Why are Earth are they here?" I said. They had their own magical source in the school. It was ancient and supposedly good. Why come here to deal with Seamus? Then again, the police officers and Father O'Flacity also had their own magic. Did Seamus gather all the magical people in Bethlahoom to enlist them for his evil plans? He would be unstoppable.

The group that had gone to the stairs began trickling back into the clearing. Two of the last were carrying a body back with them. It was Jerry. He was shot several times in the torso and left a trail of blood glimmering in the firelight. They threw him on the ground next to Flannigan.

A lone man in the corner took notice. "Jerry?" he shouted, sounding concerned. "Jerry?" He pushed his way through the crowd to where Jerry lay. When he got to him, he turned so I could see his face. It was Blane. His cheeks were gaunt and sallow. "What have you done to him? You shot him!" He cradled Jerry's limp head and rocked him back and forth. If he was not already dead, it was an act of evil to keep him alive in such a condition. The group grew quiet except for a couple of weeping women who must have known Jerry too.

Seamus stepped back into the clearing, effortlessly drawing everyone's attention. His cloak was of the same glowing green as the sky. "Did someone have something to say?" He twisted around, staring everyone down. His cloak cracked like a whip as he spun. "You'll want to be saying it now. I don't like interruptions."

The silence that followed was absolute. The women stopped crying. They may have even stopped breathing. I only heard the crackling of the fire and Deedris clenching his gun. He had not shown any restraint since our arrival. He could snap at any second. I could only brace my gun and follow him into battle when the time came. In truth, I was grateful it would not be me leading the way.

Blane broke the silence. "You killed him. You killed Jerry."

"Is he your friend, Blane?" Seamus's voice dripped like acid. "Awfully strange having a friend who's trying to kill me. You have something to say for yourself?"

Blane's mouth opened but no words came out. The guilt on his face was too strong to believe. It scared me as much as Seamus did. A man that guilty was capable of anything, and it looked like Blane wanted to kill Seamus. A glimmer of hope came to me. Blane was a wizard himself. It wouldn't be so far-fetched to think he could overpower Seamus. Seamus didn't seem to be able to read Blane's face at all. Guilt was not something he was capable of feeling. He must not have known how powerful it can be. As obvious as it was to me, Seamus would be caught unaware.

The moment passed, however. Blane did nothing. "That's what I thought," Seamus quipped.

I closed my eyes and sunk my head between my knees. When I opened them, I was looking at another flashing blue dot. One of the black boxes was positioned right below us. I still couldn't tell what it was. I pointed it out to Deedris. He had a curious reaction.

"That looks like one of the explosives from the apartment," he said. "What is it doing here?"

"Explosives?" I looked around in a panic. There were flashing blue dots everywhere. It all clicked into place. "Seamus is going to blow up the warehouse. He means to take out all the other forms of magic in Bethlahoom and claim the whole town for himself."

At last, Deedris was afraid. He trembled, softening his grip on the gun. He finally saw the horrifying power we were up against. It was only blindness that made him bold. Of all the contradictions life had shown me, this was the strangest of all.

"Well, gentlemen," Seamus continued, "it's high time the real fun starts. If you'll all be so kind to wait here while my friends and I fish our gifts out from the back. Blane, Tobias, if you'll follow me. You boys, too," he said, pointing to the small faction that had gone with him to the stairs. "If you need the restroom, ladies, now's a good time, too." All the women detached from the remaining men and moved towards Seamus. The remaining men, a few dozen of them, looked around quizzically, unsure of how to feel.

"I'll see the rest of you in a few minutes," Seamus finished and began walking out of the clearing.

This was it. If we didn't attack now, we would burn. I turned to Deedris and Babs. Both were paralyzed with fear. It was up to me. I had to lead the way. I slapped Deedris to awaken him and hoisted my gun in the air, firing a bullet into the sky. "For Jerry!" I screamed and leapt from the bulldozer. The crowd scattered. I fired a shot at Seamus, but my aim was off. It clanged off a drill far to the right of him. He didn't run like the rest. He pulled out a gun of his own and opened fire.

I leapt to the ground and rolled across the floor to a crate whose contents I could only hope were strong enough to stop bullets. The ground all around sparked from gunfire. There were more shooters than just Seamus. I was pinned.

I looked at Deedris. He was still on the bulldozer. I wanted to shoot him. "ATTACK!" I screamed.

Babs leapt first. She screamed for Murphy and fired in the direction of the police officers. Deedris jumped shortly after and sprayed bullets in a chaotic arc all around the clearing. The gun was too powerful for him to control.

The shots around the crate stopped long enough to run to a new spot with more cover. Seamus's gang scattered. I aimed for Seamus once more but missed just as badly as before. I couldn't waste any more shots.

We drove them back into the equipment. Babs raced to Murphy and untied him. They embraced and were slow to retreat. Our enemy recovered and returned fire, now hidden from view behind the machinery. We each dove behind the closest objects we could find. Deedris had a thick stump carved up like a chair. I found myself hiding behind three metal drums.

Babs and Flannigan didn't make it to safety. They hid behind the fire, but the bullets ripped through flame as easily as their bodies. They held each other close as their guts sprayed out behind them. Their bodies were limp but stayed aloft from the force of the bullets shredding them apart. Deedris's screams pierced me like one of those bullets. These were his parents. Not his original parents, but the ones he had used to forget about his real parents. Not only was he screaming for the loss of Murphy and Babs, but of the torturous reality he had used them to cover up. It was almost enough to overshadow the deafening roar of dozens of guns firing at will.

The gunfire trickled down and finally ceased. The bodies that once belonged to Babs and Murphy Flannigan collapsed into an unrecognizable heap beside the fire. They had become one.

"Is that you, Frumpkin?" Seamus called out manically. "What is it with you and hiding in trash cans?" His cackle was of an otherworldly beast. The clearing was the perfect shape to focus the echoes directly on my trash can. It sounded like there were a hundred Seamus's all seething with sadism. "You think I'm going to shoot you? You think I'd let you off that easily? I'll shoot your friend, sure. I'll shoot him in front of you. Make sure you see him die before I pluck your eyes out and shove them up your ass."

His taunts were threatening, but I noticed his voice didn't come any closer. He was afraid to approach. He told me once that wizards could be killed by guns. I had a gun. Deedris had several.

"I'm not Frumpkin!" I yelled back. "My name is Humphry Bulgerdeen, and I am a good boy!" I tipped one of the barrels on its side and jumped in. "Start shooting, Deeds!" I said while rolling towards him.

Deedris leapt up and unleashed another stream of bullets. Everyone was distracted by my maneuver, and I was able to roll all the way to Deedris without them returning fire. "Get in, Deeds. I'll roll us to safety."

He slid beside me into the barrel and we began to roll. With each turn we tumbled faster and faster to the edge of the clearing. It was exhilarating. I always knew that one day my talent for rolling would save the day. My body shape was ill-equipped for so many tasks. All of them except one: rolling.

But there was no hill to roll down. The dusty warehouse floor was flat and littered with impediments. We slammed into a rusty pile of scrap that rang the drum like a bell and sent it rolling back into the clearing. By the time we crawled out and recovered our hearing, Seamus and his crew of crooks had us surrounded. Seamus kicked our guns away before we could recover them.

"So, Humphry, is it?" Seamus sneered. His gun was pointed right between my eyes. "It looks like this is the end of the line. It's a shame it has to end this way. I really wish it didn't. Maybe if you tell me who you're working for, I could reconsider what I said about your eyes. You want to tell me and see?"

I didn't respond. Seamus's words were meaningless.

"Not going to talk, eh?" Evil flashed across his face and he slammed his gun across my cheek. I fell to the side. Blood dripped off my cheek and onto the ground. It felt like my jaw had cracked. The pain was brutal, but I forced myself back up. If these were my final moments, I would not crumble.

"Don't tell him anything," I said to Deedris.

Seamus no longer bothered to hide his true form. His eyes glowed green like the haunted sky. His cloak waved about like a great wind was blowing, though the air was stale and dead. His bared teeth were the wicked fangs of a predator. He pointed his gun at Deedris. *No.*

I opened my mouth to scream, but it was another voice that came out. A wild voice of superhuman strength. Everyone turned toward it. It did not echo. It pierced. The wild woman was coming.

She burst into the clearing brandishing a shotgun. Her hair frizzed high above her head making her stand as tall as any of the men. It sprung forward as well, casting a shadow on her face, shielding herself from the evil green light.

The woman pumped the shotgun with one hand and fired on Seamus's crew. Four men fell and the rest scattered. She pumped again and aimed at Seamus. He cursed and dove to the ground. The shot cast a wide net but spared its target. He ran to take cover before she could take another shot.

"Run, Deedris!" I yelled. We left our guns on the ground and ran as fast as we could to the edge of the clearing. We were so egregiously outmatched, our guns seemed useless. All we could do was run.

The wild woman took another shot toward Seamus, but she ran in our direction. She was quickly upon us. We could not outpace her. She pumped the shotgun another time. "To the exit!" She screamed. It was an unexpected command. She swiveled around and blew another round towards Seamus. She was saving us. "Go!" she yelled again. This time her voice was softer, more pained than maniacal. I recognized that cry.

"Mom?"

"Move!" She kicked my bottom and knocked Deedris with the butt of her gun. We obeyed.

We raced to the door, but there wasn't a clear path. The tangle of forgotten scraps snagged us every time we tried to truly run. We finally managed our way through the rubble and out the front door only to hit a mountainous snow drift outside. Countless feet of powdery snow slowed us like molasses. We were an open target. A streak of crimson light appeared across the green sky, painting the snow a bloody red as though we had already been blown to pieces.

It didn't take long for Seamus to follow out the door. A crowd of cronies formed behind him. Blane was at his side. "You see those rats out there?" he cackled to his followers. "Watch what happens to rats."

We stopped trudging and turned to face him. He hoisted a rocket launcher onto his shoulder and pointed it right at us.

"Any last words, Frumpkin?" He didn't need to yell like he did. We were so close I could have heard him whisper.

I had nothing more to say to him. I did not want my last words to be to such an evil man. I didn't even want to look at him. I looked at Blane instead. Blane, who looked more terrified than I was. He had every reason to be. He was the one who would have to live with Seamus after this. He was the one who would continue to be beaten and degraded forever more. Worse yet, he had to live with his conscience. No torture is worse than a good conscience living in sin. He would never forgive himself.

"I forgive you, Blane," I said. I don't know where the words came from. I said them without thinking or knowing of their power. A greater force was working through me. I had tapped into a magical source of my own.

Blane's face changed. The pain appeared to lessen. I had given him the slimmest bit of relief, and from that relief, he was able to see where his pain was coming from. It was the same tool Seamus had used on me. The one he was surely using on all of his followers. A tool will work no matter who wields it.

Seamus looked confused when Blane raised his gun. He reacted to it as my brother would when he caught me picking my nose. That look of disgust would stay on his face for the rest of his life.

Blane pulled the trigger. Half of Seamus's head blew off his shoulders. A cloud of blood showered down on the snow. The crimson streak in the sky flared as the green light was extinguished. The whole sky was scarlet.

For a moment, everyone was calm. Blane had done it. He had killed Seamus. He saved my life in the process. What gave me the most joy in that moment was seeing all the pain in Blane disappear. He was free for just one moment.

The other men finally reacted. The police officers and cronies were loyal to Seamus. They drew weapons on Blane and shot him down. He collapsed instantly. They kept firing, bolting him into the snow.

I screamed. I started to run to him, but my mom held me back. The trolls stopped shooting and looked up at me. They turned their guns towards us. We were still not saved.

Mom pulled me down into the snow. Deedris still stood. He pulled something deep from his coat. It was a grenade. He pulled the tab and threw it at our enemies as they opened fire. I reached out to his leg and pulled him off his feet. As he hit the ground, the first blast sounded. The gunfire stopped and a wall of air hit us. Just as it passed, a magnificent light shot into the sky. A wall of immeasurable sound and hot air pounded us. The grenade had triggered one of the explosives. The entire warehouse was full of them. BOOM BOOM BOOM....

Shrapnel flew in every direction. The blasts lasted all but ten seconds, but it felt like an eternity. The ensuing fire burned so bright it scorched the skin from a distance. The snow around us was melting. The wetness froze our faces while our backs fried. Another explosion rocked us. More shrapnel spewed. We had to get out of there.

Deedris popped up unharmed. Mom didn't move. I hoisted her up, but she was unconscious. Her back was shredded apart by the flying pieces of metal. She had shielded us when the bombs went off and taken the full brunt of the damage herself. I cried out for help, but only Deedris and I were there to hear.

I wrapped myself in her arms and cried. "Why did you come?" I whimpered. She gave no answer. It seemed she wanted to save me, but I couldn't be sure. I heard Jebediah's words ringing in my head, 'She's there because she was worried people would find out how little she cared about you.' It sounded so wrong, but it gave me doubt regardless. I squeezed her. It didn't matter if she cared about me. I cared about her. I hugged her tight. Her chest was warm. So was her face. The warmth touched my neck and disappeared. It came again, then faded. She was breathing.

"Deedris! Help me carry her!" I rifled through her coat and found a set of car keys. Deedris and I lifted her onto our shoulders. She was lighter than her large coat made it seem. We marched to the car, bludgeoned and burned, through the snow under the bloody sky.

Chapter 33

Mom spent the following week in the hospital. The doctors said she was in a coma and that there was no way of knowing if she would ever wake up. I offered to make her a nice breakfast to coax her out, but the doctors insisted it wouldn't work.

Dad didn't want to acknowledge what had happened. He grounded me for the rest of my life, but the scolding he gave me was not as severe as I expected. It seemed that what happened to Mom was so hard to deal with that he would rather pretend nothing had happened at all. He instead focused all his energy on Tabitha and her baby who was expected to be born at any time.

That Sunday at church was chaos. Father O'Flacity's fiery death was a shock to his congregation. The sudden jolt was enough for some people to question their loyalty to his convictions. The withdrawal of members from the church just before the birth of their messiah left the remaining followers indignant. In the heated confrontation, Dad became the new de facto leader and steered the remaining members into a deeper submission to Tabby and their supposed messiah. They came to the house later that day bearing extravagant gifts. One member brought the deed to his family's house. Unfortunately, the gifts did nothing to ease Tabby's ferocious temperament. If I didn't know better I would have thought her ballooning belly was filled with pure rage.

School was temporarily canceled in the wake of Principal Chewbooger's and Mr. Smellington's deaths. A city official was appointed as the interim principal and class was set to resume the following Thursday. An assembly to honor the deceased was planned for that Wednesday at the high school. The students from all the schools in the district along with their families would be in attendance. I had recurring nightmares each night in which the school blew up with everyone inside while I stood outside with the detonator.

Tabby drove with Dad to the school while I rode with Jebediah. He made sure to let me know how disappointed he was that he had to drive with me. After everything that happened, the insult made him sound pathetic. If riding with me was a problem for him, then he must be pretty weak. I saw him clearly for the first time.

I hadn't seen Deedris since that night at the warehouse. We were separated at the hospital. I was allowed to stay with my mom, but Deedris was taken into protective custody. I wasn't even sure if he would be at the assembly. I hoped with all my might that he would. I had so much on my mind and he was the only person in the world who could understand. I wouldn't even have to talk to him. He already understood. Some things are so difficult to explain or impossible to believe that only those with personal experience make us feel understood. I was beginning to think that my experiences were so unique that soon no one, not even Deedris, would understand me.

The parking lot was full. Jebediah and I had to park on the street and walk. We found Dad's car parked illegally on the sidewalk right next to the entrance. A security guard was writing a ticket that would surely be swiftly thrown in the trash.

Dad had taken four seats from the Windleson family in the front row. Greg Windleson, the father of the Windlesons, paced the aisle, trying to summon the courage to confront my dad about it. Jebediah was also angered to find that the four seats were meant so Tabby and Dad could have empty chairs on either side of them.

I didn't care much at all. I was too busy looking around the massive auditorium for Deedris. I needed someone, anyone, to share the burden of my memories. I couldn't find him anywhere. I resigned my search and moped to the back of the hall where I stood alone as the meeting started. The mayor himself approached the podium. The police chief stood behind him. As expected, he talked a great deal about how there was nothing to worry about in Bethlahoom. He was lying and it made me sick to hear.

Molly Mucasine was seated several rows ahead of me. Her eyes had followed me up the aisle. She sat on her knees facing the back of the hall, her bespectacled eyes fell upon mine. Her giant glasses covered half her head. The strength of her prescription made her face look like a squeezed tube of toothpaste. It was the most beautiful tube of toothpaste in the world.

She briefly broke her stare to creep past the people seated in her row. She stuck her head into the aisle and resumed her stare, bent over an unnerved elementary school student. Finally, she hopped up the aisle like a timid rabbit towards a head of lettuce. "Hello," she said in her squeaky voice.

"Hello," I said back. The urge to be close to her gripped me. I had to stay strong. This was Molly Mucasine after all.

"I'm glad you're back," she squeaked. "I missed you."

"You did?" *What was this about?*

She blushed and nodded. "Everybody thought you were dead. Were you? I won't tell anyone if you were."

"Was I dead?" Conventional wisdom held that when people died they stopped living. I never thought to doubt it. "I don't think so. I was just away from school for a while."

"Oh." She pulled out a collection of handmade dolls. "I thought you were dead so did a ritual to make the universe take Principle Chewbooger and Smellytown instead of you. I supposed they died for nothing."

"You did that for me?" *Why in the world would she do that? Did she want me alive so she could torture me more?*

She nodded sweetly. I stared in confusion. Whatever the reason, she wanted to be close to me, and it gave me a warm fuzzy feeling. But one question remained. *How was she so powerful?*

The mayor continued his lies. He started talking about Flannigan. He blamed him for the explosions. He said he was working with the magic cartel, spreading false rumors to hide the true identity of the cartel's leaders. It was too much to ignore.

"He's lying," I whispered to Molly, though I wanted to scream it as loud as I could.

"Of course he's lying. He's evil. You never noticed?"

"The mayor? But he's the mayor!"

"Pshh. They're all evil. That's why they spend all their time trying to convince people they're good. Evil, evil, evil." She pulled out a doll that looked eerily like the mayor. She began stabbing it with a sewing needle. "Evil, evil, evil…" Molly Mucasine was not to be messed with.

The mayor wrapped up his tirade about Flannigan and addressed Tabby. The troubling times were over, he claimed, and the birth of Tabby's baby would bring about a time of great peace. The auditorium gave a mix of polite applause, groans and uproarious cheers. I felt sick to my stomach. These people were being fooled. That baby was mine, brought into the world through Molly Mucasine's bizarre witchcraft, and these unfortunate souls were about to enshrine it as their ultimate leader. How pathetic was I that I could not stand up and tell them the truth? I could shout it for all to hear, but I was too embarrassed. Is that what I am ruled by? Embarrassment? Fear of my reputation being tarnished? I had no reputation other than as a fat little kid, and for that, I was willing to let my town be overtaken by my magical demon spawn.

The mayor called Tabby to the stage. She refused. He asked again. Dad encouraged her. Finally, she stood and took the stage, waving off the applause. The people who were cheering grew even louder. The groaners groaned louder too. My shame screamed loudest of all.

And then it was Tabby who screamed. "OWW! GODDAMN SON OF BITCH!" She clutched her swollen belly and grimaced. "What the fuck was that shit?" she asked the mayor. He was perplexed.

The cheers subsided, replaced by murmurs. Dad leapt up to check on Tabby.

"That's ok, everybody," The mayor said. "Just a little hiccup. These things happen with the mothers of messiahs."

"GOD DAMN FUCKING SHIT FUCKERS!" Tabby clutched her stomach again. This time everyone was silent. Everyone but my conscience.

This must end. The demon baby was possessing Tabby and once it was born it would rule the town with the same fiery rage. I had to warn the people. I looked at Molly. She would try to stop me. I looked at her and braced for the full brunt of her mind control efforts, but she was staring at Tabby with as much confusion as everyone else. *How could that be? Surely she knows what's going on.*

"JESUS FUCKING CHRIST!"

I had to do it. I had to warn them. I stood to my fullest height. I cleared my throat. I would tell them all it was really my baby.

Another boy stood and shouted before I got the chance. "It was me! I am the father!"

The audience gasped. *Why did he say that?*

"No, it was me!" another boy stood and exclaimed.

"I'm the father!" shouted another.

A chorus of boys stood and proclaimed themselves the father.

"Settle down, settle down," the mayor chided. "We know who the father is. It's God and we are all here to obey his word as expressed through me, the mayor."

"COCK SUCKING JESUS FUCKERS!" Tabby yelled again, clutching her belly.

The whole auditorium erupted in boos. An older lady stood up and shouted, "Oh for God sakes, get her to the hospital! The poor tramp's in labor!"

"TITS AND DICKS!" Tabby shouted while being carried off the stage. The audience became an unruly mob. Some of them shouted at the stage. Others stormed out of the auditorium.

I was stunned. I looked at Molly. Her eyes were so wide that they appeared to be of a normal size behind her preposterously powerful prescription lenses. "That was odd," she squeaked.

"Did you do all that?" I asked.

"No. I just cast a spell to make the Mayor poop his pants. I'm not sure if it worked."

We turned to the mayor. He smelled the air a few times and checked his pants.

"So you are a witch!"

Molly blushed. "That's very kind of you." She smiled a smile like I had never seen anyone smile before. It was so bright and beautiful. How could she keep such a beautiful smile from the world for so long? It was like a glacier had melted and revealed a field long forgotten. And from that field grew a flower. And for the first time in a thousand millennia, a flower bloomed. I cared not for anything but to hold that flower close. It was not a curse that made it so, but love. I realized then for the first time that I was in love with Molly Mucasine and that maybe she loved me too. Love is the most powerful magic on Earth. There was only one thing I still wanted to ask her. Just one thing that kept my heart at bay.

"Can I ask you something, Molly?" I took a step closer. Her smile widened. My heart fluttered.

"Yes, Humphry?" She twisted on her toes like a daisy in a gentle breeze. Such a beautiful daisy.

"Did you cast a spell on me to make me get my sister pregnant?"

"What? Eww! Why are boys so weird?" Her smile wilted into a frown. It was the first flower in a million years and I stepped on it. Molly drifted into the unruly mob, gone from me forever. I had everything in the world and so quickly did I falter.

I stood and watched the crowd disappear out the doors. Jebediah walked up to me without a care to be seen. "Hey turd breath, let's go. We're meeting Tubby at the hospital."

"You mean Tabby?"

He swiped me across the head and left for the car. I followed.

Jebediah played the radio as loud as it got. It was usually enough to keep us from talking, but I had too much on my mind to keep it all to myself. I turned down the radio to Jebediah's shock.

"What do you think you're doing, buttface?"

"I have to ask you about Tabby. You told me that I was the father. I need to know how you found out and how it happened."

"What are you talking about? Tabby slept with the whole football team. Who knows who the father is?"

"But you said it was me..."

"And you believed me? What a dummy!" Jebediah started laughing. He laughed all the way to the hospital.

A rage brewed inside me. It roiled and boiled like a hot bubbling cauldron. The pressure built and built until I could take it no more. I pulled out the knife I was keeping in my sock and pressed it against Jebediah's face.

"You think you're tough? You ever cut someone up with a knife? Huh?" The fear in his eyes emboldened me. "You don't know who I am or what I've seen. I am death. I've seen the life drain from a man and I'd take your life right now if it was worth a single penny." I sliced a line across his cheek and watched it bleed. He whimpered like a dog. I smelled the air. Blood and urine. His lap was wet for he had peed himself. "Don't ever mess with me again or I'll slice you up like salami."

I slammed the door on my way out and stuffed the bloody knife back into my sock before entering the hospital. I went straight to my mom's room. She was still there. Tubes stuck out from every limb. The steady beat of her heart pinged on the monitor. Her life teetered on the edge because I was dumb enough to believe a lie.

I sat alongside her. The longer she lain, the less likely she would ever get up. *What would she say to me if she did?* She tried to find me. According to Jerry she had been scouring the neighborhood for days, even weeks, but Jebediah said she didn't love me. *Could it be true?*

"Do you love me?" I whispered.

The lights above me flickered. The bed rattled. My mom's eyes shot open as she inhaled half the air in the room. I would have screamed but my voice went missing. It was like we traded places. I was paralyzed and she was awake.

"You don't think I love you?" she asked. Her voice was weak and pained.

I could give no response.

"How could you ask that?"

My voice briefly returned. "Jebediah said that you only pretend to love me because you're ashamed about how much you really hate me. You never want to spend time with me so I thought it might be true."

Mom scowled. "Next time you tell that lying little shit to shut his lying mouth."

"Yes, mam."

"You listen to me. I loved you with everything I had. We spent every day together for years and years until you were finally old enough to do things on your own and decided that's what you wanted. I let you. You went off to play just like Jebediah and Tabby, and once you did you forgot about all the time we spent together. As far as you know, your life started when you were in grade school. It didn't. You had a whole life before that and my love was the only thing you knew. All you remember is me in my room, too exhausted to come out. I was exhausted because I loved you so much. You and your little shit siblings. I was a goddamn saint and the only witnesses were little shit kids who forgot every minute of it."

The light started flickering again. Mom's eyes closed and the heart monitor flatlined. A surge of energy flowed through me. The buzz blew me off the bed. The floor was cold and hard like the truth.

I got to my feet and looked at her lifeless body. She had given her life to me. I wasn't sure if she had really woken up. I didn't know if the lights had truly flickered. It could have been my mind playing tricks on me. What I did know was that she loved me and died to save me. Those were facts and they were cold and hard.

Nurses scampered in from the hallway, pushing me aside to perform their fruitless medical tricks. I drifted out the door knowing they wouldn't work. She was dead and she had loved me.

I left the hospital unsure of what to do or where to go. The sun was out in full and all the kids frolicked and played in the fresh snow. They had snowball fights and sledded down hills. They were all so carefree and happy. I had gunfights and shredded bodies on my mind. I would never be carefree again, or so my emotions convinced me. I would never be one of those kids again. I was ruined.

I wandered for some time. I eventually found myself in Betty Plumpkin's neighborhood. Once I knew where I was going, I picked up my speed.

I saw her as soon as I turned the block. A man was helping her out of a car. I ran the rest of the way but slipped on the slick sidewalk and slid to a stop at their feet.

"Little Hippo? What are you doing here?" Paulo the gardener asked from beneath the flabs of Betty Plumpkin's arms. Betty was just steadying herself on the ground.

"Is that you, Humphry? I thought you might show up one of these days." Betty sounded as carefree as the children playing in the snow.

"I have a question for you," I said.

"Well shoot, why don't you get off the ground and ask it?"

I got to my feet and brushed off the ice from my bottom. "How am I supposed to live with myself? The things I've seen and done are too awful to believe. Every day that goes by I see them clearer, and the clearer they get the more horrifying they become. How will I get through tomorrow and the next day when things just get worse? I've done so many horrible things. Things that killed people I loved. My own mother is dead. I thought it was all for a good purpose. I thought I would make a difference. I was wrong. All I did was bring death and destruction. What do I do now?"

Betty Plumpkin was unfazed. She patted my head as though I told her I was afraid of monsters under my bed. "Now, now, you'll be alright. You just had a rough couple of weeks is all. And don't get yourself worked up about saving the town or whatever. That boy Seamus was a real trouble maker and you put a stop to him."

"But dark magic is still out there and Frankie Fourfeet is as powerful as ever. I did nothing."

Betty Plumpkin smiled. "You did a lot more than you're giving yourself credit for. The worst thing that can happen is a change in power. Everyone gets all these fancy ideas about revolution, but the truth is that stability is the best thing we can have. Whatever gives us stability is good. You wanted to start a revolution and instead, you stopped one. I'd say that despite your intentions, you did a great thing. That's the trick to a good society. Getting people with the wrong intentions to do the right thing. Let's say you're an unfeeling maniac who likes to cut people open. So be it. You can be a surgeon and we'll pay you a fortune for it. That's the secret to being in power. You have to make everyone work for you, even the ones who think they are working against you.

Now, as for how to get over all the death and whatnot, I think you'll just have to leave town. I had to do the same thing once upon a time. Paulo too." Paulo nodded. "You've seen too much and you'll never unsee it. You just have to move on to something new and hope it makes you forget."

"You should listen to Ms. Plumpkin," Paulo said. "She is wise."

"You're so sweet," Betty said. "Now take me inside and let's clean my feet. Goodbye, Humphry. Thanks for all your help."

The two left, walking in lockstep, Paulo supporting Betty like a cane. Their footprints in the snow appeared as one person with four feet.

. . .

I left her house more distraught than before. My hopelessness spiraled into a bottomless pit of despair. I had to leave town, Betty said. I knew she was right, and the only place I wanted to go was wherever it was people went when they died. I wanted to be with Mom and the lovely Marlene. I wanted to see Jerry and Murphy and

Babs. I wondered if Blane would be there too. Something told me Seamus went somewhere else with Principal Chewbooger and Smellytown, but Blane was with Marlene waiting for me.

I walked to the creek, heading for the igloo. There were guns that we left there when we went to Flannigan's house. If a gun could kill a wizard it could certainly kill a little boy.

The sunlight was strong enough to melt the snow from trees. Some of it evaporated in the dry air while the rest dripped off the branches. Icicles and larger chunks of snow sloughed off all at once. It was like the whole world was crumbling away. It made me wonder how much of the world would be left after I was gone. Every person I knew who died took a little piece of me with them. *Did they take other things with them too?* I didn't think I would be taking any part of a person. Maybe I would take the igloo or a trash can somewhere near the Shank.

I found the igloo. It had shrunk since the last time I had seen it. There were footprints outside that looked new. I entered cautiously. I was afraid even though I had already decided to die.

Inside was a bare-bottomed boy covered in beans. "Deedris!" I exclaimed. "What are you doing here?"

Deedris tossed his beans in the air and covered himself. "Oh, hey, Hump. I ran away from foster care and didn't know where else to go. What are you doing here?"

I couldn't tell him. I realized who I would take with me to the grave. It was Deedris. I would never do that to him. "I ran away, too," I said. "My mom died and I don't care to stay with the rest of my family. I figured I'd come here to get supplies and then skip town. Do you want to come?"

"Out of Bethlahoom?" Deedris's eyes widened at the prospect. He licked some bean juice off the back of his hand while he thought it over. "We could go anywhere!" he said at last. He rose to his feet.

"Come on, Deeds. Your dangles!"

"Oh, sorry, Hump."

Deedris put on his pants and coat. Together we swept off the ice-caked tent, disassembled it and stuffed it back into its carrying case. We gathered as many of the other supplies as we could. It was mostly just beans. We decided to leave the guns. If we could go anywhere in the world, it certainly wouldn't be somewhere we needed those. We would go somewhere where we were welcome. Somewhere we didn't have to pretend to be someone else. Somewhere it was okay to just be a couple of boys with a bag of beans.

The End.

Epilogue

Humphry finished deep into the night when all was quiet and still. Just one of the dozens of candles remained lit. It flickered about, fast consuming its dwindling puddle of wax.

Merideth clutched a pillow in her arms. She had never heard such a dark story. Drugs, murder, corruption, the story had all of it and more. And all of it came from an unassuming, dull, grotesquerie of a boy. But maybe he wasn't so dull after all, Merideth thought.

Humphry, as though hearing Merideth's thought, sat up and met Merideth's eyes with his. His pupils were as big and dark as his story, though the candlelight lit them aflame. In the candlelight he wasn't so grotesque either. He even looked like a man, Merideth thought.

Humphry seemed to hear that too. He tilted his head in wonder like he couldn't believe what he was seeing. He drifted towards her. One of his hands planted itself on the back of the couch above Merideth's shoulder. The other reached out to cradle her head. Merideth's heart pounded. The pillow slipped from her hands. Humphry leaned in to kiss her. Merideth slammed her freed fist into his face and followed that with a foot to his chest. "Get off me you freak!"

Humphry yelped as he was thrown to the ground. "I thought we were having a connection," he groaned.

"Eww. You're gross," she said while rubbing her tingling fist.

Humphry's head sagged low. "I'm sorry," he said. "I'll go now."

"Don't go," Merideth blurted out.

"Don't go? What, do you want to hit me again?"

Merideth was quiet for a moment. The truth was that she also felt a connection, even an attraction, but it did not come at the expense of her repulsion of him. "Of course I don't want to hit you," she said. "I don't want to touch you at all." She immediately regretted her choice of words. "I mean that I like you, I just don't like you like that. You can sleep on the floor if you want."

Humphry took little time to reject her offer. "Good night, Merideth," he said and walked out of the room.

The brief draft coming in from the open door blew out the last candle. Merideth lay still in the pitch-black room and wondered why with all that was happening in the world, she suddenly cared most deeply about a dull, grotesquerie of a boy.

Acknowledgement

The stunning artwork on the cover and title page of this book is by none other than the most talented artist in the world, Yvette Gilbert, who also illustrated my previous book, The Great Ooflan from Corplop. These books, in fact, are primarily a medium to express Yvette's giftedness. Nothing else in my life comes with such importance, for, without regularly expressing her brilliance, Yvette's bottled talent would erupt in pure calamity.

This knowledge burdened my conscience. From the moment we last departed I was plagued by thoughts of the coming destruction. Unable to focus on my work, I took the long flight to Northern Ireland.

I picked up her trail near the pub where I last saw her. For months, I followed her scent across the North Channel and down the British countryside, arriving in an open pasture where her distinct smell seemed to come from all around. The local herdsmen told stories of missing sheep. I was close.

I stood watch that night on the roof of a barn overlooking the fields. The full moon gave ample light to see. The flock of sheep huddled close together in hopes of warding off predators. Yvette was undeterred. The sheep fell one by one.

The night was long and tiring, but the screams of sheep kept me awake. When at long last the herd had been culled, I set off to find her.

She lay in the field, temporarily made docile by the consumption of an entire herd of sheep. I approached with caution nonetheless. "Is that you, Yvette?" I asked wearily, though I knew of no one else with such a stench.

"Beep beep. Bop boop." It was her alright. It still boggles my mind that someone can be so talented that they can only speak in beeps, boops and bops.

I pulled out a sheet of paper and a pen. "Draw Humphry," I said, clear and direct, "And Blane, too."

"Bop beep. Beep boop," she said and began to draw.

The motion of her hand was mesmerizing. So powerful were her strokes that they cast a strong wind that twirled around us. It picked up the stench and carried it far away.

With every dash, her skin grew clearer. With every stroke, her beard wore thinner. Finally, she set the paper down, revealing the most beautiful picture ever drawn. She stood, not as the frightening creature of before, but as a woman as dazzling as her art.

"Thank you," she said, ruffling my hair as though I were a small child.

She then danced a joyful jig. She danced that joyful jig right on out the field and to places I will never know. Thank you, Yvette, wherever you are.

Also by Charlie D. Weisman

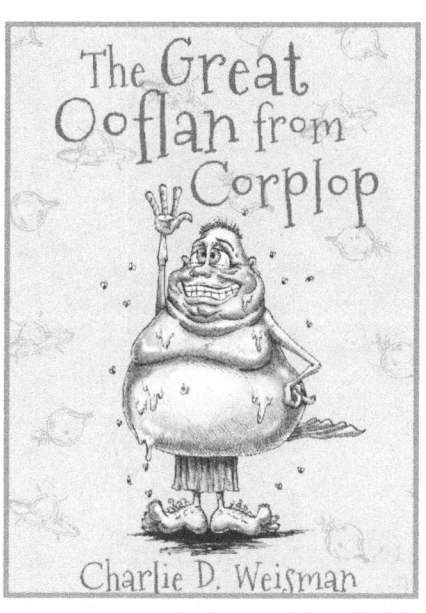

The Great Ooflan From Corplop

After a lifetime of wandering the galaxy, Charlando, a love-sick alien from the planet Corplop, lands on Earth to find Janet, a homeless alcoholic passed out on a park bench. Believing Janet to be his long awaited soulmate, he eagerly learns the intricacies of human courtship, all while braving the full might of Earth's military defenses. Love knows no bounds.

Made in the USA
Monee, IL
15 October 2024